BIG BEAR, LITTLE BEAR

BIG BEAR, LITTLE BEAR

DAVID BRIERLEY

CHARLES SCRIBNER'S SONS • NEW YORK

Copyright © 1981 David Brierley

Library of Congress Cataloging in Publication Data
Brierley, David.
    Big Bear, Little Bear.
    I. Title.
PR6052.R4432B5   1981   823'.914   81-9343
ISBN 0-684-17301-8   AACR2

3 5 7 9 11 13 15 17 19 F/C 20 18 16 14 12 10 8 6 4 2

Printed in the United States of America.

This one's for Ju
Who professes psychology
As if she knew
My in and outology

Author's Note

This is a work of fiction whose characters live only in
the imagination, with one exception. I have used the
novelist's license to let General Clay walk through
these pages. I should like to record here my thanks to
the Indiana University Press for permission to quote
from *The Papers of General Lucius D. Clay*.

PART ONE

It is true that liberty is precious—so precious that it must be rationed.

Nikolai Lenin

21 February 1948
Prague

"*Promiňte.*"

"*Ano.*"

"*Muzete mi doporučiti dobry vinárna?*"

His face came up, a furrow of puzzlement between his eyebrows. He seemed to have a drunk's trouble with his mouth, rubbing with the back of his hand at loose lips, and then he jerked his head across the square.

"*Doprava, u Mecenáše.*"

"*Je to příliš drahé.*"

"*Drahé?*" The man swung back, the furrow deeper, and Orris knew in the instant that it was blown. The man leaned forward to peer closer into his face and Orris half-turned to move away, as much to avoid the man's breath as keep his features hidden.

"*Děkuji vám.*" Orris fumbled at the collar of his coat, turning it up against the wind and the man's eyes, and started to walk away.

"Are you American?" the man called out suddenly, and as Orris passed beyond the spill of lamplight into the shadows he shouted: "Do you know Chicago? Indianapolis? Philly?"

Orris mumbled under his breath, soft curses. The man was going to run through a whole bloody railway timetable. Now he'd even begun to follow; Orris could hear footsteps, sharp on the frosted paving. There was the sourness of fear in his mouth because the man was at the precise spot at the precise time and he was not the contact.

"What's the matter? *Mluvíte anglicky?*"

The metal tips on the man's heels stopped tapping but the footsteps continued and Orris knew without turning that the man had broken into a shambling run. A drunk, his luck to run into a bloody drunk, full of dark beer and garlic bread, arm round the shoulders and sharing stupid confidences.

"Hallo friend, wait. What are you? American? English? *Deutsch?*"

A bloody farce and the sweat broke out on Orris's face. If he'd realized the man was drunk, maudlin drunk, wanting-a-pal drunk, he'd have acted out the charade differently from the outset. Humoured him, taken him for a walk arm in arm, put his thumbs to the arteries under his ears. Because the drunk had been at the right place at the right time, and that was a coincidence. Only pups believed in coincidences and Orris was an old fox. Four years in this field and you were an old fox or you were dead.

"Come friend, we have a drink together. Good wine at the Mecenáše."

The man, Orris noted, had a very Czech way with the initial 'd' of *drink*. Or he was genuinely tanked up and slurring. Orris never paused, because the drunk wasn't the contact.

He heard a shout from behind and a sound that might have been a scuffle and finally Orris broke into a run. You never ran, because that drew attention to you; you only lengthened your stride, because that passed unnoticed. But if they were watching now it was already too late and so he ran. At the corner there was a lime tree with a sturdy trunk, winter bare with lamp light coming through the tracery of branches, and as he swung to the left and made for the river he glanced behind. The drunk lay on the cobbles of the street, feet in the gutter, rubbing at an elbow.

No one else in sight. But there were a lot of shadows, doorways and windows, and he couldn't penetrate the depths.

He walked a little down the hill, crossed the road and checked the car that was parked half over the pavement. Volkswagen, wartime model, dull sandstone paintwork. Nobody.

The lights of an approaching car bounced over the cobbles and he watched it from cover. Large, black, American, heading towards the legation, with a U.S. Marines driver in front and a fat man in the back. The interior light was on, the passenger read some papers, a fat man with a fat cigar.

The night quietened again and he checked his watch, the luminous dial turned inwards on his wrist. Two minutes had elapsed, the hands showing just past eleven.

Orris returned up Mostecká Street, limping as an excuse for the slowness of his walk, and at the corner he looked for the drunk. The man was shuffling across Malostranské Square waving his arm. Easing the pain in his elbow? Two policemen appeared from the entrance porch of the church and stopped in front of him. The drunk made exaggerated gestures with his bad arm while he talked, his audience standing very still in the way of policemen. Orris couldn't hear what was being said. A late tram came up the street, banging its bell at the sight of pedestrians, turning left across the square, passing in front of the little group. When it had gone Orris saw the drunk wandering away about his business and the two police walking in step, like soldiers, the length of St Nicholas's and vanishing.

Another tram clanked down the street carrying no more than half a dozen passengers, hunched into their coats.

Orris abandoned the square and moved to the river, stopping part way across the bridge to stare into the water. The west bank wore a veil of mist. Half the lamps on the bridge were doused for reasons of economy. He rested in one of the recesses where the statues stood in menacing shadows, unmoving as sentries.

He waited. There was nothing to do but wait in the cold. And think.

When he reviewed the last half hour, there were three areas that worried him.

The drunk might have been no more than a drunk. Even though he'd been at the rendezvous at the right time. He'd switched to speaking English as if he knew Orris wasn't Czech, though with a Czech mother and a childhood in Karlovy Vary Orris's accent was faultless. So why the switch? Unpredictability of a drunk? Because Orris seemed a stranger, asking for a tavern? Or because he knew Orris's identity and was setting a trap? Then he'd run until he tripped on the cobbles and given up the chase. That was the action of a drunk. Equally, if the man had colleagues watching, it might be pointing the finger at Orris.

Then again: when Orris had doubled back to check the man had been approached by police. Was that because he was drunk? Or was he making a report? There was no way of judging. Orris found a scrap of comfort that they were uniformed men. Agents from the *Bezpečnost* branch would have worked out some cover. Like playing drunk.

Steps echoed on the walkway of the bridge. Man and woman, arms round each other, her head on his shoulder. He listened to their talk, something about the lock on his mother's wardrobe. They were gone.

The third thing was the matter of surveillance. There were few cars and, being Prague, an absence of taxis. Not many pedestrians either as if the news had swept them all off the streets into the safety of their homes. It was just feasible to use trams for surveillance, getting on at the stop before Malostranské Square, alighting past him. But that relied on the sporadic light evening service and so there'd have to be more. If he was blown, there would be eyes in unlighted windows. Almost certainly there would be a van with an aerial somewhere near.

It was time to smell his own sweat.

He returned to the square and keeping the cupola of the church on his left began a circuit of the small streets surrounding it. He drew blank. No vehicle that didn't breathe innocence. There was one closed van he couldn't clear absolutely. He watched it for five minutes before approaching, quiet in his rubber-soled shoes. He rapped with his knuckles on the side panels, three shorts and two longs, as if it might be a signal. His right hand held the grip of the pistol in his coat pocket. Nothing happened.

The fallback time was 12.12. Blank.

Again at 1.24. Blank.

At 2.36 Orris acknowledged it to himself: his contact was prevented from coming. It had begun to snow softly again.

Orris walked with quick light steps to Kampa park on the bank of the river. Benches offered the comfort of frosted wooden slats and he ignored them. He turned in under the trees, to where last autumn's leaves lay gathered in a vast snow-covered heap. He burrowed in, no better than an animal, fearful of the predators that waited in the night, the leaves sheltering him from cold and from curious eyes, waiting for dawn.

He slept fitfully. Mostly he worried about Palacký. Why hadn't he come?

22 February 1948
Prague

This is the revolution. He came awake with the thought.

It was the voices of children that roused him, two boys throwing a ball and whooping.

One of the boys shouted: "But why?"

The other, older, replied: "Mama said something enormous had happened and it's shut for today. Maybe a whole week."

"But why?" His voice was plaintive, not understanding how his childhood world could be so upturned by grown-ups' waywardness.

There were people talking in groups, quite unlike a normal workday, faces tight with passions, sudden sharp movements, a fist in the air, gestures for history. The men looked much like Orris, unshaven, bristles darkening their pale faces, clothes drab. Orris brushed at the mud and leaves that clung to him.

Now full daylight had come there was more traffic, buses and trams, three dustcarts going in convoy over the bridge. The sky was heavy, clouds echoing the purple of slate roofs.

His body felt tired, cold and hungry. Part of his mind still wondered about Palacký's fate. Mostly, like an old fox, he was concerned about how it affected him.

He made a detour and climbed the hill to the castle. The flag hung limp: the President in residence. Beneš must be a worried man. Orris joined a short queue, holding back for the third tram, a number 22. He pushed forward through stocky men with broad shoulders and tired faces and women with shopping bags. Orris stood to the front of the tram because it gave him a view over the driver's shoulder.

The tram wound its way down from Hradčany. Orris turned up his collar and stood with one hand scratching a cheek, gazing ahead and down sidestreets and up to second-floor windows.

He saw them.

An iron fist gripped his belly and he felt the sweat break out under his shirt and he thought: Dear God, poor Palacký, poor bugger.

The little Škoda was parked eighty metres from where the rdv should have taken place. As the tram went past with a petulant clanging, Orris saw the two men in the front seat, raincoats and grey felt hats, sitting and watching, waiting.

Poor bugger, poor bloody bugger.

For secret police, even for Czechs, they were very conspicuous and that was a puzzle. Not just badly trained, not just indifferent. It was as if they wanted to frighten him into carelessness. They hadn't been there the night before but they were there now and that meant sometime during the dark hours Palacký had talked. He knew nothing of Palacký, not even his real name; just that he worked in the Ministry of the Interior and was passing on information that London was panicking for. But he'd been caught with documents or betrayed by nerves or fingered by a friend and during the night he had broken and this was the proof: two men in an unremarkable Škoda, waiting, impassive.

Orris didn't speculate on the manner of his breaking: by fist or metal or electrodes, or simply bright lights and noise and confusion. No one is invincible: it is simply a question of finding the thing that is intolerable. Orris had been told that for most men it is unbearable to watch a woman being hurt, and possibly Palacký had a wife. Others will endure agonies to their body but

16

their imagination catches fire at sounds from the next room. Orris himself, as the Third Reich was in retreat, had questioned a Captain from one of the Wehrmacht's infantry divisions; it was a matter of discovering German troop movements so that sabotage would be most effectively directed. The Captain had been called Fischer, Orris remembered that, though for three years he had tried to forget; Fischer had been a true believer, a tough nut who wouldn't crack. Orris himself had vomited in a corner, because he had been a young pup then. An older man, a teacher of Latin, had solved the problem of making the Captain talk: he'd put a metal bucket over the Nazi's head and beaten with a wooden broom-handle for twenty minutes. It had needed no more than a schoolmaster's trick and all Fischer's suffering had been unnecessary. The Wehrmacht Captain had wept, the tears trickling pink on to the bruised body that had refused to give. Between sobs he had talked.

As Palacký had talked. After the last of the fallback times, the poor bugger had talked.

The tram crossed the river and Orris got down by the National Theatre. *Národní Divadlo* in Czech. And wasn't *národní* the same word in Russian too? It was a language he would need. Another enemy, another language.

Two men and a woman got down at the same stop. The woman carried a shapeless bag and she turned away, muttering. One man carried straight ahead towards Nove Mesto. The second man seemed to hesitate.

Orris bent to his shoelace.

He was distracted by someone running along the pavement from the direction of Nove Mesto. He was young and shouting as he came and people turned at his words.

"We've won the radio station."

He had a gaunt face, pinched by cold. Orris noticed his eyes, the white showing all round the iris, like a boy enraptured with a Christmas present.

The second man who'd got off the tram was now going down a street parallel to the river Vltava. He wore a dark overcoat with

17

thick padded shoulders and old battered leather boots like a countryman come to town. Sensible. Snow lay packed into heaps, dirtied from the city grime; from the look of the sky there was more to come. Orris followed. Nothing about the man was suspicious, nothing to mark him out as a streetwalker tagging Orris from the front. But since Palacký had missed the rdv, Orris accepted nothing, checked every face, double-checked doorways, was alert to movements reflected in shop windows.

Smelling your own sweat: Little Eric's phrase for it.

They were approaching the Charles Bridge when they ran into the roadblock. The open-backed truck was slewed across the street and a group of men stood in front. They wore ordinary workclothes, each with a red armband. Their collection of guns was motley, Czech, Russian and German, and probably half had no ammunition.

When Orris reached the truck a young man in a cast-off military greatcoat thrust out a hand.

"So, your papers, comrade."

Orris fumbled at the buttons of his coat and pulled out the wallet from his inside pocket. The identity card was creased and worn, the crudely-lit photograph making his nose more prominent than it was. Petr Sladký, born Karlovy Vary 1920, occupation Waiter, Unmarried, scar left thigh. The scar was correct. Probably the Unmarried. She'd said the marriage was blown to hell and he couldn't dispute that because she'd slammed the door on the way out.

The young man in the greatcoat inspected the photo, checking it against Orris's face. He read the description, his lips moving, and turned the document over and studied the reverse side. He took his time, savouring the taste of petty power, no different under the skin from any Nazi *blockwart* or *gauleiter*.

"You live in Karlovy Vary, comrade?"

"Yes."

"Why have you come to Prague at this time?"

"I've come to visit my sister. She's not well. The winter, you know, it affects her chest."

"So how goes it in Karlovy Vary, comrade?"

18

"The town is no longer empty. Families have moved into many of the houses vacated by the Germans. Still not many visitors. The Hotel Pupp, of course . . ."

The young man in the greatcoat had a fixed stare and a deep line between his eyebrows that gave him a look of anger.

"I'm talking of the revolution. How does the revolution go?"

"It was quiet when I left," Orris replied.

"So when did you leave?"

"Yesterday morning. I came most of the way in a lorry full of cabbages." Orris rubbed at the mud on his coat.

"There were roadblocks?"

"A number. But I was hiding in the back. You know how it is, comrade. When you are a working man, you assume every hand is against you. That is how the working class survives."

The story came pat. *Oh, you lie so easily*, Valerie had said, *I look in your eyes and they always protest it's the truth. You should be a politician, not a . . . whatever it is you do*. Orris was careful not to say too much; never volunteer information to a man with a gun; nor to a woman.

The man rubbed the yellowing identity card between his thumb and forefinger, as if he could feel its texture through his glove. "All right, comrade, you may proceed." He handed back the card.

Two other men who'd been checked were passing the truck. Wanting to leave a gap, Orris took time putting away his wallet.

"Why is the roadblock necessary?" he asked.

"Because the life of the city is threatened by fascist elements and counter-revolutionary bandits. So the people must increase their vigilance."

Orris looked at the man with interest. It was unusual to hear someone speak the language of propaganda as if it were natural. Give him the Manifesto and he was a revolutionary. Put the Bible in his hands and he would be a missionary. The eyes stared while he repeated what he had memorized.

"It is fortunate you had weapons."

"We were given them this morning when we turned up for

work. Last week we were workers at the Bata factory. So now we are the people's militia."

Orris fastened the top button of his coat. The two men had turned the corner. Somewhere in the distance was the sound of a police car. There was nobody else in sight but two boys throwing snowballs. Time to move on.

He was clean, he was absolutely sure of that. No one off the tram had been tagging him; the man at the roadblock had been savouring power, no more; no drunks wanted to be friends. He doubled back round the Philosophy faculty and spent time staring at reflections in bookshop windows. It was more difficult than usual. There were people about, students, talking and arguing, gesticulating, turning abruptly because of anger. It was that which made it difficult. A sloppily trained agent will give himself away with some hasty protective turn, but here half a dozen people had to be rechecked.

He was uneasy, the mood of the city affecting him.

People thronged the street in front, some openly carrying rifles. There'd been nothing like this yesterday: it was growing in urgency by the hour. Police stood, half blocking the pavement, doing nothing about the guns on display. The crowd flooded out into the road and moved east towards Old Town Square.

There was a café on the corner. He was tired of walking and needed time to breathe without watching his back. He ordered coffee, rye bread and cheese, and there was no bread.

"The bakers have gone on strike."

Orris sat at a table against the wall with a view down the street and convenient to the passage that led to the toilet. A café always has a back way out by the toilet. The morning was dark and the central light had been switched on. How long before the power workers came out?

A truck came down the street, heading west. It had khaki canvas hooding the back, and at the tailboard the first soldiers Orris had seen. Going to Hradčany to arrest the President? The loyalty of the army fluctuated with the political colour of the commanding officer at the garrison. And the C.O. depended on who was in charge of the Ministry. Orris spread a newspaper on the wooden table but couldn't concentrate. His own situation was now critical.

It had been late yesterday when the order came from the Depot in London: priority, from Beamish. Contact Palacký and collect the latest information on police appointments in Prague. If Palacký missed personal contact, Orris must clear the dead-letter drop at noon. If there was nothing, if his face and cover were known to the security police, then bloody get out. Except Beamish hadn't said that: Beamish wasn't sheltering in a café from a budding revolution.

The coffee when it came contrived to be both weak and bitter. He drank in slow sips, cupping his hands for the warmth. It was cold in the café; only in the evening would there be a fug of body heat.

The official way out was through one of the consular staff, a pompous Surrey exile called Woodburne, who smoothed the hair at the back of his head while he talked and made no attempt to hide his dislike of Orris "and those of your ilk". Instructions from London detailing Orris's escape procedure would come to Woodburne via the legation radio. Orris could not imagine what Woodburne found to do with his time all day. Possibly that was why the man was so full of resentment: Orris spoiled the symmetrical beauty of an otherwise empty day.

The drop-point was on Slovansky Island. Orris had never been happy with the arrangement because crossing the footbridge over the Vltava exposed him on all sides. He'd wanted somewhere away from the city centre. Woodburne had protested, with the vehemence of the lazy, that he hadn't the time to "go traipsing into the bush".

The island had a huddle of buildings, an old concert-hall looking run-down and neglected, a statue of some woman whose plaque Orris had never read, a strange contrivance that was reputed to be an old water-tower. The rest was given over to grass and paths, stark trees, a gardener's hut. The paths had been swept of snow; elsewhere it lay trampled by children's games.

Some sort of uniformed official stood outside the locked concert-hall, stamping his feet against the cold. A young woman walked hand-in-hand with a much older man who glanced over his shoulder. Smelling his own sweat, Orris decided, in case his wife suspected. Boys whooped round some bushes.

Orris walked along the path by the river until he came to the place. A low wall protected him from scrutiny while he bent to his shoelace and reached inside the drainpipe. He knew from the moment he had to brush away snow that there'd be nothing.

For the second time that day there was the clutch in his belly. Something had gone very wrong. He was at the frayed end of the rope, in the midst of a revolution, with the security authorities hostile to him, totally isolated. He was certain, without needing to check, that there'd be police or army outside the British legation. Perhaps that was where the truck of soldiers had been heading.

Now he sat on a bench, breathing slowly to relax the tension, listening to the sounds of the city: sirens, a few car-horns, chanting from a distant crowd, the grinding of a heavy engine going uphill on his left. No tram bells, why are there no trams? Have they come out? A plane droned overhead making for the airport in the north. The clouds were leaden but the snow had held off. There was less smoke in the sky than usual; the factories in Karlín and Vysočany had emptied on the streets.

He used a newspaper as a shield for his face and an excuse for sitting. His eyes focused on a photo of Zorin. The caption was vague: the Soviet Deputy Foreign Minister was visiting Prague "for consultations". Yes, there were consultations taking place right now, in police cells and screamproof back rooms all over the city.

Orris knew he couldn't reach the legation. The official way home was closed. He'd get out on his own. It was better that way.

George Orris, the boy wonder, Valerie had taunted, *do everything on your own, can't you, except one thing.*

22

He spent ten minutes on the bench reviewing options: the wind off the river made it too cold to sit still longer.

He crossed back over the footbridge and started to walk, avoiding the main streets with their people's militia and police and crowds. He had to cross Václavské Square and paused to eat a sausage from a stand. Only three stalls were open for business and they were thronged: even in a revolution people had stomachs.

The press of people divided to let an ambulance through. It was a military ambulance and he worried briefly about the significance of that. Soldier hurt? Army helping out? Army preparing? He'd heard no shots. Might be smuggling Soviet officials up to confront the President—nobody queried who was in the back of an ambulance.

Orris dropped his *Rudé Právo* in a bin and continued towards Masaryck station.

Every agent has his style: blazing lights and champagne in the Sixteenth arrondissement; bowing servants in Beyoglu; a slim houseboy in Tangier. Orris had a poky room in an old building and there were things he needed: a second set of papers, ration book, money, a different coat. His bolthole had been carefully chosen, the building being on a corner with entrances in two streets, the actual room on the third floor having windows on both sides.

A block away he hung back until a group of demonstrators came on their way towards Old Town Square. He fell in with them, chanting for the resignation of Gottwald and Nosek.

Orris had the gift of anonymity, of being one of any crowd of ordinary people, an art that concealed his art. His eyes were— grey, was it? Even Valerie would be uncertain now, though she'd often searched for the truth in them. Hair dark-brownish, a mouth that was a mouth. Only the nose was a little prominent, drawing people's attention away from the rest of his features. He merged into the group of men, raising an arm when they shouted, and nobody noticed that his eyes were on the third-floor corner window, and that he lost the rhythm of the chant.

It was bloody gone.

The man next to him in the crowd linked arms and at the

corner Orris muttered something about "... shoelace ... catch you up down the street ..." and disengaged himself.

The jar with the two pencils had been on the ledge inside the window in front of the net curtain and it was gone. Knocked over, moved out of the way, tampered with.

Bloody. Oh bloody bloody bloody.

He made three left turns and approached the other corner window until he was some sixty metres away and stood, his outline obscured by the jutting edge of a shoe shop. Five minutes, six minutes. Then he caught the movement of dark grey behind the light grey of the net.

A shimmer, gone.

Someone was waiting for him. It made Orris very angry, that sudden gushing anger of betrayal. Somehow, somewhere, there had been the mother and father of a cock-up.

Palacký had been arrested and Palacký had talked. But not about this. Palacký was in a completely separate compartment and had been reporting to London by some other obscure route until the crisis had blown up.

Possibility: someone had mentioned Orris's bolthole to Palacký and during the course of the night it had been part of the information bled out of him. Who could have told him?

Woodburne was the only one who knew the address. Woodburne could have told Palacký. Or might have committed it to paper and filed it in some insecure registry in the legation to be turned up by a clerk. Or transmitted it to London and then God knows half a hundred people in the Depot might share the secret.

Result: a shadow moved across the curtain.

Orris turned and walked away with apparent casualness.

There were police in the railway station and Orris felt sudden shyness about his face. He sneezed and lowered his nose in his handkerchief and drifted out.

It was three-forty by the station clock but outside the winter's day was closing in, darkness falling from the sky and rising from old stone buildings.

24

They came round the corner without warning, two or three hundred, young men with small moustaches, older men with threadbare faces, a few women with those fierce Czech eyes.

Orris followed because this was the kind of thing Beamish fed on: "How many of them? What reception did they get? Did they make converts?"

They marched into the broad expanse of Václavské Square, the crowd falling back in the face of such discipline. They halted and a man with a strong square face and a heavy fist made a rousing speech. Did they want the old order back, he cried out, the landowners and moneylenders, traitors like Heydrich who'd co-operated with the Nazis? He appealed for solidarity, for social democrats to march shoulder to shoulder with their comrades in the communist party, to solve their problems together, to fight the exploiters and not their own brothers.

Orris turned and walked slowly away. There was, he felt convinced, going to be a communist government in Czechoslovakia. It might come abruptly, as in Yugoslavia. Or gradually as in Hungary and Romania, with complaisant left-wingers co-operating until the communists swallowed them. The signs had been there, growing day by day. Now they were growing hour by hour and he had to reconsider his position.

Suppose the revolution succeeded. Then Orris was no longer a danger, merely a minor irritant. Not worth looking for. It was better, he decided, to lie low and not try to get out. By tonight London would realize he was blown and slip another man in, one who wasn't compromised. He, Orris, simply had to go to earth until the new régime settled down.

To his knowledge Jiří Brouček was the only other man the Depot used in Prague. He called himself a publisher though he was no more than assistant to an educational editor. Orris couldn't remember which publishing house but he had his home address. Brouček had a back bedroom he could use. He had no wife, only a grown-up daughter who'd emigrated to America.

It was almost dark. Orris was there when it happened.

There is a breed of men that covets this kind of thing, the dross of their nature setting them apart from others. They go about their work in half-light, the dawn raid, the dusk call. They shun the exposure of day, fear the complicity of full night.

They came out of the apartment block in tandem, one with his arms folded round books, the other toting a carton jammed with papers. Words, especially written words, were powerful, a danger to the totalitarian twist of mind. They were police, Orris presumed, dark uniforms, a van at the corner. He pressed into a doorway.

Brouček followed after a moment or two, a man in a sombre coat at his side. There was a trickle of something dark from Brouček's mouth.

They treated him like some black-market spiv, a man of his age, one of the patriots who'd been in the uprising of May 1945. He'd run a little printing press, literally an underground press, in a cellar under the shadow of the Old Town Hall. When Nazi soldiers came to flush them out Brouček had made one of his scholarly little jokes: that there were certain occasions when a wise man recognized a sword was mightier than a pen. He had used a rifle from a first-floor window, though his glasses had got broken in the scramble. The fighting was intense, the partisans resisting the Germans with fierce pride. In the confusion, with the Old Town Hall in flames and mortars being brought up against the Czechs, Brouček had escaped through the labyrinth of passageways and cellars, swimming through one that was flooded.

His hair was finest silver in the half-light. A hand on his shoulder helped him into the back of the van.

It was like the way Brouček's wife had disappeared in 1943, in the back of a Gestapo car. She had never been seen again.

A man can always get a bed for the night.

"For the whole night? You're a strong one."

"You have a place of your own?" Orris queried.

'Usually a gentleman prefers to go elsewhere. I know a hotel where they don't rob you. It's quite clean."

"Your place." In a hotel he'd have to give a name, show papers. With the city in turmoil, the police would be sifting hotel registers for names. "What sort of a place is it?"

"It has a bed. You're not expecting to swing from the chandelier, are you? Or do you mean the other stuff, ropes and so on?"

"No family, I mean. No neighbours poking their noses in."

"You're a funny one," she said. "What are you edgy about?"

Orris kept silent.

She started to walk, her coat swinging, caught by the wind, displaying thick ankles. "The trams aren't running, but it's not far." Orris stood still, peering across the road where he thought a man was watching. He was sure someone was there, a man with a hat pulled down. She came back and took his arm. "Come on. I thought you were so eager."

The street lamps weren't on, though lights glowed yellow from some of the windows. There were men's shouts in the dark behind them and the sound of breaking glass. The woman shivered and tightened her grip on his arm. In the distance was a loudspeaker van: it could have been a call to arms, a proclamation, propaganda, ordering a curfew. It was too indistinct to catch the words.

There was a rush of footsteps without warning behind him and Orris spun, freeing himself roughly from the woman's clutch. Two men ran past, one shouting, his warning caught by the wind.

"Come on." Orris grabbed her arm again.

There was cheering from the centre of the Old Town, suddenly quite loud on the breeze.

"You're hurting," she complained. Her voice had already begun to grate on Orris's nerves. It rose at the end of sentences, querulous, a voice that would always find something wrong, never expecting happiness in life.

The lights of a vehicle swung round the corner behind them, bouncing off the walls of the houses. Orris abruptly forced the woman round.

"Kiss me."

27

He fixed on her slack mouth, a red gash of cheap lipstick traded in God knows what black market. The chemical cosmetic taste almost drowned the staleness of a mouth that never knew toothpaste.

The lights grew brighter. It sounded a big-engined car, going slowly. Orris bobbed his head down to nuzzle one of her ears, her fluffed out hair filling his eyes and nose. One hand gripped her shoulder, the other smoothed over her hip to her buttocks.

"You take liberties, you know that? You haven't even paid yet."

The car passed, tyres thrumming on the cobbles. Orris didn't know who was in it.

"How do I know you're not just hoping to get a feel for free?"

"Shut up."

Orris walked on without her. She had to trot a few steps to catch up. They continued in silence, apart, before she took his arm again, not wanting to risk losing him.

"Nearly there. Can't wait to get stuck in, can you?"

She lived in a depressing street off Peter Square. The building had grey walls, streaked with weather, decorated with a flyposter for a circus and faded slogans for a national front. It was pitted with old bullet wounds, uncommon in a city that escaped the worst of the war.

She went ahead of him up the stairs, fumbling for the key. There were four doors on the landing and for a moment Orris was disorientated, hearing a domestic drama broadcast by some German radio station. A smell of cabbage and drying laundry hung in the air.

She locked the door behind them.

"All snug now."

She dropped the key in her bag and stood square in front of Orris.

"I always insist on cash first. That way there's no misunder-standing."

Her talk was a curious mixture, brisk professionalism giving way to a domesticity she could scarcely know.

Orris gave her the money and she put it into the top drawer

of the dresser, locked it and took the key next door into a hutch of a kitchen. Orris heard the chink of a jar: to retrieve the money, it would take all of thirty seconds to locate the key.

He went to the window and pulled the curtains closed. His eyes flicked round the room because it was ingrained in his nature. He could see why her gentlemen preferred to go elsewhere. A damp patch grew in one corner, edging up the wall in successive waves of dark grey, flaky white and pale green. A painted wooden dresser, a mirror with its reflecting surface spotted and tarnished, a wooden cross on one wall, a coloured picture of two kittens, a couple of chairs, and on one of them an outsize doll with a pink-and-yellow dress. A wooden letter-rack on the dresser held brownish photos: two girls in traditional costume in front of a village church, an old man with a pipe, a photo of the woman herself but younger and laughing at a soldier. The soldier wore a Wehrmacht uniform.

On the bedside table was a dirty cup and a bottle that had once contained perfume. She had the reluctance of the poor to throw anything away.

When the woman came back she found him slumped on the bed.

"What's your name?"

"Karel," he said.

"I'm Sophie."

She took off her coat and hung it with care on a hanger on the back of the door. Now she was in better light, Orris took in how unattractive she was. Her body was heavy, her hair ruined by harsh setting, her cheeks covered in powder, creases in the skin of her neck.

"Don't you like the name Sophie? Exciting, a teeny bit naughty." She put a hand on her hip and made a travesty of a provocative walk across the thin carpet, humming a few bars of something vaguely French.

He said: "For God's sake wash that muck off your face."

"Here, what do you mean?" She stared down at him, uncertain again.

"Wash it off. I'd be stinking for days."

29

She hesitated, pouting, and went back to the kitchen. He heard the sound of a tap.

He hadn't moved when she returned.

"Aren't you going to undress?"

The white had gone from her cheeks, grey taking its place with a pink flush where she'd rubbed with a towel. Even without make-up it was hard to judge how old she was. Twenty? Thirty-five? She seemed not to have grown up, just aged. Despite the hard usage of her life, she had a child's eagerness to please.

"Where's the toilet?" Orris asked.

"Across the landing." And when Orris didn't move: "You can use the basin next door if you like, provided it's not . . . you know."

"Later."

"First things first," she said, cocking an eyebrow at him.

Her blouse unbuttoned down the front. She took it off and turned her back, not out of modesty. "Unhook me, will you?"

Orris fumbled with cold fingers at the fastening.

"Nervous?"

There were marks on her back where the tight bra had bitten into the skin. A scar showed across one shoulderblade, white on white.

She kicked her shoes off, one after the other clattering against the wall. "I feel quite excited tonight," she said. "It's in the air, isn't it?" And then unexpectedly: "I like you, you know that? Some of the others are all over you the moment we're through the door." Her skirt slid to the floor, then her knickers, dun-coloured and mended at one side and unarousing. She stood in front of him, her heavy body freed of restraint, arms above her head, pivoting like Giselle.

"Something a man can get hold of. Not like those broomsticks." She cupped her breasts in her hands. "Get your hands full." She spoke dispassionately, as if it were not her body at all.

Orris sat on the edge of the bed, fully clothed, staring with dull eyes. *You're a randy little bugger, I'll say that for you,* Valerie had said, *always wanting it.* All he wanted was to sleep, exhausted after a night heaped over with leaves and a day of mounting tension. It wasn't so simple; there were prostitutes who took out insurance by becoming police informers, dropping word of someone who was merely seeking shelter.

"Are you only going to look?" She put her head on one side. "It won't cost extra to do something." She came and ran a finger down his cheek. "Don't tell me you've never had a woman."

"Christ," he said.

She slipped her hands inside his jacket. "Don't be shy, Karel. I'll help."

"Leave me alone," he said, furious, shrugging her hands off.

She stood back hastily and watched with dark eyes while he took his clothes off. He got between sheets that felt clammy.

"Jesus, it's cold."

"I'll warm you," she said, slipping in beside him, leaning her breasts over his face.

The sound of machine-gun fire woke him. He stayed rigid in bed, breathing through his mouth, greasy with sweat. It came again and a hoot, eerie in the night. His brain told him: goods train, the couplings between wagons. His imagination said: they're lining Palacký and Brouček up against a wall.

He lay still, dark in the room, dark thoughts. Someone had betrayed them; someone in Prague or someone in London. A traitor had sold every one of their names.

Sophie stirred and mumbled "Darling" as he swung his legs out and bare-footed to the window, parting the curtains with his fingers. It was a moonless night. He could see the dreary building across the street, the top of a tree. There was a powdering of fresh snow. Sometime recently there'd been a brief thaw and icicles had formed at the top of the window, half a dozen ghost fingers.

Somebody whistled in the street outside.

"What are you looking for?" she asked from the bed.

The silence ran on while Orris stared at the dark. He said: "There's a damn revolution coming. Aren't you worried? Aren't you scared?"

31

"Come to bed." He heard her stir among the blankets. "What does it matter? Different men on top but men all the same. They'll want a woman underneath."

She clicked on the light.

"You'll freeze to death. Come to bed."

She eyed his naked body as he walked back. "I like a man who cares for himself. Too many men let themselves go, beer and dumplings, and they crush the breath out of you. What's that?"

Orris pulled the blankets up and turned away. She slipped a hand over his hip and when he didn't respond she pulled the covers back and knelt on the mattress, her hair sliding over his belly.

"What are they?" With a stubby finger she traced the outline of three scars on his inner thigh.

"Scars."

"How did you get them?"

"Gestapo."

She went very still. Orris could feel the beat in her chest as she leaned over his body.

"They look like cigarette burns," she said. When Orris didn't respond she whispered: "Mother of God."

At first light Orris dressed. She watched from the bed. *Why do men like to watch a woman getting in and out of clothes?* Valerie had asked, *they're so childish.* Sophie seemed to find some interest in it.

"Do you want to borrow a razor?" she asked. "I've got one, a man's. The blade's quite sharp."

He shook his head. Not how he was going. A shave would be as out of place as a silk cravat.

"Have you anything to eat?" he asked. When she hesitated he added, "I'll pay."

"It's not the money," she answered, then shrugged. "There's bread next door."

She wrapped her coat round her shoulders and went with him to the cramped kitchen. It had a solitary gas ring and a cold-water tap above the sink. There was dark bread and a jar of plum jam. She made two cups of camomile tea. Orris could feel it clearing his head.

"What part are you from?" he asked. It wasn't the silence between them that worried Orris; there was comfort in hearing of normal times.

"Moravia," she told him. "A village called Adamov. Do you know it? Not far from Brno."

"I know Brno." Yes, and knew it better in the English form, the home of the Bren gun.

"Have you been in Prague long?"

"Since the war." She took several sips from the cup, the steam rising in her face. "I had to leave home."

She said nothing further. Orris remembered the photo of the boy with a German cross on his uniform. When the conquerors had been driven out she'd brought her peasant body to the city, where all sins are overlooked.

"You're going early," she said. "You don't have to leave so early. I won't expect anything, you know, extra."

She seemed to have formed an attachment for him. Or perhaps it was reluctance to face another day on her own. He put on his coat and she went with him to unlock the door.

"Don't forget little Sophie," her voice called after him. "Come back and see me."

Sophie and Karel, he thought. Remembering each other by names that weren't their own.

26 February 1948
Bohemia

There was no shimmer behind the net curtains.

An hour or more he kept the farmhouse under observation. Because of Prague, because of the trickle of something dark from Brouček's mouth, because of two men in a Škoda. Nothing stirred except smoke from the chimney, rising in a column in the still morning and flattening with a current of air from the north-east.

It was the fourth day after quitting Prague. He had left the city centre in the early morning and walked north through desolate suburbs until he reached the river port of Liben. There an old man with a bottle of plum brandy had ferried him across the Vltava, muttering as the current swung the bow of the ramshackle boat, raising his bottle to salute a man on a rust-streaked coal barge.

Orris found a local train that was little more than a tram, halting at places that were not stations but raised hummocks of earth with wooden signs. At Slaný there was a station and he got off when he saw police boarding the front coach. He jumped down on the side away from the platform. A band of people's militia stood in the main square but the town seemed otherwise normal.

For two days he had travelled slowly by tractor and farm cart, walking sometimes, a market-day bus once. The land lay locked under the snow, there was no work in the fields, farms appearing deserted as if the population had fled an invading army. He slept in barns, ate cabbage and onions stacked in sheds, and once some soup and boiled eggs from a farmer's wife.

Now, on the morning of the fourth day, Orris sat on the iron-hard ground behind a farm cart and watched the house. It was built of stone, very solid, plastered inside and out. At some time long ago a stook of wheat had been painted on an end wall. Inside, the plaster was painted cream. He knew the inside well because the Stamic family had been part of the network that harried the Wehrmacht at the end of the war. Antonín Stamic had travelled in each Tuesday and Friday to his part-time job as café waiter in Karlovy Vary, Karlsbad as it then was, returning at night with information on troops in town, movement of armour, gossip going round the municipal office, reports from a railway signalman, recruits among the local inhabitants. And for three weeks, when some scare had thrown the local German commander into a fury of activity, Orris had hidden in the space under the steep-pitched roof. He had literally been boarded in, with food and water passed in at night; there was no window but he had

34

removed one of the big tiles to let in daylight. Soldiers came to search the farm buildings, questioning Stamic's wife Ludmila and daughter Josefina (the son Vojtěch already being two years away in the High Tatras to escape conscription); Orris had heard a shot and when he spoke to Ludmila through a gap in the boards she was numbed with sorrow: "They killed the pig and took it with them."

Orris remembered. He remembered it with vivid clarity. It had been home to him, Ludmila replacing his dead mother. And of course, Josefina: he hadn't seen her in three years.

Ludmila came out of the kitchen door carrying a basket and walked in her stiff way to the henhouse. Orris crossed the yard and followed inside as she stooped to collect the eggs from the nests.

She turned, surprised at the door opening.

"Jiří." She leaned forward in the gloom of the henhouse. "It really is you. Jiří, how long has it been?"

Orris took the basket from her and set it down. He placed his hands on her shoulders and looked into her face. A part of his life lay there, short but intense.

"You're in trouble," she stated.

"Yes."

"I suppose it's the times. Come into the house."

"No trouble here?"

"For us? Or for you?"

"Is there any difference?" Orris asked.

She let out a breath, shaking her head. "Three years and you haven't changed."

She'd always see him as the boy with quick eyes and nervous hands who arrived in the dying months of the war; like a mother who is blind to the grey in her son's hair.

"Things are all right?"

"Antonín has been gone three months."

"Gone?" he repeated, and felt immediately foolish. "I'm sorry. And Fína?"

Ludmila gathered up the basket, picking out straws that had stuck to the eggs. "Fína missed you. I don't know about now, I

35

don't know about her." She walked away, shaking her head again. "You're a wicked man, Jiří."

He followed, not knowing whether he was wicked to have gone or come back, or because of what he did in the war, or whether the wickedness was in connection with Josefina. He was too exhausted even to think until he had slept.

They sat in the kitchen.

Night had closed in suddenly with the arrival of heavy snow clouds. The wood hissed as it burned in the range and when the wind veered to the east it rattled down the chimney like an old car. The range was backed with blue tiles showing a line of geese marching to the right. Did geese really march like Hitler's battalions on parade? Strings of dried red peppers hung against the wall. There were three copper saucepans, old and heavy, reappeared from their wartime hiding place in the yard. There was no electricity; the paraffin lamp suspended from a hook gave out a dazzling light.

Ludmila kneaded dough in a brown bowl. Later there would be dumplings and vegetable soup, and Ludmila had asked whether he'd like *Spiegel Eier*. She'd used the German; Orris's presence had brought back the feeling of the German days.

Orris lit a cigarette, the first for days, since he'd waited for Palacký.

"So the President has bowed his head," Ludmila said.

"He has agreed to the terms," said Vojtěch. "It is quite legal." He'd been into Karlovy Vary most of the day because there was trouble about a new ploughshare. They had no tractor and Orris couldn't picture this man with his small feet trudging behind the plough.

"He has bent the knee," Ludmila insisted. "Gottwald has won. What about the election? What did they say of that?"

"I don't know." It was Vojtěch who had heard the news in town.

"Oh yes, they'll have an election. The world will watch for a little so they'll have an election. Vote for Gottwald. Vote for your comrade. There'll be no choice."

Orris followed the movements of her hands, dipping into flour, thumping the dough on a board again and again. Who had told him: Only a Czech woman can make dumplings; no one else is so angry with the world? He said: "It won't be like that. We'll help you."

She stopped and looked at him, standing awkwardly because of her back.

"You'll help like you did before?" She was slapping the dough down again, emphasizing each point. "Nobody helped in 1938. Nobody will help us now in 1948. Nobody will help us in 1958 or 1968. The Russians will swallow us up and nobody will lift a finger. If we were invaded tomorrow, do you think America or England would help?" She shrugged. "You think I'm bitter. I think you're a child."

Her eyes had the steadiness of a mother's. Orris met her gaze and then looked away at the big blackened kettle and the row of plates on a shelf and a bowl of grey-skinned garlic.

Vojtěch watched them, an outsider. He had his own memories of the war, when he'd joined the only real resistance fighting in the east. There were no shared hardships binding him to Jiří Horaz, as his mother had introduced him.

"Get him a drink," the old woman said to her son. "Give him wine, the Mělník your father bought before he died."

She ran her son, would run him even when she was too crippled to do more than rock in a chair by the fire.

They sat, without conversation, waiting for the bus to bring Josefina back from the school where she taught. Orris had most of the wine; it was dry with a strong taste of the fruit.

When Josefina came in through the door, with snow on her boots and the shoulders of her coat, Orris was suddenly uncertain how to greet her. He could hardly kiss her in front of her mother and brother. To shake hands was so formal. He felt the guilt of secret love.

She paused, framed in the open doorway, with snow swirling behind her.

"Have you heard the news?" Her face was glowing from the cold. And then she caught sight of Orris as he stood up. She ran to him, clasped one of his hands in both hers. Her eyes were sparkling. "Jiří, what are you doing here? Have you heard—the reactionaries have been defeated. Isn't it wonderful?"

"Close the door," Ludmila said, "unless you want half Siberia in the kitchen."

The first time he heard the movement Orris stopped breathing, concentrating everything on isolating the noise in his room. It came again, tiny feet, mouse. And the other sound was the pounding of his heart. God, he was all nerves. He'd been too long in the field, living his days of deception, watching the world grow cold. He needed England with its queues and prefabs and wot-no-marge and packets of five Woods and the Brains Trust on the wireless and the King in the palace with a ring painted round the bath so he didn't use too much hot water. Orris felt the urge to share; a man can be solitary too long.

He wanted England, though he'd spent a childhood in the town only eight kilometres away. This country was no longer his. "A faraway country of which we know little." Josefina had thrown the politician's words in his face.

The passion of the evening echoed inside him.

Mother and daughter had confronted each other while the two men had been spectators. The evening was one engagement in some longer struggle. In the end one woman's writ would run throughout the house.

"What'll you do if the Americans come in?" the mother had taunted. "Fight them with pitchforks?"

"Do you imagine we want the help of the West?" Josefina had a trick of shaking her head when she posed a question as if the other were an imbecile to disagree. "They're the ones who walked hand in hand with Hitler before the war, giving us as a dowry to the fascists."

Orris was in wonder at Josefina. In three years she'd changed radically. She'd never married and the revolution was now her child, to be cherished and helped to grow.

Orris slipped the covers back and crossed to the window. It was something that had grown to be an obsession: to look out, see that nothing menaced. The snow had ceased and the fields stretched white and silent to the hills. Beyond the line of hills was Karlovy Vary. Beyond that more hills and the frontier.

It was while he stood at the window that Josefina came to his bedroom. He heard a floorboard creak and the nails of her hand draw across the wood before she grasped the doorhandle. She saw him holding back the curtain.

"What are you looking for?" she asked. "Do you have friends signalling you? Agents spying on our socialist revolution?"

Bitter words, as they had been with her mother, but the tone was listless.

"Fína."

He went and put an arm round her shoulders.

"You're shivering."

"It's the cold. This north room was always cold."

It wasn't that. When they were in bed there was a blind desperation in her embrace, a hunger as her mouth devoured his, her tongue struggled with his, her hands snatched at him, wanting to touch and press and reclaim every part of his body.

"Jiří, Jiří, Jiří."

She panted as their bodies stumbled together. There was a wildness in every action that had never been present before, biting like a vampire at his neck, her breath hot, her fingers digging into his buttocks to drive him deeper inside. At the end she arched her back, sobbing "*Ano, ano, ano,*" shuddering as she tipped over the edge, falling, falling through the rainbow of her senses.

She lay still. When he kissed her cheek it was wet and salty. The tears had doused the burning inside her.

She lay with her head on his chest.

"I can feel your heart."

"I can feel your eyelashes. They tickle when you blink."

She smoothed a hand down over his stomach and lost her fingers in the curl of hairs.

39

"I'm sorry. That wasn't for us, that was just for me. There was too much dammed up inside me and the whole of my body came in a rush. I had to have a man's body, like men say they have to have a woman's body, and yours was the body that was available. It was shameless."

His skin was hot and moist where her body touched. He stroked her hair and on down her back.

"You have nobody else?"

"No."

The way she answered wasn't right. Orris put a hand under her chin and tipped her face up and kissed her.

"Who was he?"

"He was married."

"Someone I knew?"

She turned her face away.

"I'm sorry," he continued. "I've no right."

"It doesn't matter. In the end everyone knew. You can't keep a thing like that to yourselves in a place like this."

"You can never keep a thing like that to yourselves," he said. "Once you've loved someone you act differently and it's obvious to the whole world."

"Everybody knew," she said, her voice little more than a whisper. It was private, not a bed-whisper, Orris hardly catching it. "But still there was no one I could talk to about us."

She didn't give the man a name. Orris didn't ask because a name would make the man more real. She swallowed before she spoke again; Orris felt the movement, like a small bird against his chest.

She spoke again, for him: "He'd come to the school from Plzeň. It's only a village school and we shared the teaching. We were thrown together a lot after class, correcting exercise books, arranging the play, fixing the syllabus, you know how it is. We taught arithmetic, reading, literature, history, and he gave piano lessons. No German. He wanted to teach the children Russian but neither of us knew any."

"And he's gone?"

"Yes, gone. Someone told his wife and she made him choose.

40

How can he be happy with her? Tell me, how?" She sounded puzzled, the bewilderment of the hurt. "His wife doesn't love him, she's in love with a respectable marriage."

"But he went."

"She was a shrew. She knew how to draw blood."

Orris had nothing to say to that. His hand made small movements, stroking her body, perhaps comforting her.

Josefina went on: "I think she told the wife." She gave a little jerk of her head.

She meant her mother. The gossip in a rural community would have hurt Ludmila. Perhaps the man had been a Party member, responsible for the change in Josefina.

She drew a deep breath, forcing out the memories. "It's nearly three years and you never came back. Why are you here now?"

"I'm making for the border, crossing over into Germany."

"Why don't you take the train?"

"It's not always safe."

She raised herself on an elbow, trying to see into his face. "You're doing the same thing. Spying, stirring up trouble, right here in our country. Didn't they tell you the war's over?"

"Fína, try to understand. I work for my government, in the foreign service. I don't go round blowing up bridges and assassinating union leaders. I write reports, act as interpreter. They even sent me to the trade conference in Moscow."

"Moscow. Tell me about that, Jiří."

"What do you want to hear? Red Square, the Kremlin, GUM overflowing with milk and honey, happy workers dancing in the squares, secret police helping old ladies across the road?"

"Shut up." She got on her hands and knees to crouch over him. There was just enough light to see the stab of her eyes, the shape of her breasts behind the curtain of hair. "You're poisoned. All of you, all the spies and capitalists and bourgeois parties. You're afraid of what history has in store for you. You see nothing but evil."

"Sshh. They'll hear."

"What does it matter? Your snivelling bourgeois morality. Are you married too?"

"No."

He didn't know. Could it be finished without his being told? *What gave you the idea of marrying me? Love?* Valerie's face distorted as she screamed the word. *If I thought that, I'd get a divorce just to hurt you.* What had he done to make Valerie hate him so?

"Why are you afraid?" Josefina asked.

"Your mother would be upset."

"Not that. Why are you running?"

"Someone was waiting for me in my room in Prague."

"And you were afraid? The writer of reports and interpreter was suddenly afraid?"

"They were waiting," he replied shortly.

"One of your girls."

"I don't have girls in Prague." He wanted to say something to soften her, bring her close again; but his mind was filled with the image of a girl with sagging breasts and paint on her face pirouetting in front of him. He said abruptly: "Come with me."

"What?"

"England. Come and make a clean start."

"You're mad. This is where I belong. I'm not running away from disaster, this is the revolution we've been struggling for. This is the dawn. This is Day One, Year One."

"You're letting freedom slip away."

"Because I won't run away with you to a foggy dying little capitalist island?"

He was suddenly drained, hearing the tarnished phrases, even here in bed.

He said: "Lie down, Fína. You're letting in the cold."

She stretched by his side, a knee and shoulder touching. He put an arm across and her body was unyielding.

"I'll go in the morning."

"It would be no good," she said. "You do see that? If you'd come during these three years it might have been different. Maybe. I don't know. But three years and you never thought of me."

42

"I did, but it wasn't possible. There was no time to come and see you."

"In three years there was no time." She kept quiet for a little. "You know, there was always somewhere inside you I could never penetrate. You must make a good spy."

"Stop calling me a spy."

"A very good spy. Shall I tell you why? Because money wouldn't buy you. And you have no faith to lose. All you have is that secret core, a little dark box inside you. And if anyone ever succeeds in prying open the lid to discover your secret, to turn you into a traitor, do you know what they'll find inside that little dark box? Nothing."

"What are you talking about, a little dark box?"

"In here," she said. She tapped his chest, where his heart was.

In the night Orris started up, frightened from a dream. The dream slipped away, leaving him with the memory of a shadow moving, like a sea creature through seaweed, threatening him.

He reached out to feel Josefina. He moved closer, pressing against her back, putting his hand over to caress her breasts. Full of sleep she called him, "Eugen".

Orris thought: She didn't want me, or that other man; she wanted to make love with a revolution.

He ran a finger round a nipple until he felt it harden, clasped her tight little belly in his hand, stroked her thigh. She came gradually awake, turning to him.

They made love, without talking, without passion, as if they'd already said good-bye.

Ludmila gave him hot milk and bread and apricot jam.

"Did you ask her to go with you?"

"Yes."

"She said nothing this morning. She went off to her school or her revolution."

"She thinks she's going to help build paradise."

43

"She needs a husband, a home, children of her own. She needs more than a man for the night."

Orris stirred at the hot milk.

"She needed more than someone else's husband, rutting on the floor among the chalk-dust and broken pencils. How did she get like that, my daughter?"

"She grew up in the war . . ." Orris began.

"I grew up in the war before. Children have always grown up during wars or in slums or during famine or depressions or with a mother dead or a father drunk. Why did it have to be my daughter?"

Because she was alone, because she was desperate, because I deserted her, because it was a kind of love. Orris couldn't think what would ease the old woman.

She came to the door to watch him leave. She stood with her hands twisted in her apron, back hunched, waiting for him to pass out of sight.

Half way to the track there was a sound like a gunshot. A shutter had blown loose. The old woman secured it and went into the house, closing the door without waving.

Orris felt cold. It was the end of something in his life.

PART TWO

For many months, based on logical analysis, I have felt and held that war was unlikely for at least ten years. Within the last few weeks I have felt a subtle change in Soviet attitude which I cannot define but which now gives me a feeling that it may come with dramatic suddenness. I cannot support this change in my own thinking with any data or outward evidence in relationships other than to describe it as a feeling of new tenseness in every Soviet individual with whom we have official relations.

General Lucius Clay
U.S. Military Governor, Germany
5 March 1948

7 March 1948
London

And it was a cold homecoming.

Orris was standing in the cramped hall, his shoes among a spew of buff envelopes and copies of the *Daily Express*, months old and yellowing. He was quite still, testing the air for an alien smell, listening for tiny sounds, head turning, absorbing the atmosphere, feeling the ghosts in his home.

No, this place wasn't home, it was dead. An agent carries his home with him and perhaps that had always been the trouble.

It was twelve months ago that Valerie had run out, the door slamming behind her like a coffin lid. *You don't want a wife, you're incapable of sharing.* Valerie's face had been tortured into ugliness by the scream. *You're a baby, clutching at any skirt in reach.* Perhaps that had been the trouble too. But in the field you lived as a hunted animal, snatching comfort and shelter for the night where you could. Valerie could never understand it, never imagine the days gauging the look in other men's eyes, the nights when there was no relief from the worse enemy: loneliness.

He hung his coat on the hook. The hall was dim, walls papered brown to waist-height, orangey cream to the ceiling.

Scooping up a handful of letters, he passed through to the sitting-room. *Why do you have to call it the lounge?* Valerie had said, the inflection dipping at the end of the sentence, not a question but a criticism. Because a lounge is what the hotel his father managed in Bohemia had had. Perhaps that had also been part of the trouble: childhood in the shifting world of a hotel, creating his own secret life among strangers, never giving friendship.

He tore open an envelope and found he owed Chas Morton, Newsagent, the sum of 4/11d. "Kindly oblige—final time of asking" was written in a careful rounded script. Another envelope, another tradesman. Another envelope, a typed letter headed Bosman, Wilkie, Procter and Partners, Solicitors, and it was his divorce that saved his life.

Orris didn't want to read about it, didn't want to know the death of his marriage nor the revenges clothed in legal Latin. He wanted to banish the echo of her voice, her sneer, her squirrel eyes. Stooping abruptly to dump the mail in the grate, some thought of a funeral pyre of his past, he heard the window past his left shoulder shatter and there was the thunk of a bullet burying itself in the wall. A little plaster drifted down.

For a grotesque instant, his mind in the grip of the letter lying in the fireplace, he protested that this was not the way English solicitors undertook divorce proceedings.

He tumbled sideways in a desperate roll, ending up under cover of the windowsill, while a second bullet smashed into the ceramic surround of the mantelpiece. He huddled, his knees bleeding from the broken glass, the back of his neck aching for the next bullet. There'd been no sound of gunfire, silencer, very professional, very dangerous. His mind registered it while he took the first deep breaths to control the sprint of his pulse.

Through the broken window came the sound of distant traffic, the racket of a District Line train, the idiot chatter of sparrows. But no voice, no shout to give himself up. Because it was his death they wanted, whoever they were.

That was what Orris intended to discover. There were other urgent questions too: how the man had known Orris was returning, how he knew the address, who had instructed him. But first Orris had to escape from the deathtrap of his flat.

It is said that some people are ice-cool when threatened by acute danger. But the effect of fear is sweat and that is cooling. The sweat had sprung to Orris's forehead and the back of his neck and under his arms. A chill had come into the room.

Who was out there? What was he doing?

Orris selected the largest piece of shattered glass and used his sleeve to clean away the London grime. He edged the jagged glass above the sill, angling it to catch the shadowy reflections of the buildings across the dreary yard.

It took him some time to isolate the hiding-place, and then only by eliminating the chimney-stacks, the ridge of the roof, the dormer windows. The skylight of number 38, directly opposite, was wedged open with a stick. There was a movement, like the shimmer behind the net curtain in Prague, and he pieced together the outline of a head and shoulders. It was very faint, a ghostly silhouette reflected in the glass. Where the face would be, he could see only a pale nothingness. Except it looked misshapen, as if it had a monstrous nose. It was pointing down at his window, unwavering.

It had been, of course, Little Eric who first called the building in Queen Anne's Gate the Depot.

At one time there had been one of those little brass plaques that proliferate in the back streets round Whitehall: Ministry of Land (Administration). It was during a weekend in the previous summer that this had been removed and in its place appeared a plaque of identical design that read: Department of Overseas Payments. Why? There'd been no warning or explanation; several of the older staff who'd worked from the address throughout the war had been particularly upset. At one stroke some unknown and more powerful servant of the Crown had obliterated their heroism and sacrifice. It was a symbol of the change and retreat from moral standards they saw all round them.

As an acronym, DOP had sounded facetious; Department too unspecific. Little Eric, doodling unprofessionally on the agenda during the longueurs of a meeting, had inserted the "o" into the abbreviation "Dept". So Depot was born. It seemed perversely appropriate, even if the Depot stored nothing but files and dust and dirty secrets.

On this afternoon Little Eric burst open the door marked with the prim white card: A. R. Beamish, Eurcon. He was ready to do battle with the daunting Miss Lambert. The Civil Service had a curious rule that when a woman married she must resign. The ones who remained grew old, absorbing tea and suspicion, and were treasured for their knowledge of the Whitehall machine.

Miss Lambert had never married. "*Senex et harrida* is our motto," Beamish had murmured once, out of hearing of his secretary. He had been a Cambridge man "in my honest days", as he put it.

But Little Eric found himself standing over a thin-faced young girl from the pool whose name he didn't know. She gazed up, startled. He barked: "Is he in?" Without waiting for a reply, unthinkable when confronted by Miss Lambert, he pushed through the further door to Beamish's own office.

Even in Little Eric's turbulent state he noticed Beamish looked terrible. It could be the end of winter. It could be the flu that had laid low Miss Lambert. It could be nerves or a bad conscience. It could be the situation in Czechoslovakia—he had heard from Tombs, the doorkeeper, that Beamish had arrived at the office in the middle of the night, making Tombs limp his way to unlock the Registry.

Without any greeting, Little Eric burst out: "We were supposed to discuss Dorothy this afternoon. The meeting has been cancelled. Your diktat."

Eric Johns was a burly man and inevitably called Little Eric. His presence filled any room. There was often a problem containing Little Eric, and Beamish, looking up, recognized one of these occasions. Tired from the night's vigil, uncertain of himself, he shrugged. "As European Controller I decided against discussion."

"It has been rolled up, like a Turkey carpet. Rolled up, bloodstains and all, and taken away to the cleaners. The whole damned Dorothy Network. And there's to be no discussion." The faith burned brightly in Little Eric. He was very angry.

"Policy decision." Beamish was bland. Little Eric was the poet-warrior, the buccaneer, the one with the bright-coloured language. Policy was alien.

"I was there after the war. I helped sign them up. Bronstein and Martinu were my choice. I coaxed them out of their warm little jobs and gave them the King's shilling and now they're dead."

"I made a policy decision," Beamish repeated.

"You call it policy: I call it people spilling their blood for us. Why the censorship?"

"The reason must be obvious." There were files on the desk and Beamish squared them up, nothing so blatant as concealing them. "The Dorothy Network has been destroyed. Czech Security is not lively enough to do that unaided. Now, you and I are above suspicion—at least, I hope I'm not being over-chivalrous." Beamish tried a little smile that was not returned. "Similarly, I think we can trust Polly, Dayton, Glenning and the others who would have come to the meeting. But the fact remains that Czech Security received help. It is my responsibility to trace that leak. The less speculation, the more likely our man will relax his vigilance. It's not censorship, Little Eric, it's security. And plainly there's been too damn little of that."

"The whole bloody Dorothy Network."

"With one exception." Beamish raised a limp hand and let it drop on the desk. "And wasn't he one of your star pupils?"

He had no weapon but his wits.

It takes more than physical strength to slip past the snares of the field. Orris was resilient, resourceful, suspicious, reliant on himself and nobody else. He was a survivor: only in marriage, his private war, had he lost.

He was acutely aware of the seconds passing.

The man with the rifle at the skylight opposite had made no move. He was relying on Orris to panic and show himself. Or he was waiting for an accomplice to go and finish Orris off. That was the frightener.

Orris tried the old trick. He squirmed out of his jacket, rolled it into a ball, knowing that from across the yard it would look like the hump of his back. With infinite caution he edged the bundle above the sill and moved it across the window.

The jacket twitched with urgent life, the fabric bursting with a puff of dust, the bullet burying itself in an armchair across the room with an off-key metallic twang from the springs. There was a brief cough from the rifle.

Orris dropped his jacket.

He was trapped.

It was a poky room, with a single door leading to the hall. So far as he could judge, the assassin had an angle of fire that covered the entire floor area in front of the door. Also he had a quick trigger-finger. Orris had just proved that.

The gunman was content to play a waiting game because he had time on his side. There'd be a colleague walking round the block, making for the entrance of Orris's building, up the stairs, smashing a panel in the door to the flat, taking his time while he raised his pistol, aiming at the figure cowering by the wall under the window.

How much time did he have? Five minutes? Two minutes? Was the other at the bend in the stairs already?

There's always a way, always something to fight with. You never huddled and waited for death.

There was a settee he could have up-ended to block the window but he could only reach it across the no-man's-land in full view of the window.

There were no curtains. He could have dragged curtains across the window to shield the moment he made his dash. Valerie had taken them with her. Valerie would be the death of him.

Suddenly, switching tack, Eric Johns said: "There's a rumour about operational changes. By God, a real stab in the back. I know we're a bloody secret service, but it's different when the blood's your own."

The poet's leap, as if he'd changed metre. Come to that, Beamish conceded, the warrior's sidestep, as if to skirt danger.

"Little Eric," Beamish chided gently. His nickname was always used when he was to be mollified. "Operational changes do not refer to operations in your sense, of moondrops and muscle. You remain D/Ops, worldwide. The changes are structural, they apply only to Europe, they benefit mainly me. Do sit down. You look so physical standing over me."

Little Eric subsided into a chair, brooding behind his black beard and dark eyes, power in his deep chest, a quiescent volcano.

"It's a minor miracle how news travels," Beamish continued. "I saw the D-G yesterday and today you're threatening me with hellfire and brimstone. To borrow your phrase, we may be a bloody secret service, but we can't keep our secrets." A tired smile worked its way up Beamish's face. He fixed his gaze on Little Eric and in the end was rewarded with a nod.

As Director of Operations and European Controller they were at the same level on the Whitehall greasy pole. But Little Eric nodded to Beamish, deferred to him. It was unvoiced but the feeling throughout the Depot was that Beamish was somehow above the rest of them; that Beamish spoke easily to the Director-General, and the Director-General spoke only to the Prime Minister and God.

"I remain as titular head of Europe Desk, as Eurcon. But the day-to-day control of stations is split: Dayton takes West Europe, I take the East. East Europe is possibly the more onerous zone, so it is right and just I should take it: I am grey-haired with experience in the wicked ways of the world. In some small recompense, I shall deal with the French less often."

He raised an eyebrow, world-weary.

"Germany?" Little Eric asked.

"We bow to *Realpolitik*. Dayton takes the West, I take the Soviet zone of occupation."

"Berlin?" Little Eric persisted. "I'll need to know."

"Berlin being physically surrounded by the Soviet zone falls within my province. But you're not setting up a Berlin party, surely?" His voice contained a trace of anxiety.

"If currency reform comes, the Russians will hold the party. There'll be no request-the-pleasure sent to us. When we go in it'll be as gatecrashers."

Little Eric's arms were folded across his chest, the hands clenched tight. His big fists, Beamish thought, were like bunches of pork chops. Yet there was nothing unattractive about his extravagance. Everybody loved Little Eric, everybody.

Like everything in the flat, the linoleum was cheap and shoddy. It was dark green with the appearance of being mottled by disease.

Orris manoeuvred the whole width of the strip, working with feverish fingers to unstick the lino from the floorboards. The old glue gave way with dry whimpers of protest while Orris muttered under his breath: "The bastard's coming. He's turned the corner from Haversham Terrace. He's not running, he's whistling as if he hadn't a care in the world. He's got bloody murder in his heart." It was encouragement of a sort.

He ran his hand under the lino as far as he was sheltered by the windowsill, loosening it. Then he gripped one edge in both hands and jerked with brutal force. It ripped across the entire width. He was left with a piece as tall as himself, roughly in the shape of a coffin.

He jammed it upright against the window, using a straight-backed chair as a prop, and was immediately rewarded by a bullet punching a hole. A second bullet smashed through the lino. There was a pause. The gunman was reassessing, maybe counting his ammunition.

Orris stood upright, foot braced against the wall short of the fireplace, at the extremity of the rifle's angle of fire. His route to the door was now concealed by the lino, though it provided no armoured shield. The gunman could put bullets through the lino at will but couldn't see his target.

It was going to be a gamble, but the best odds he could devise. Better than the dead cert of a second gunman coming through the front door.

He waited, counting the seconds trickling away.

Another bullet through the lino, burying itself in the wall, and imediately Orris launched himself, sprinting for the door and safety. The gunman might have anticipated the move, or seen a blur through one of the holes in the lino. A bullet gouged a track by Orris's foot and then he was through to the safety of the hall. If more shots came, Orris wasn't aware of them.

He pulled open the front door, stumbled on to the landing and heard a noise more terrible than footsteps on the stairs.

He heard the footsteps stop. Below, someone was waiting.

Beamish was alone again.

Whenever Little Eric left a room, there was the sense of some humming piece of machinery being switched off. There were some, and they were principally across St James's Park, who dismissed Johns as the pyrotechnics of a volcano. He rumbled, might erupt unpredictably, sweeping everything away in an awesome display of destruction. Perhaps, the more malicious hinted, his vehemence was to conceal something. Of course, across the park they found emotions embarrassing to handle.

What the Director-General said had the ring of truth: "Without Johns we'd turn into some damned Women's Institute." He saved them from degenerating into the Foreign Office's poodle, trotting obediently to heel. Among the research and reports and meetings, he throbbed with life.

It was an extraordinarily hot day for early spring and Beamish suddenly found the stuffiness unbearable. He opened the window and a breath of air blew a paper on the carpet.

Picking it up, he noticed it was the blue-note from the Foreign Office with the report from the Prague legation. It concerned Woodburne.

Beamish closed his eyes for a moment, feeling a little sick.

He was exhausted, that was the trouble. They'd woken him at two in the morning with the news.

Woodburne had been a bachelor. Thank God there was no Mrs Woodburne to be told.

If the day had been rainy, he'd have had no hope. Orris jammed the skylight up and manoeuvred through, swinging himself round to let his feet fight for a grip on the slates. Slates were slippery enough when dry.

Another piece of luck: his skylight was on the opposite side from the shadowy gunman or he would have been picked off at leisure.

Crablike he moved along the roof. It was terraced housing, put up by a speculative builder in the 1860s. Each house was marked by its cluster of chimneys and a skylight. If he could reach the next skylight he had a clear escape route.

The sun was hot on his back. City noises floated up. He tried not to think of the three-storey drop to the concrete below. His hands were sweaty against the slates, his progress slow, agonizingly slow.

The noise made him jerk round and there, half out of the same skylight he'd used, were the head and shoulders of his pursuer. It was grotesque. The man wore the cap and uniform, high-buttoned to the collar, of the Salvation Army. In his hand was a collecting box. He opened the box, took out a pistol and began to screw on a silencer. The man was deliberate in his movements, not looking up, and Orris knew he'd never reach the safety of the next skylight.

Orris changed direction, crawling up the slope with desperate urgency. The ridge of the roof was his one hope for he could shelter behind the chimney-stack from the gunman with the rifle opposite. The reprieve would be temporary. He slithered over the ridge and down the opposite side, terrified until he came to a jarring halt against the chimney.

He raised his head over the top of the roof to look back at his pursuer. The pistol caught the sun, gleaming dully. Why the Sally uniform? Orris wondered. Because it was a storyline if he were found in a strange building? The man began to crawl in pursuit, hampered by the gun in his right hand. "Pox on you, Sally," Orris whispered.

He felt in his pockets. No gun, no knife. A handful of coins. He flung them and they rattled down the roof, making Sally pause four or five seconds.

He came again, awkward in his movements, the gun rasping across the slates. He wouldn't let the gun go. That was his power source.

Orris dug at the slates and the third one came away in his

56

hand, its peg corroded by weather. He hurled it, missing his pursuer, and it sailed over the edge of the roof into the abyss below. Sally advanced diagonally up the roof, the fingers of his left hand splayed out, his shoes scraping across the slates, his right hand encumbered by the gun.

Another slate. Orris hurled and it buried itself in the shoulder of the Salvation Army uniform. The man jerked his hand to rub at the pain and Orris knew what was going to happen. He watched and felt no pity. Sally's shoes grated as he began sliding down the slates. He fought to stop himself, finally dropping the pistol, his hands and feet scrabbling to find some purchase as his body gained momentum.

The cry was wordless, from his terror, as he slipped faster, his arms reaching out as if imploring for help. He slithered to the very edge of the roof, fingers grasping the guttering, the whole rotten structure tearing away. He was shrieking as he disappeared from sight, out into the void, down, his voice spiralling away into infinity.

From below rose the sound of milkbottles smashing down the steps.

Another scream, a woman's.

8 March 1948
London

Beamish looked up. The girl who'd taken Miss Lambert's place stood just inside the room. She had a pinched South London face and shifted her body restlessly, as if shrugging off a boy's advances.

"The Director-General is asking for you."

"Now?"

"Well ..." She gave a sniff, shrugged her shoulders and disappeared.

Beamish had quickly grown to accept her half-swallowed

sentences and twitchy body. Her sniff was not severe like Miss Lambert's eyes.

His bulk was almost blocking the window as he stared out across St James's Park. We conclude that people who talk slowly must think slowly, and they're careful not to disabuse us. The Director-General spoke without turning, brooding like a statue.

"I'm booked to dine with Ernest Bevin tonight. Shepherd's Pie and Newts." The Foreign Secretary was partial to one particular red wine and it was the duty of someone from his Private Office to interpret Nuits St Georges to wine-waiters. "There is a division at the House at ten, which is a mercy. Dorothy. I need to be informed so the Minister can be informed."

"Our late network in Czechoslovakia," Beamish told him.

"I'm aware of that," Standing said. "Every man-jack of them?"

"With one exception."

Standing was a heavy man who was not light on his feet. He came away from the window slowly, his eyes turning on Beamish like twin gun-barrels swivelling.

"Put me in the picture."

"Palacký in the Interior Ministry. Brouček, a functionary in a publishing house. Martinu and Bronstein, communist party provincial officials in Pilsen. Pascha, the Union of Chemical Workers. And two days ago Woodburne, our vice-consul in Prague."

"Ugly business. What details have you?"

"Nothing much. Woodburne was concerned about the Dorothy Network being broken and went to Orris's room, the man who's gone missing. There were stories of shots in the room and two men left."

"Who were these thugs?"

"Someone from the embassy went to identify the body and talked to a neighbour. She said just men in coats and hats who glared at her and stomped down the stairs into the street."

"Police? Security? Beria's boys?"

"Well, no one's owned up." Beamish smiled and the Director-

58

General didn't join him. He sat like Buddha, in silence. Gaps were another feature of his speech. You were left wondering whether he was making connections of supreme importance or had lost the thread of his thoughts.

At last he said: "These chaps who wander round the city with rifles . . ."

"People's militia."

"Could it be them? Can't we give the Prague police a boot in the backside?"

"The police deny they control the people's militia. A spontaneous manifestation of revolutionary zeal is their description."

"Good God." The twin barrels bored into Beamish. "This chap from the network who escaped . . ."

"Orris."

"Is it good or bad he escaped?"

The two men stared at each other. The silence dragged on.

"I see." Standing drew breath. "You think it's like that?"

Beamish said: "When an entire network, with one exception, is caught, and that exception disappears from view . . ." He raised a hand to finish the sentence.

"Orrible Orris. What manner of man is he?"

"Mother was Czech. British father who was an hotelier in Karlsbad before the war. Liaised with the Czech partisans from the autumn of '44. Also worked in Germany and Austria because he has faultless German in addition to Czech."

"But what's Orris like? As a chap?"

Ah, Beamish understood, was he the sort to go into the jungle with. "Very simply, the best man in the field we have. He has the skills, the inner resources. He has the instinct for self preservation—it's an animal sense, nothing civilized about it." Beamish could have said more, for he'd thought hard about Orris. There was the question of motivation that was so puzzling. He doubted Orris ever looked up to see what was happening in the wide world. He wasn't driven by hatred of dictatorship. He wasn't passionately for King and Empire. The second-rate and the insecure continually dust off their philosophy, polish their motives to admire themselves. Orris had simply embraced the occupation of agent; he accepted it, like breathing, as natural to his life. There was no profit in disputing it. You pointed Orris in a certain direction and he marched. As an enemy, implacable.

Orris would have to be found. There was no need for the Director-General to tell him.

Standing poured madeira and slid the silver cigarette-box across the desk. On the lid was etched: *To General J. F. Standing D.S.O., from the Officers of the Fifth Royal Ghurka Rifles, to mark the occasion of his retirement, 28.ii.1939.* "The fornicating Fifth," Standing had called his old regiment, "because of the barnyard morals of its officers."

"Kordorf," Standing announced, as if it were another heading on Orders of the Day. "I hear you're going to see him."

He heard a lot, Beamish mused. President Truman had set up the C.I.A. the previous year and Kordorf was Station Head in London. Beamish thought of Lou Kordorf as quintessentially American: bright, energetic, direct, arm-round-your-shoulders. He had a tubby face, a crewcut and tortoiseshell-rimmed glasses. He was thirty-six or -eight years old but you could still see the boy underneath, with his snub nose and freckles. Kordorf was a perfectly good man: he simply lacked the Old World capacity for despair and betrayal.

"Kordorf suggested the meeting. 'Cross-fertilization' was his term," Beamish replied. They were going to have to accommodate themselves to trans-atlantic jargon and enthusiasm. "He's worried about Germany."

"How serious do we consider Germany? I haven't spoken to Polly."

It had been Little Eric, again, who'd christened Houghton "Polly". Officially he was Political Evaluator. Beamish took his time, considering his answer.

"Potentially, very. It is in my opinion the break-point with Russia. They will not give up Germany without a struggle, maybe not without a fight. They will push to the limit, possibly right over the edge."

"Not the view of the chaps across the park. You seriously believe the Russians would start shooting?"

"If we provoke them by setting up a West German government, yes. Watch Berlin. It's a barometer of Russian intentions."

"They wouldn't dare march into West Berlin."

"What's to stop them? They could take Berlin while General Clay was in the shower one morning. Anyway, there's no need. All they've got to do is cut rail and road communications from the west and Berlin couldn't survive. No food, no fuel, no medicines, no raw materials for industry. Berlin would die."

"Damn it, the Russians wouldn't starve them. It's inhuman."

"I thought it was part of our philosophical baggage in the West—or is it mere propaganda—that Stalin was a monster and quite capable of starving two million to death if it achieved his objective."

Beamish tasted his madeira. A distressing drink he found it. Standing began: "I cannot believe the Soviet Union . . ."

"D-G, it's not a question of the Soviet Union. This is Mother Russia, something much older, afraid of attack across her western frontier. Napoleon invaded, Hitler invaded, and Russia desperately wants friendly states as a buffer. They see a united Germany as a potential threat to their security and in the case of national survival all nations become unpredictable. If we provoke Russia, yes, there could be war."

"War, eh?" Standing understood war. He understood it not as a politician, who declares it; nor as a boy, who is sent to the anguish of it; nor as a woman, whose son dies in it. Standing had come to be sickened, as old soldiers sometimes are, by the delusion of one final war to settle things for good. "You're unusually vehement."

The Director-General continued staring.

"Tell the Foreign Secretary about Berlin's coat of arms," Beamish said. "It shows the *Bärlein*, the Little Bear. If we push too hard, the big Russian Bear is going to squeeze the Little Bear until something goes pop."

18 March 1948
London

Once you've been at the wrong end of a rifle, everything changes. For days after you see colours more vividly, the outlines of familiar objects are sharper. Orris felt some drug had got into his bloodstream, fear or anger.

He took violent exercise at the gym in Clapham, working out his rage on the punchbag the heavyweights used. His rage wouldn't leave him: he could put no features to the punchbag.

Every day he walked: across the river, up Whitehall, swinging left at Trafalgar Square. A lonely man finds a certain comfort in routine. He couldn't indulge himself. He varied times, avoided too rigid a route: Admiralty House, The Mall, or along Horse Guards to admire the glitter and pride of a column of Household Cavalry.

At some point he cut into St James's Park. It was easier in the park to smell your own sweat. At a line of wooden palings he contrived to turn sharply, though there was only the churned ground of old gun emplacements to hold his interest. Then he dawdled by the pond, watching the mallards. One morning he saw a duck at the water's edge, drowned, victim of the ruthless ardour of the gaudy drakes.

He grew to like the park. Not for the flowers and the ducks and the swing of girls' skirts. This was the still heart. Orris was far from romantic but he had a sense of the city sprawling miles in every direction, its empire beyond embracing a quarter of the globe. It was hard to reconcile this power with the small building in Queen Anne's Gate and the ordinary mortals inside. One had betrayed the network in Prague and tried to have him shot in London.

The rage wouldn't leave him. But he tamed it, made it work for him.

It took Orris a week.

He didn't feel the time wasted. He had a stubborn cast to his mouth and would take however long it needed: week, month, year. He would track down the traitor and kill him. It was a simple decision.

Reflecting the British class structure, there were two entrances to the Depot: one in Broadway for junior staff, visitors, tradesmen; the other in Queen Anne's Gate for the high brass, section heads and above. The Broadway entrance had new doorkeepers, a fact he filed away. He watched the Queen Anne's Gate entrance until he was certain of the doorkeepers' shifts there.

Queen Anne's Gate had handsome gas lamps that left great pools of darkness. After dusk the street was largely deserted, which gave it a melodramatic air, in a Victorian way.

There was a bobby with a pushbike who came just before midnight. His routine was rigid: dismount, palm the handle of the Christian charity three doors down, walk with the bike, boots sharp in the night, use his torch over the windows of the building with the architect and the antiquarian magazine, slowly past the Depot, remount, pedal away with ponderous policeman's dignity.

It was a timetable. Like a bloody stopping train to Didcot, Orris had decided. Or Little Eric's verdict: "Policemen and agents are entirely different animals: you're the carnivore."

So on the seventh night, at a quarter past midnight, Orris set fire to the dustbin in the area outside the Depot. He doused newspapers with paraffin and put a match to them. They burned with hungry flames, and when he clamped down the lid, acrid smoke escaped. Metal railings (God knows how they'd escaped being melted down during the war) and an iron gate enclosed the area. He'd brought a padlock which he used to secure the gate behind him.

Orris stood back in the shadowy doorway of a building further down the street. There was no impatience in him. The fumes would drift into the Depot; he was sure no veteran of the First World War could ignore them.

The door to the Depot opened. Tombs came out, spotted the

source of the smoke and made for it. He remembered to pull the door shut behind him. Tombs limped down the steps, turned right at the bottom and found the gate to the area unaccountably locked. He had been wounded in the knee at Gallipoli ("One of Mr Churchill's orphans," he called himself) and found it impossible to clamber over the metal spikes.

There was the explosion of a bottle and a tongue of flame slipped over the rim of the dustbin. Tombs limped as fast as he could back up the steps, disappearing inside the door, which again he closed.

Orris counted the seconds. If this didn't work, there was always another way.

It worked.

Tombs reappeared in the doorway. In one hand he held a bulky fire-extinguisher, in the other a chair. For a moment he hesitated, feeling the tug of discipline. A fresh spurt of flame came from the dustbin, licking at the paintwork of a window, and discipline was discarded. Tombs was now too hurried and too encumbered to shut the door.

He propped the chair against the railings and clambered over. While he dealt with the flames, Orris trod softly up the steps. The Depot was open to him.

For a moment he hesitated. If this was the holy of holies, he was about to commit the sin of sins. He felt a breeze from the open door behind him. It was like the little breath of cold air on the back of his neck he'd felt in his flat; that had come from the grave someone had dug for him.

Anger mounted again. Get a bloody move on. The killer got his orders from here.

At night, apart from duty officers and Signals, the Depot was largely deserted. Someone was whistling in the distance, which would have been unthinkable during the day. Orris hurried past the abandoned doorkeeper's desk to the stairs. Archives was in the basement. Personnel was on the first floor, through the connecting door into the new building in Broadway. He'd go down to Archives first.

The easy route out was through the new building, where one or two unfamiliar faces were always around on business. Orris followed half a minute behind a pair of cypher clerks.

Whistle, never mind the dry mouth, bloody whistle, you've put in a good night's work too, and nod to the doorkeeper, and keep going, use your shoulder on the door, push out into Broadway. Nobody ever bothers with passes on the way out.

There was early morning sun. His shirt felt as if he'd rolled in the dew.

22 March 1948
London

Beamish was furious with Adamson. It showed in his punctilious behaviour.

"Mr Adamson, please take a seat. Would you care for a cigarette? Perhaps I can prevail on that girl to forage for tea. Now, I understand you have seen, actually spoken to, our errant lamb Orris."

"That's right." Adamson eased himself into his chair.

"When would that be?"

"Wednesday evening. No, I tell a lie, Wednesday is bell-ringing, must have been Tuesday."

Adamson was a dull young man whose wife believed he worked for the British Council, something to do with appreciation of ecclesiastical art. He encouraged these pious notions with church activities.

"Last week?" Beamish, despite the control over his emotion, leaned forward. At any other time he would have made some courteous reference to campanology—Had Adamson read *The Nine Tailors*? His long mandarin face was steady, only the flicker of an eyelid betrayed him. "We're talking about Tuesday of last week?"

Some sharpness in the tone alerted Adamson and he took his time, checking back.

"Yes sir, last Tuesday."

"I see." There was a terrible pause while Beamish looked over the other's shoulder, gazing into a troubled distance, his fingertips together, like a priest contemplating some weakness of the flesh. His eyes adjusted by degrees back to Adamson's face. "We don't employ fools," he announced, no charity in his voice. "Fools in the field dig their own grave. And we have no use for fools in the Depot because they endanger the man on the far end of the rope. But we employ you. If not a fool, a what?"

Adamson had gone white, from anger or fear, and opened his mouth. Beamish was quick with his hand.

"No. Listen to what I have to say. The recruiting of the Dorothy Network was a matter of some delicacy in which I played a part, and Johns, and Hendricks who was something commercial in Prague before he went to Hong Kong. All along your role has been peripheral, minor, junior; but the regret is we cannot do without juniors. We can only do without rogues and fools. Certain transactions had to be paid for, and you supervised the money flow. Certain information came not via Woodburne but from ad hoc pick-ups and dead-letter drops; here too you played a part. You knew about Dorothy, knew the whole network had been swept up—except for Orris. Orris the ghost; Orris who dematerialized; Orris who returned to London but has been shy of his old chums. Perhaps because they are no longer his chums. Query against the name of Orris. No, you hear me out, young man, you do me the courtesy of hearing me out."

The eyelid flickered and Beamish rubbed at it, angry that it signalled some form of weakness.

"Six people are dead. Our wells in Czechoslovakia have completely dried up. The man we want to talk to has been playing peekaboo with us round London. And yet I hear in roundabout fashion that you have seen him, talked to him, spent a jolly evening in his company. And more, you have not seen fit to report the matter to anyone with a sense of responsibility at

66

the Depot. And that, Adamson, is what is completely beyond fathoming."

When he stopped, Beamish had to cover his left eye for some seconds, hiding the shameful flicker. And then he dropped his hand in astonishment when Adamson spoke.

"I don't understand you, sir." Adamson's tone was clear: Are you all right? By the twitching of your eye, I think you've taken leave of your senses. "Orris had your note of hand authorizing him to make inquiries."

The eyelid stopped in the instant.

"My note of hand?"

"You can't have forgotten, sir. You signed it. Turquoise ink." Beamish didn't respond and he added idiotically: "Two dots over the 'i'."

"I see." Beamish considered the mechanics of forgery: Orris must have some document with his signature as a specimen, the right ink, contact with a criminal forger. To what end? For the first time Beamish seemed truly disconcerted. "Tell me about the meeting. Treat me as a seven-year-old, tell it in words of one syllable."

Adamson regained a certain confidence from the collapse of Beamish's authority. "It was on Tuesday evening, as I said. I was crossing the road to Victoria Station to catch my train, the stopping train to Brighton calls at Redhill, and he ..."

"One moment. What time was this?"

"Something after six-thirty."

"Almost dark." Beamish could have been speaking to himself, visualizing Adamson loping towards the grimy tired façade of Victoria. Then more sharply: "Almost dark, in other words."

"Yes. Is that important?"

"Of course it's important," Beamish snapped, impatient at the other's dullness. "If it were light he might have seen you from a distance: it could have been a chance encounter. In the dark, he must have been waiting for you. Please continue."

"I felt a tap on my elbow and when I turned it was Orris."

"How did he behave?"

"He was quite open, nothing furtive if that's what you're driving at."

"What did he say?"

"Not the sort of thing that sticks in your memory. Something banal." Adamson considered. "Something like: 'Well I never, Roger old boy, long time no see.' "

"Well I never, Roger old boy, long time no see." The deadpan repetition made the words even shallower. "He used your first name?"

"Yes, he did."

Beamish stood up and paced to the unlit fireplace, resting his hands and forehead on the mantelpiece, in the attitude of someone on the rack. He came forward again, his head protruding like an aged tortoise, the skin of his neck hanging in folds.

"Would you consider yourself on first-name terms? You were hardly bosom pals. He was a field man and you were one of those bastards with a cushy number back home. I'm putting it in Orris's terms."

Adamson had one of those very white London complexions with full red lips, as if a sculptor had taken a chisel to his face. A lock of black hair fell forward and he stabbed his fingers at it, eyes fixed on Beamish to see whether the barometer rose or fell.

"To be honest, the thought never struck me. I was surprised to see him, after his disappearance I mean."

"But you did nothing about it. Attracted a constable's attention, for instance."

"But he seemed so normal. He insisted we go for a drink at the Green Man."

"Is that near the station?"

"More like four or five streets away."

"So you passed other pubs en route, lights and laughter beckoning. Still nothing struck you as odd: here was Orris lying in wait for you, claiming friendship with you, and now steering you to this backstreet public house."

Adamson was sweating. "Well, we were chatting . . ."

"Did they know him at the Green Man?"

"The landlord said good evening."

"Think hard. Did Orris talk to any of the staff or customers?"

"He told me to grab a table. I had my back to the room. He said he'd get the drinks, put them on exes, nudging me in the ribs." Adamson opened his mouth in a vacuous grin, hoping that sharing this schoolboy wickedness would give him favour. "When he sat down he produced your signature under some form of words."

"What did it say? The precise words."

"I don't remember, to swear to. Something about affording George Orris every assistance in his inquiries."

Beamish shook his head in wonder.

"The point was," Adamson explained, "that it was deadly secret. Even the note of hand must give nothing away. You had verbally instructed him to find the leak in the Depot. He said your expression was *put a finger in the dyke*. It stuck in my mind that; I reckoned it was just the way you'd put it."

"It struck you as plausible?"

"He was so open and above board. Brazen I suppose, with the benefit of hindsight."

Adamson continued. Orris had been drinking Guinness, a shabby raincoat sort of drink, he joked, but it was a shabby raincoat sort of inquiry he was engaged on. He wanted to know who had access to the Dorothy files, who had been showing interest. Who in Ops, who in European Desk, who in Archives, so forth. Adamson had volunteered three or four names and then Orris had begun to press, taking the sections one by one. He'd made a list of possibles in a cheap, lined notebook.

Beamish was as still as blotting paper, absorbing it all.

"And me?" His voice was soft. "Did he show interest in me?"

Adamson shuffled his feet.

"Damn it man, you sold the rest of the Depot. Would you stop short at me?"

Adamson broke his sulky silence. "He asked if you'd been involved in recruiting all members of Dorothy."

"What did you tell him?"

"I said yes."

"Did it never occur to you," Beamish's voice came from an icy distance, "that that was an extremely off-beam question?"

"All the questions seemed odd . . ."

"I mean," Beamish broke in, "he put himself forward as working on my behalf. Yet he's nosing round, asking about my access. Did it never flash through what passes for your brain that these two facts are incompatible?"

Adamson had no answer to give.

"Did it never occur to you," Beamish was relentless, "to report this bizarre meeting to me?"

Adamson was reluctant to speak. In the end he looked up and Beamish's eyes held his until he felt obliged to. "He said there was to be no discussion within the Depot, not even with you, because of the danger of microphones."

"Did it never occur to you that I could have taken Orris to Joe Lyons and simply given him all the secrets he prised out of you? That the business of inquiring into defectors within the Depot is not entrusted to some thug from the wilds of Czechoslovakia? That I am not in the habit of issuing notes of authority to pry into affairs of state over glasses of ale in the grubby backstreets of Victoria?"

Beamish heard it then, faint, a band marching away towards Buckingham Palace playing some wretched tune from a Broadway show. He sighed. It was quite wrong, as if the King's soldiers owed allegiance across the ocean.

Was Orris a saloon or public bar man? He was too self-contained to be accepted in the public bar, had the air of not quite belonging on the saloon side. But no, it wasn't a question of social niceties, Beamish decided. It would depend on mood or cover.

Beamish looked first into a nearly deserted public bar and then went round to the saloon bar door of the Green Man.

It would have been much the same time of day that Orris and Adamson had been in here.

The saloon bar was more popular, the watering hole of people willing to pay an extra penny for a patch of carpet, dinky lampshades on the wall, an absence of labourers' boots. At a glance there were a dozen office-workers not yet gone home, a solitary in a blazer with a handkerchief at the cuff, two corseted old women, an unshaven man who looked vaguely familiar.

You think it's gone for ever but your body soon remembers: unease touching you with its ghost fingers. You're in the field again, a voice whispered inside Beamish. You're moving into alien territory where Orris could have friends. That man with the familiar cast to his face . . .

Beamish ordered a drink from the landlord, who had a wizard-prang moustache. Beamish detested the moustache on sight. There was a barmaid with too much of everything, too much auburn hair, too much powder, too much bosom showing, too much of a laugh.

Beamish watched the unshaven man in the mirror, working back through his past until he'd pinned down the memory. San Sebastian. Early years of the war. It had been Beamish's last foray in the field (briefly he had been seconded to Room 900, the *nom de guerre* of the people who set up the network which brought home downed Allied fliers). The unshaven Basque fisher-man who was the last link in the chain had been seen talking to a known German agent. The decision had been Beamish's. It was inconceivable this unshaven man could be the same. Beamish didn't believe in ghosts.

He drank. The eyelid was tremoring again. So much to remember.

He sat at a bar stool with a diagonal view past a toucan-lamp into the public bar. He waited, adjusting to the feel of the place. Of course Orris might be a stranger, using the place once only. But the district was perfect for a man on the run, a wide choice of cheap lodging-houses, a transient population, shabby lives that nobody questioned.

Problem: what would Orris call himself?

Beamish caught the barmaid's eye and ordered a second Guinness.

"And yourself?"

"I don't mind if I do. I'm partial to a sweet sherry."

71

"You're sweet enough as it is." Beamish could bring out the cliché as if it were new-minted.

"Get away with you." She turned her practised barmaid's smile on him while her cruel eye took in his age, his mackintosh, the pinched look of his face, the hair arranged over the bald spot on his scalp in self-defeating vanity. Beamish knew he'd been classified: middle-aged man, business trip away from his slippers and humdrum spouse, looking for adventure for the night. Safe adventure, mind.

He felt the quickening of his pulse, not because of the nearness of her flesh, but because she provided a reason for Orris to use the pub. Orris the compulsive womanizer, with his dark look, his eyes that took possession of a girl, he would be circling round this gaudy moonflower.

From the public bar there was the banging of an empty glass on the counter and a voice calling without rancour: "What about the workers, then." Beamish welcomed the break. While he sized the barmaid up he fiddled with cigarettes and matches. "Remember you're actors, you create illusions," he'd heard Little Eric drum the lesson into the new scouts. "A good actor always has a bit of theatrical business up his sleeve because if you lack business on stage you die the death." The poet-warrior had paused for effect. "In our chosen theatre you'll hear no applause: it's the theatre of survival."

"Bit quiet tonight."

"It gets livelier later on," the barmaid said. "People like their tea first and then they come out for a couple."

She fetched her glass and sipped some of the dark sherry, saying "Chin, chin," over the rim. She made small talk (Beamish calculated one sherry was worth four or five minutes) about the clothing ration, about Blackpool's chances in the Cup, about Beamish's occupation (he was a Southampton shipping agent). Her look went over Beamish's shoulder when the door opened.

"Let me guess," Beamish said. "I would hazard he was tall, dark and handsome."

"Dark and handsome? What are you on about?"

"Your boyfriend. The one you're waiting for."

"You must be joking. I don't wait."

"The clerk from my office was up in town last week. Dropped in here, Roger Adamson, do you remember him. That's really why I've called in tonight."

"Liked it here, did he?" Her eyes were restless again, bored with Beamish.

"Roger got chatting to a chap. In fact, between you, me and the bedpost, they went on and made a bit of a night of it. You know how it is, all lads together, gather ye rosebuds. The thing is this, dear." Beamish was suddenly confidential, leaning over the bar. "Come closer a minute."

He laid a hand over hers, squeezing it absent-mindedly. She raised a lavish eyebrow at this forwardness but leaned in. She brought a smell of Woolworth's cosmetics with her.

"Down the docks, you know how it is," Beamish confided, and his soft voice had slipped a long way from its usual patrician tone. "Things sometimes fall into our laps. I'll say no more. But my clerk Roger, he's a good lad really, when he was in here last week he promised this chap a bit of . . ." Beamish sucked his lips in and scratched his nose, ". . . a bit of booty. This is strictly hush-hush, you understand. Nylons."

Beamish's eyelid fluttered and he was content to let it appear he was admitting her to the seamy side of shipping. Nylon stockings were black-market stuff taking half a week's wage packet, when you could find them.

"Nylons?" She looked up through heavy eyelashes.

Beamish patted the briefcase on the stool next to him. Her glance dropped.

"I don't know what this other chap fixed up for Roger. Better not to ask, if you take my meaning. The thing is, dear, Roger was half seas over by the end and he lost the chap's address. Except he seemed quite at home in here. Got a room near by most likely. I promised I'd try and deliver the goods. You'll never believe your ears. A dozen pairs." Beamish was aware of the resonance of his voice and it sounded false. But she was absorbed.

"A dozen?" Such riches.

"Sssh." He squeezed her hand. Give her time, he decided. Let her greed grow. "Let's have the other half."

There were more customers in the public bar. Irish voices calling out for refills. Everybody seemed to be drinking Guinness that night, except the barmaid with her sweet sherry. It was some minutes before she could return, leaning forward as she set the glasses down.

Beamish was careful not to hold her hand again. But she leaned across and laid her fingers on his sleeve.

"If he's a regular here," she said carefully, "I could help you. What's his name?"

It was turning out nicely, Beamish thought. He hadn't lost his touch. It was a question of never rushing fences. Her mind was full of nylons and how she could acquire them. If she wasn't Orris's friend already, she planned to be.

"Another problem," Beamish admitted. "No name either. As I said, Roger got as pissed as . . . Oops, pardon."

She squeezed his arm and smiled; she appreciated he was really a gentleman who didn't use vulgar language.

"He's got a hazy notion it might be George Somebody-or-other. Can't be sure. Young chap. About your age." It would be George or similar, Beamish was certain, in case Adamson had called out to him.

"George? George Grey?" she suggested.

"What's he like?"

"About the right age. Works on the Tube. He's a driver."

"I don't think so," Beamish said. He fed another scrap of information. "Bit of a rolling stone, he is. That's why Roger is so concerned to get this fancy parcel to him in case he moves. Spent a lot of his life abroad, Roger remembers. And like me, he drinks Guinness."

"Not George, Geoff." There was a look in her eyes that said she knew Geoff.

Beamish grunted.

Strong he was. And tallish. And something dark about him. Brooded as if his past held a terrible secret, or someone had done

74

him wrong. His eyes—well perhaps it was different with a man, the barmaid hinted—but his eyes seemed to bore right into you. Geoff Orbach was his name.

She smiled to herself. Some recollection, some plan.

"That sounds useful," Beamish said. "I'll call round and check. If he's the right one, I'll deliver my cargo." He let his hand stroke the briefcase.

She smiled again, fiddling with the material at the plunge of her dress.

"Where's he putting up?" Beamish asked. "Did he tell you?"

Leaving the Green Man Beamish turned left into a district of mean businesses, secondhand booksellers, shop windows stuffed with drums of flex and metal tools whose functions eluded him. Other windows displayed unstylish clothes draped over spindly wire frames. A café had a faded sign: Hot Bovril prevents that sinking feeling.

Full darkness had come. The lamps showed buildings where the plaster rotted and the paintwork wept. He passed along a street of tall terraced houses, some boasting mock pillars by the door. Cards in windows advertised vacancies. Timber baulks propped up walls where a bomb had left its mark.

Too old. The palpitations in his chest told him.

On the far side of the road a man turned abruptly and disappeared up an alley. Wasn't there something familiar about the unshaven features? But then (Beamish had to be stern with himself) who in Victoria indulged in the luxury of a shave each morning?

He stopped for breath, gathering his coat more closely round him.

Too old to be in the field. He hurried on again.

The Endlicott Private Hotel would be cold comfort to a lover if Orris had brought the barmaid here. The woman who answered the bell gave him a room with reluctance, insisting on 11/6d in advance because he had no proper luggage. The name G. Orbach was in the register which Beamish signed. The landing was redolent of institutional disinfectant.

Beamish gave the woman time to settle back in her basement lair and made a silent tour of the building. One bedroom to the front had murmured Scottish voices and he ignored that. Four rooms showed no chink of light and he put them mentally in reserve. That left five other doors and he knocked at them one by one, holding a half-crown in his hand, asking for change to feed the gas meter.

Orris had a room that overlooked the bus depot, garish under sodium lighting. He stood at the door in stockinged feet while Beamish peered in, anxious lest there be another person. Orris appeared to have been sitting in the straightbacked chair which he'd pulled close to the fire. Sheets of paper lay on the floor.

Beamish felt a moment of panic as he stood in the wedge of light from the bedroom: that the spring of Orris's violence might suddenly snap. Then, catching sight of the socks, a surge of relief: one wasn't afraid of a man without shoes. Finally, the recognition of the ridiculous nature of that reassurance and he smiled at Orris.

"I was going to ask for a bob for the meter, George."

Beamish came into the room, shutting the door. He looked round at the bolthole Orris had selected. How much did one ever remember of a place like this the next day? It had a Utility chest of drawers, a tarnished mirror, a Thames-coloured rug in front of the bubbling gas fire. Above the basin in the corner was a notice forbidding the washing of clothes. A pair of socks was drying on the towel-rail. On the bed the orange cover of a Penguin paperback was a splash of life.

Beamish swung round to confront Orris and the whole of their relationship was in his words. "You're in deep water, my boy."

Orris hadn't moved from the door. He opened it, looked both ways into the dark corridor, shut it again and turned the key. He crossed to the window, peering out into the night.

"Should I have brought somebody, George?" The smile had deserted Beamish's face. "Should I have brought muscle?"

"So who betrayed me this time?" Orris rounded on him. "Or have you been doing your own dirty spying?"

"Don't use that kind of language. . . ."

Orris wouldn't let him finish. "Afraid I've got chums in the next room?"

Oh sweet lord, Beamish reproved himself, I've been away from the field a long time. I never thought to check for that. He felt the tremor in his eyelid.

Orris turned on both taps in the basin. Their conversation continued to the complaints of the plumbing.

"I have taken the trouble to hunt you down," composure had returned to Beamish's voice, "because the game of hide-and-seek has become childish. I don't particularly object to your being A.W.O.L.; nor to your buying beer for the office fool. But I will not tolerate your being free and easy with my authority, conducting witch-hunts in my name, letting my subordinates believe I am incapable of pursuing my own inquiries. Lastly, I will not tolerate your questioning my loyalty."

"Don't lecture me about loyalty." Orris moved with quick steps to Beamish. "They put Palacký up against a wall. They took Brouček away in a van. They snuffed out the whole network. They were waiting in my room in Prague. When I got to London they had two killers staking out my flat. But don't ask me who they were, don't ask who gave the orders, and keep bloody quiet about loyalty."

In Prague Orris had worn his hair swept straight back. Here he had brushed it into a parting and a lock bounced across his forehead in anger.

"Do you question my loyalty?" To his dismay, Beamish's eyelid went out of control: perhaps the other would imagine a wink as good as a nod.

"Oh, everybody's loyal," Orris snapped. "Just, somebody along the line is loyal to a different master."

"But you question *my* loyalty?" Beamish knew how absurd he must appear, his scrawny neck thrust out, burning spots on his cheeks, the eyelid convulsed in a spasm.

Orris stared at him, his old Controller, the one who'd plucked him out of a hundred thousand sodden tents the week before D-Day, the master who'd emery-papered the soldier's skills and taught the beginnings of subtlety for the secret war, the one who'd shown compassion for his foibles, praised his successes, used irony on his failures, had dined him at the Garrick before parachuting him into the midst of the enemy. Orris stared, and hesitated.

Beamish worked the silence, seeing the doubt steal into the other's eyes, choosing his time to speak again.

"For the third time: do you question my loyalty?"

"No, I . . ."

"By God, that's just as well, or I'd have had the witch-doctors look you over."

The tension suddenly eased and the room was filled with the sound of water gurgling through the pipes. It seemed like silence. They were both aware how much their voices must have been raised in anger.

Sullenness shadowed Orris's face and Beamish smiled to gain his confidence.

"At least there are two of us, two certainties. Though I may say that not everyone in the Depot shares my faith in your sterling worth."

"Who?"

"Don't bridle, George. It's natural. There is a *prima facie* case against you because you don't show your face at the Depot."

"Some bugger has put a bloody great X against my name. I'm not coming in to have arsenic slipped in my tea."

"For God's sake, George, stop indulging yourself. We can't afford anger, it's a luxury, it's against the spirit of the times. We're living in the age of austerity; morality is strictly rationed." Anger was a deadly emotion, Beamish reminded himself, almost as destructive as love. It was time to be practical. "Your notes, are they?" He nodded to the pages torn from an exercise book. "What have you found out?"

"He's not Czech-side," Orris replied. "He's one of us."

"You can't be certain."

Orris shook his head. "There were two of them waiting for me

78

in London with guns. They knew about the flat. They were expecting me, knew I was coming. As if there'd been a tip-off from Dover Immigration."

"Prague could have sent word."

Orris was emphatic with his head. "How could the Czechs have known I'd passed through Dover? They wouldn't know the name on the Depot documents I was travelling under. The killers knew the exact time; I had a bloody reception committee. Nobody in Prague—not even Woodburne—knew my London address."

Beamish stooped for the sheets of paper and held them like a poker hand while he perched on the hard chair. Orris slumped on the bed.

"Little Eric." Beamish looked up. "The frost really got into your soul."

"I'm not playing games," Orris snapped, and for a moment it seemed the anger would boil again. "I've got no favourites, no protected levels. These are all people who've shown interest in me, who've marked out the files, who had something to do with recruiting Dorothy. I fined it down to six. Funny," he finished, his voice dropping to show he found it anything but funny, "it was six who were killed."

Beamish read the case against Johns, D/Ops, who had visited Plzen when Martinu and Bronstein had been recruited, who'd shown interest in Orris's early years, who controlled the kind of killer who could scramble across a roof to point a gun at Orris, and who had spent a year in Spain during the Civil War when it was notorious that Soviet agents had been hunting for recruits among the committed.

"Hope-Tarrant," Beamish read. "You imagine Operations is a hotbed of defectors."

"They have the opportunity."

Beamish made no comment on any other name: Suzman, Falcon and Ulyett (who everyone acknowledged was the Foreign Office snoop in the Depot). The last sheet was headed Beamish.

His face betrayed nothing: no flicker of emotion, no granite set to his features. "A good indictment," he said at length, his voice soft against the music of the plumbing. "Possibly you lean too much on my Cambridge days. Youth is in a hurry to change the world. But by and large you make nothing of motive and I'm glad. There are only two motives: gold and love. As for gold, you'd receive scant help from the bankers of Zürich. As for love, in which I include political love, we never understand that. Rely on facts. The bloodhounds of Scotland Yard are right: one dropped bus ticket is worth a ton of psychological cant."

It was an odd little speech but it had its effect, soothing Orris. He made no response.

Beamish ran his fingers down the sheet of paper, stroking it. "You've had considerable access: dates of travel, leave-rosters, life-files."

"I went and had a look."

"Ah, quite so." Beamish considered the bald admission. It was unlikely Orris had an accomplice or he wouldn't have needed to question Adamson. "But George, there are possibilities you haven't considered."

"One of those names." Orris was not going to be shifted. "Who else had knowledge of Dorothy *and* knew my flat *and* knew I had returned to England?"

"You're self-centred, George. That's not a condemnation. It comes from being responsible for staying alive in the field. You occupy your skin and are pre-occupied with saving it. I'm disturbed by the larger picture. If Dorothy was betrayed from within, what is the likelihood it was an isolated instance? Very small. Won't there be other betrayals? How about Samson in Bergen last November. Tripped on the ice, the harbour police said; provisionally accepted at the time; should be reopened now. And other Desks: mischief in Tehran, K.L., Montevideo. It's bigger than you, George. Which you, in your obsession, cannot see."

"If people have been knocked off like flies, why hasn't something been done? Six people dead in Czechoslovakia. How many more do you need?"

"There's been no pattern. Your disappearance, for instance, made you favourite for betraying Dorothy."

"That's monstrous. They were out to shoot me in Earls Court."

"You hadn't seen fit to tell anyone that. You were the prime suspect. Your security clearance was nullified. I did that, George, what choice had I?"

Beamish's voice was hypnotic against the rush of water. The belligerence had finally drained out of Orris. "Well now you know." There was grumpiness there, like a schoolboy chided for carelessness.

Beamish said: "You're not the kind of man to waylay the D-G on the steps to his club and thrust your researches into his hand and mutter, 'Here, you do something about nailing the Judas.' You're a practical man, an old fox in the field. What did you intend to do?"

Beamish gestured with the sheets of paper, drawing the answer out.

Orris spoke promptly. "Show myself to the dogs and see which one hunted me down."

"And then?"

"Then I'd have killed him."

Beamish didn't react outwardly, though he was mindful his own name had been among the suspects.

"Shall we do without the plumbing for a bit? We don't want Mrs Thing to believe you're obsessive about washing your socks."

The silence was absolute. Beamish thought for some minutes.

"Let us accept that your talents lie elsewhere and that playing Sherlock is more in my line. Let me set up one or two tripwires within the Depot for anyone nosing after you. Let me at the same time search the files for traces of a wider pattern. For your part, go into the field and show yourself, draw the hounds. But I think you'd do well to get right away from London, make your man break cover."

Beamish tapped the sheets of paper square, folded them and tucked them into a pocket. He rubbed his hands together and held them out to the fire. "Don't come into the Depot to see me. Don't alarm our man. You'll need money, papers, that sort of thing. Let me arrange that and we'll meet."

"Which particular field," Orris asked, "should I run across?"

29 March 1948
Soviet Zone, Germany

Winter had swept back a few days previously. Snow suited the flat plains of northern Germany, masking the worst of the destruction. Village after village had had its heart torn out in bitter fighting and now they huddled round their broken churches, oddly beautiful, the shattered spires gaining a lightness they'd never shown before.

Orris, watching through the window, saw the lorry move across the car-park, bouncing over unseen potholes. The snow lay in muddied heaps, like new-dug graves, where soldiers had shovelled it aside. The lorry halted beside a car painted in khaki waves, futile camouflage in the snow. The driver, a Corporal, jumped down from the cab. His lips were pursed with whistling, his breath showing in a thin grey stream. He walked with his shoulders hunched towards the Naafi roadhouse.

The building was the usual prefabricated construction, low, satanic-coloured, steam on the windows like net curtains. There was most of a platoon, waiting for lost transport, tipping their chairs back, bored with Jane in the *Daily Mirror*, ignored by the two girls behind the counter. Beyond, visible through a hatch to the kitchen, a German skivvy washed dishes. The place reeked of sweat and burned fat. A notice on the wall advertised a dance with Roy Davies and his Swashbucklers. Another notice was headed: Emergency Procedure in case of War.

The Corporal stood at the counter, rubbing his hands.

"Brass monkey weather, innit."

"What would you like, dear?" The thinner of the two girls spoke without troubling to look at him.

"You know what I'd like, sweetheart."

It was a ritual, not raising a smile let alone an eyebrow. The girl waited, finding the urn more interesting than the Corporal.

"Cuppa tea and a wodge," the Corporal said. "What jam've you got?"

"Red or green, dear."

The Corporal sat at the table next to Orris, shifting a bottle of brown sauce and a tin ash-tray. He gave full attention to the bread and jam, chewing as cows do, looking nowhere. He drank tea with his mouth full, softening the bread.

"Got a light?" Orris asked him.

The Corporal fished out a box of matches.

"Want one?" Orris offered the cigarette packet.

"Cheers. You with that mob?" The Corporal gestured at the squaddies.

"No," Orris said. "On my tod. My transport packed in." He nodded in the general direction of the car-park.

"Which way are you headed, squire?"

"Berlin."

The Corporal looked him over. Orris was in civvy clothes, with an awkward army haircut. A well-travelled suitcase was by his chair. "Reckon I could fit you up. Not a bloody Kraut, are you?"

"Do me a favour."

"No offence, squire. Just checking."

After ten minutes they left. It was bitter in the cab of the lorry and Orris sat hunched in his thoughts.

Johns, Hope-Tarrant, Ulyett, Falcon, Suzman, Beamish. Six names in block capitals on sheets of paper with dates, duties, access, knowledge. One had betrayed the Dorothy Network and Orris would kill him. He'd written in blue ink, marking inconsistencies and queries with red bars in the margin. Suzman had two thick red bars: he was away at the time the gunmen had staked out Orris's flat (a week's leave in the west country, according to the contact address he'd entered in the roster); and he'd been Duty Officer in Signals during that weekend in February when Dorothy was put in the bag. If Orris sent a signal to the Depot now, it would likely pass through Suzman's hands. And then there was Beamish himself.

They bounced across the potholes, through the security gate

83

where no one bothered whether they'd pinched the teaspoons, and rejoined the Autobahn. Two minutes brought the lorry to the checkpoint with the candy-striped pole and the Union Jack bright in the grey day. The M.P. held out his hand for the papers.

"Checked your fuel, Corporal?"

"Yes, Sarge."

He transferred his attention to Orris.

"Military or civilian?"

"Military."

"May I see identification?" He checked the photo on the I.D. card against Orris's face and saluted. "Thank you, Major."

Orris caught the Corporal's sidelong glance at him: aggrieved because an officer had tricked his way into getting a lift. The pole lifted and they drove forward slowly.

"You never warned me you was an officer. Strewth, what were you doing in the Naafi?"

"It doesn't matter," Orris said.

"Are you one of the specials?" Barracks gossip had it that a lot of specials were going through.

Orris might not have heard.

There'd been a final meeting with Beamish while they tramped over Hampstead Heath, dodging kite-fliers exhilarated by the lion-like March day. In the shelter of a changing-hut by the ponds Beamish had handed over money, military papers, a wallet with engraved visiting-cards giving addresses in Hampshire and two ticket stubs to the Haymarket Theatre, a nicely-thumbed British passport, a German identity card in the name of Kellermann, and a travel warrant for R.A.F. transport from Northolt to Gatow in Berlin. Orris had accepted it all. He'd simply ignored the plane ride. There was going to be no quiet little man standing against a pillar noting his arrival in Berlin.

When Orris considered the possibilities, Beamish was still among them. Despite their talk. *You're an old fox*, Beamish had said. And Orris had told him what he intended to do: *Show myself to the dogs and see which one hunts me down.* Beamish had sat still for some time, thinking. It gave Orris the chance to think too. One thought: if there were six hounds, one had already sniffed him out, in the back room of a Victoria lodging-house. On the sheet of paper with Beamish's name there'd been no red bars in the margin. No point. Like D/Ops, Beamish's position gave him absolute knowledge and opportunity.

A white line had been painted across the tarmac. A sign read: You are leaving the British zone. The Corporal asked: "Have you crossed before?"

"No."

"We stay put at the Russian post. Only Krauts get out to have their papers stamped. We're ally-pallies, you see." There was the briefest of pauses and he added: "Sir."

The Hammer and Sickle snapped in the wind and the lorry came to a halt at the red and white barrier. The Corporal put on the handbrake and switched off.

"Now we wait. One of their bleeding games, trying to make us get out to show our papers. Started playing silly buggers at the beginning of the month."

After five minutes two soldiers walked out of the hut, adjusting assault rifles over the shoulders of their double-breasted great-coats. Their grey fur caps had red stars in the centre. As if it were something to aim at, Orris thought.

The older soldier spoke in Russian and the Corporal smiled pleasantly at him. "Sorry, Ivan. No good parley-vooing me because I don't speaka da lingo."

The second soldier said: "You are required to show your papers to the Border Regulation Officer in the hut."

"Fuck that for a lark, as Shakespeare wrote. Listen, old son, we're British Occupation Force. We stay in the lorry."

The second soldier moved his hand up to the strap of his rifle.

"The Border Regulation Officer does not come outside in the winter weather."

"Bully for him. Me neither."

The Corporal opened the locker and produced a series of documents, handing them through the window. "Personal identification. Driving licence. Vehicle registration. Military Transit Authorization. *Kommandatura* registration. Cargo manifest. That's your lot."

85

The Lieutenant came from the hut. He wore the same great-coat but with gold buttons and gold shoulderboards with blue piping. Numbers, times, dates and descriptions were entered in a beige book.

"What are you carrying?"

"Dutch caps for the nurses."

"You will open the back of the truck."

"No, squire."

"Your refusal is in violation of Soviet Military Regulations and will be noted."

"Suit yourself."

The Lieutenant moved to Orris's window. He stood very close, his hand raised. Orris noticed the curious arm badge: a sword with a floral decoration. "Your papers."

Orris stared through the windscreen while his identification was scrutinized.

"Your photograph looks different. You will get into full light so that we can verify you."

"You'd think they owned the fucking country," the Corporal said. "Pardon my French."

Orris said nothing.

"Why are you not in uniform?"

"It's in my bag."

"We do not believe you are a member of the British Military Force. There are stories of thugs and pirates with stolen documents."

The Corporal got suddenly very angry. "Listen, you peasant. He is an officer in the British army. A bloody Major too, superior to you. Show a bit of respect."

Orris felt the sweat start under his shirt. A border incident was the last thing he wanted.

A Soviet scout car came down the Autobahn from the east, turning round by the border hut. It waited, its engine idling: Orris could see the blue-grey haze from its exhaust. Two soldiers sat in front, one with a Shpagin submachine-gun across his knees.

"Very good. You are authorized to proceed to Berlin. You may not leave the Autobahn. You may not stop on the route except in case of emergency. You will obey the legitimate instructions of the Soviet Military Police. You will not pick up any German civilian. You will make no attempt to communicate with the civil population. You will take no photographs. Is this understood?"

The Corporal started the engine. "We are legitimately proceeding to Berlin in accordance with our rights of occupation." It was a phrase he had committed to memory.

The lorry moved off. There was silence in the cab until they'd passed the desolate village of Marienborn. The Autobahn ran beside the railway track where wagons stood rusting in a siding.

"They're following, sir. The scout car."

Orris had noticed. An ugly little doubt had set itself up in his mind: Suppose the new cover was blown? Suppose the scout car was following for a purpose?

"They do that sometimes," the Corporal added. "Sniff down your exhaust, try to make you piss your pants."

They drove without speaking through a dull uniformity of pine trees, the land featureless, the only relief where old shell craters exposed the light soil. Silence was a void to be filled. The Corporal hummed, against the competition of the engine, "Roll me over in the clover."

A man, a woman, two boys and a dog walked along the side of the road heading west, carrying bundles.

"They'll turn north before Marienborn, cut across country and try to cross the border at night."

"Do they catch many?" Orris asked.

"They'll nab them if they don't get off the road by Marienborn. If the man's got a skilled trade, they'll stop them. Otherwise, four less stomachs to fill."

The Corporal hummed a bit. They passed more trudging figures.

"Bloody Krauts," the Corporal said. "Your first time over here, guv'nor? They don't give us much trouble, not considering. We're pretty safe because we're the conquerors, see. They understand that. If a Kraut does something naughty we'll trample all over him and the Krauts don't like that. They been used to trampling over other people and they don't like taking it. I wouldn't say

Herr Kraut loves us but he knows better than to get into a barney. Otherwise he wakes up in the morning behind wire with boot-marks all over him and no front teeth in his fag-hole."

They passed a field where women bent, turning over frozen clods, searching for potatoes.

"Course, you get a bit of bother with thievery. Keep your eyes open, my advice. If a Kraut can eat it, smoke it or shag it, he will." He hummed a bit and added: "Another thing. I can't stand smoking in the street. Krauts stare like you're burning money."

That seemed to exhaust the Corporal's wisdom about Germany. They drove in silence. Towards Magdeburg the pines gave way to arable land, winter bare, ridges of ploughed earth poking up through the white mantle.

The Corporal was humming again.

They crossed the River Elbe over a wooden U.S. Army bridge. Soviet Military Police controlled the sparse traffic and the Corporal showed their papers again. The Russian officer looked down a sheet of paper, ticking names off.

"We're famous, see. They'll know all about you at Karlshorst. Know anything about the set-up?"

"No."

"Well, Karlshorst's the Soviet headquarters. Right bloody fun palace. Posted to Berlin long?"

"Depends."

The Corporal glanced at him. Orris didn't elaborate. Bloody queer officer, the Corporal decided. All the specials were odd bods.

"I'll tell you, guv'nor. In Berlin everything's in short supply, but there's one commodity that's completely vanished: elastic to keep the girls' knickers up." Orris made no response and the Corporal sang under his breath: ". . . me over, lay me down and do it again."

Coming in past Lehnin the traffic thickened, mostly buses and military transport. Orris had counted a dozen cars in thirty minutes. They crossed an unnamed river, passed through a desolation of wartime fighting, the Autobahn dividing at a sign that read: Potsdam 13 km, Berlin 21 km.

"Welcome to Berlin," the Corporal said. "Biggest bloody building site in Europe."

Beyond a cluster of Soviet soldiers and a T34 tank, Orris saw the tall finger of the Siegessäule in the distance. Some victory.

"Drop me here."

"You said you were going to Gatow."

"I've just changed your orders, Corporal."

"Sir."

Orris stood at the broken kerb in Charlottenburg while the lorry disappeared towards the Olympic stadium. He looked, very slowly, all round him.

At the end, Hitler had willed the destruction of Berlin. The German people had failed him and the vanquished deserve no quarter.

Nothing had prepared Orris for the scale of devastation. He stood numbed at the edge of the road. There was a taste in his mouth, of damp mortar and fire and secret decay, the taste of the fallen city.

PART THREE

First I'm going to skin this bear, then shoot it.

Marshal Vassily Sokolovsky
Soviet Military Governor, Germany

31 March 1948
Berlin/Washington

Telecon reference TT-9286
Classification: Top Secret—Eyes Only
Present Berlin: Gen Clay, Commander in Chief, Europe
Present Washington: Secretary of the Army Royall
Gen Omar Bradley, Chief of Staff
Gen Lawton Collins
Lt Gen Wedemeyer, Director Army
Plans and Ops

ROYALL: Please give us the Russian note verbatim.

CLAY: Dear General Hays, I hasten to bring to your attention certain supplementary provisions with respect to the régime governing the lines of demarcation and communication between the Soviet and U.S. zones of occupation in Germany which will be put into effect from 1 April 1948 . . .

(As wars have become more terrifying, military leaders have gone to earth: Churchill to the War Room, Hitler to his bunker, Clay to the telecon room. This bleak room was in the basement of the U.S. military headquarters in Kronprinzenallee, and if no one had actually declared war yet, the pessimists pointed out it was an oversight that could soon be corrected. While the teletype operator continued the transmission, Clay walked to the door with neat steps, followed with smaller but equally neat steps by his scotch terrier. "What is it, Les?" Major Les Garn of his political staff was one of those military men who speak as if standing to attention: face, eyes and hands quite still. "Trouble with the spooks, sir." "Big trouble with the spooks,"Clay asked, "or do they just want their hand holding again?" "Trouble with the chief spook in London, sir. Big enough to have brought Wrea panting up to your office." Clay sighed: like everyone in Berlin,

93

he was ill at ease in the shadow of the C.I.A. "Give him coffee. I've got my own load of trouble with Washington right now. One crisis at a time. I'll come up when this is finished." Clay returned to the worktable. The letter from the Soviet C.I.C. was lengthy and Clay smoked a cigarette down while the transmission was completed. The demands were for all employees of the U.S. Military Administration crossing the Soviet zone en route for Berlin to produce papers; for freight to have a permit from the Soviet Commandant; for all personal belongings to be searched.)

... You are requested, dear General, to bring all of the aforesaid to the attention of the appropriate organizations and institutions of the U.S. Military Administration, and of other agencies in your zone so that persons entering or leaving the Soviet zone of occupation may be duly informed with regard to procedure applicable when crossing the line of demarcation. Respectfully, Dratvin.

ROYALL: What does that mean—that the British will not permit a search? Will they resist by shooting? Will they run trains?

CLAY: The British reply means at the moment that they will run trains. I think their decision relative to shooting depends almost entirely on our own. I doubt if they will shoot although Robertson has agreed to do as we do.

ROYALL: How many trains do you run daily, freight and personnel? How many trucks per day? How many C47s needed to supply you?

CLAY: We run one passenger-train daily each way between Frankfurt and Berlin. We also run several freight-trains per week for our own supply. However we have thirty-two paths daily for Western powers to meet our own needs and to supply Germans in Berlin. We have one daily scheduled air round-trip augmented as needed. We run few trucks and those not on regular schedule. We could supply ourselves and meet passenger needs by airlift for a while but not the Germans in the city. Moreover this action would be most damaging to our prestige and would be met by new acts. I believe this is a

94

bluff but do not wish to bluff back as the British may be doing unless we mean it. Urge I be permitted to proceed on my judgement.

(The teletype machine said "Wait" and Clay recognized what was coming. When Washington vacillated, you could feel the weakness half way round the world.)

ROYALL: Realizing that any incident involving shooting or other heavy violence might precipitate war, some consideration has been given here to the President sending an immediate note to Stalin informing him that the requirements of the Soviet Berlin commander are a violation of the existing agreements and stating that traffic will continue to move pending discussions as to any proper regulations. In that event traffic would start moving in the usual manner after twenty-four hours, even if no reply has been received from Stalin. What do you think of that procedure? Another suggestion is that trains move but in no event will there be shooting. What do you think of this?

CLAY: Any weakness on our part will lose us prestige which is important now. If the Soviets mean war, we will only defer the next provocation for a few days. For that reason I do not think that either suggestion is realistic. I do not believe this means war but any failure to meet this squarely will cause great trouble. I realize our train resistance would be token. I am convinced it is the only course of action.

ROYALL: But if you had to choose between those courses, which would you prefer?

CLAY: I would prefer to evacuate Berlin and I had rather go to Siberia than do that. . . .

On the desk was a wooden plaque with four gold stars and the inscription: General Lucius D. Clay. As if anybody ever forgot.

Some generals, like Washington, have seized power. Others, like Eisenhower, have been elected. General Clay had political power forced on him by virtue of being CINCEUR. The work was overwhelming: the German economy was shattered; the population sullen; food pitifully inadequate, and with the food shortage came a general lassitude; the problems of de-nazification were immense, for it wasn't merely a question of punishing the guilty but of finding untainted men to resurrect the country from the ashes.

Above all, Clay was faced with the problem of the erstwhile ally, the Soviet Union. Entire factories had been shipped east; and still Russia demanded reparations out of current production. The U.S. Commandant in Berlin, Colonel Howley, said Germany was like a cow: the West fed the cow at one end, the Soviet Union milked it at the other. Down the long headquarters corridors the wags called him Howlin' Mad.

And now Berlin had become hot.

In Washington, London and Paris the politicians had no plans. The crisis was literally unthinkable. Let the men on the spot sort it out and kick them if they got it wrong.

"We are going to run trains," Clay said. It was an affirmation of faith, as if by repeating it he could impose his will first on his colleagues in the room and thereafter on the scheming Soviets. "We have to run trains. Has anybody dreamed up any alternative to running trains?"

Four men faced Clay: the wooden-featured Garn and Chuck Lucas of the political mafia, Philippides from Military Intelligence, and Dan Wrea from the C.I.A. Wrea looked anything but a spook. He sat bulky and still, only his eyes flicking from face to face.

"Well, we have limited spare capacity in barges," Lucas said.

"Chuck, it would take the Soviets five minutes to pull the plug in the canals," Major Garn said. "We're left high and dry."

Lucas shook his head. Earnest little glasses caught the light and flashed with a passion that was totally lacking in the man. "I doubt they'd do that. They need the canals to haul freight just as much as we do."

"So they simply refuse us permission to navigate."

"They can't do that. We have a right of access to Berlin."

"Chuck, they can do it. We have a right of access by rail but they just halted our trains. They're out to control our lifeline. If we're not good boys, they'll cut it. Give it a month and you'll find yourself on your knees each night saying a dozen Hail Marxes. Don't be naive."

"Enough, gentlemen." Clay finished the argument. There were spots of colour in Lucas's cheeks. "We are going to run trains. There is no question of going to Dratvin for permits. Nor will I permit any searches of our trains." Clay glanced at the wall where twin clocks showed Washington and Central European time. It was 22.35 in Germany, eighty-five minutes to the Soviet deadline. "What paths do we have overnight?"

Lucas, the one who could always be relied on for small things, told him: "One military train, two food and general freight-trains."

"Les, orders from the Military Governor." Garn was poised with a pen over his pad. All four men waited, hardly breathing. This was the first act and none was sure how it would end: the trains halted by force, shooting by the Red Army, war. It was Clay who drew breath and dictated: "To the commandants of those trains by name—check that out. Also standing orders to all in transport command. Message commences: Proceed through the Soviet zone as per previously agreed regulations. Allow no repeat no Soviet inspection of trains, no repeat no inspection of freight, and no repeat no querying of U.S. military or civil personnel. Signed, etc. Make sure it gets to those three train commandants before they reach the wire."

Garn got up to leave the office. He stood by the open door, with the sound of a typewriter and voices coming down the corridor.

"And if the Soviets won't budge, sir?" Garn asked. "Are you sanctioning force?"

General Clay smoothed the edges of the stack of files on the desk. Again the four men waited.

"Gentlemen, we have a long night in front of us; a long day tomorrow; nothing but long nights and long days. At this moment we are not going to settle what happens if things go wrong." Clay was not a theatrical man but he swivelled in his chair to point at the Stars and Stripes that stood on a pedestal behind him. "This flag was brought here by right of the American armed forces defeating the armed forces of the Third Reich. We are not going to be muscled out. We have an absolute right to run those trains and I am not having that queried. Once we shoot, the outside world forgets we had a legal right and sees only we're trying to do something by force. Now get that order out to the trains."

Clay laid his pack of Chesterfield on the desk next to his lighter. He fiddled with the glass ash-tray and pens, rearranging them all in a straight line. To Lucas, it looked like a child's representation of a train; to Dan Wrea, the spook, it was the nervous tic of a worried and exhausted man.

"Okay, Alex." Clay looked up at the military intelligence man.

Philippides was an orator who gestured constantly with both hands as if conducting a conversation with the deaf. With his movements came wafting a smell of after-shave.

"I have had two meetings today with the French. *Plus ça change, plus c'est la même chose.* That's how it goes with them. There is no consistent French policy. It depends who you talk to, what the political jockeying in Paris dictates, who is pushing for position in the Quai d'Orsay. General Ganeval is simply evading the need to make any decisions: he says the Russians would never do such a cruel thing as blockade Berlin. He spreads his hands," Philippides aped the movement, "and exclaims, 'Only a monster would contemplate starving two million people.' In short the French cannot be relied on."

Clay nodded. The French wanted Germany dismembered so there would never again be any danger of war. "The British?"

"A similar story. They can't agree what to do. Some of the British Cabinet want to send a tank force down the Autobahn and then run in goods by truck."

"Gentlemen, tip your hats to a smart idea; a couple of hundred British tanks ploughing up the Autobahn so nothing else can get through."

Nobody pursued the idea. Clay tapped a cigarette out of the

packet and lit it. He gazed through the cloud of smoke as Garn returned to the office. "Those instructions go out?"

"Yes sir."

"Alex has been telling us the British are getting belligerent."

"Correct," Garn agreed. "Churchill wants to drop atom bombs on Leningrad and Moscow."

A voice from the end of the table said: "Churchill is not Prime Minister." It was the first time Wrea had spoken and they shifted in their chairs to look at the C.I.A. man.

"I apologize for not coming to you sooner," Clay said. "As you see, we're in a situation where everything has to be done at the same time, and preferably yesterday."

"I understand, General."

Wrea was a big man, an ex-Marines officer who'd fought and lost in the Pacific, and then fought and won. By the end of the war he'd transferred to the O.S.S., and skipped into the C.I.A. when Truman set that up in 1947. He said bluntly: "The British won't fight."

"Mr Wrea, what do you know and how do you know it?"

Wrea angled his face towards the General. At Okinawa a piece of shrapnel had taken a diagonal path across his left cheek; to Germans of a certain caste, it resembled a duelling scar. It caught the light, gleaming white against a fine net of red veins.

"Our Station Chief in London is a guy who goes by the name of Kordorf," Wrea said. "Kordorf is nobody's fool and he doesn't panic easy. He filed a report to headquarters after a meeting with a top British Intelligence man. The Englishman was putting the facts of life to our man about the Allied posture in Berlin. In short, if Stalin has decided to blockade the city we have two choices: go to war or get out. And the British are too weak to fight."

There was general consternation but Garn was the first to break out. "Jesus wept," blowing his lungs at the ceiling. "Just like the English to run scared. Ran out of India, ran out of Greece, running out of Palestine. Now it's turn-tail time in Berlin."

"Limey, slimey, I wouldn't throw two-bits to them." Philippides kept dark angry eyes on Wrea.

"'I have been in touch with Robertson all day," Clay objected. "Nothing is further from his mood than cutting and running."

"With the greatest respect, General, the decision will be made in London. Philippides, how many divisions do the British have in Germany?"

"Three."

"And the Russians?"

"That's beside the point," Philippides objected. "They've always needed a high garrison because . . ."

"Chickenpiss. The Soviets have always needed a high garrison," Wrea rode in over him. "Twenty divisions. So why are they bringing in new troops? How many are stationed here now? Thirty divisions? Forty? What's the latest military estimate?"

Philippides made a dismissive gesture. It was Lucas who supplied the number: "Thirty-eight divisions, counting border troops." Lucas had never liked the smell of Philippides's aftershave.

"The Agency doesn't advise the military how to fight its battles," Wrea said. "But if we hear your allies are going to steal away in the night, we'll sure as hell tell you."

"Mr Wrea," Clay tapped his forefinger on the desk. "I do not believe the advice about withdrawing from Berlin has been accepted by the British government. I don't even believe it's been given. If it had we would see evidence here: Robertson would tell me, we'd see British dependents going home, there'd be all sorts of rumours. Gentlemen, it's now five minutes to midnight." He broke off for a moment, as if the phrase had unpleasant undertones. "Let's come to all our problems fresh in the morning."

1 April 1948
Berlin

Cable reference CC3681
Classification: Top Secret
From Gen Clay to Gen Omar Bradley, Chief of Staff

Three of our trains entered Soviet zone at midnight. One train commandant now under investigation apparently lost his nerve and permitted Soviet representative to board train, and this train passed through Soviet zone. Remaining two trains were stopped and Soviet representatives insisted on boarding trains. They were denied access and did not attempt to force access. However the trains could not have proceeded forward except by use of force, and with traffic control in Soviet hands could not have proceeded very far even with force. Two British trains have entered Soviet zone stocked with rations for several days. These trains were likewise stopped and Soviet representatives refused entry. Our two trains have been backed out of the Soviet zone.

For the present we have cancelled military trains and have laid on airlift which I believe will meet our needs for some days.

2 April 1948
Berlin

What the Lancasters and Super Forts had begun, what Joe Stalin tanks and howitzers had continued, the Berliners themselves had finished. In the winter of 1947, bitter beyond memory, they had sawn down the last of the grand old trees in the Tiergarten and chopped them for firewood. They had even prised up the roots. It was a question of survival.

"Each family has ten kilos of coal a month. Can you imagine that, old boy?" And Munden turned to look in Orris's face. "Scarcely enough to boil a kettle. I mean to say."

God, another one, Orris groaned. The war had been fought and won to make a world fit for the old-boy brigade to live in. Let them sing the Red Flag in the House of Commons: the old boys had picked themselves up and dusted down their blazers and were doing very nicely thank you. *You sound such a red-hot bolshie*, Valerie had spat out, *why don't you join them instead of spying on them?*

"When did you arrive exactly, old boy?"

They walked side by side and Munden turned his head at every question, as if Orris's face would betray a secret.

"A few days ago."

"Ah yes." Munden adjusted his hat. The snow of winter had given way to a cold drizzle that laid claim to their faces. "Knew you were coming, of course. Got a consignment note from the Depot. Must admit, I thought you'd be checking in with me straightaway."

"I had things to do." Unbelievably, the man was even worse than Woodburne, Orris decided. How could the Depot choose such a fool as Resident? "I wanted to find a shake-down, have a look round."

"Quite. Where are you staying, as a matter of fact?"

"In the city." Orris stooped to pick up a pebble and toss it away. He glanced back, smelling his own sweat. He'd told Woodburne about the Prague bolthole and look what had happened: a face behind the curtain. There was nobody following. In front a skinny nag pulled a cart with a few sticks of furniture. An occupation car passed, cruising slowly. Friend of Munden's?

"What? Oh quite. I could have helped you with a billet, but not to worry." Munden wore brown leather gloves and he took one off to tug at an earlobe.

They turned down a muddy path in silence, past a dispiriting muddle of barbed wire. The path led to a narrow piece of water, the arm of some once-ornamental lake. There'd been a proud little bridge, reduced now to jagged stones and humps of rubble. They crossed in single file and as Orris stepped on to the path Munden asked: "And what is your impression of Berlin?"

"Disgusting."

"What?" Munden stopped short at the violence in Orris's voice.

"They're rats running over a garbage tip, nosing round for rotting scraps. Pointy faces and shifty eyes. They were cock-of-the-walk when the Nazis were on top, strutting round Europe, puffed up by the screams of a madman with a cowlick and a jutting arse. They were the blond heroes and we were the scum, the degenerates, the mongrels. The Gestapo had me for two days and a night in Czechoslovakia and do you know what they called me?"

Munden stood, mouth slack, eyes round as a whiting's, appalled at the torrent of venom.

"They called me 'Slav shit'. 'What were you doing, Slav shit? Why were you in the café on that evening? Speak, Slav shit.' There was one with a fat neck, Porten, I've got his name filed away, come the day. 'Do you smoke, Slav shit? Here, try one of our good German cigarettes. Look, there's smoke coming out of the Slav shit's arse.' Rolls of fat on his neck, bulging cheeks, his eyes swallowed in the blubber when he giggled. Let me run into Porten now, ten minutes with him alone, I wouldn't need two days and a night. Is he still fat or is he a skinny rat like the rest of them? God, we hammered them into the ground and now they scuttle from one dungheap to another."

"Old boy," Munden plucked at Orris's sleeve, "you mustn't let personal feelings get the better of you. We're professionals, we've got a job to do. Who knows, if the boot had been on the other foot . . ."

"Personal feelings," Orris shouted. He was filled to bursting with corrosive emotions: hate for the enemies of wartime, hate for the enemies of peace, hate for the wife who'd left him, hate for the betrayer of the Dorothy Network, hate for the conquering Russians. Sometimes, hate for himself.

The tirade finished and Orris was silent. He'd let all the pus drain out and was empty inside. He strode away, Munden hurrying to catch up.

"Old boy, I know how you feel but the war's over now, no Jerries left to fight. You shouldn't kick a chap when he's down. And Berlin was always different. Hitler never trusted the Berliners. They were to much of a mixed bunch, too tough, too—what's the word—cocky."

"*Schnoddrigkeit.*"

"Bit of a mouthful, that. Truth to tell, my German is a mite creaky."

"*Schnauze mit Herz.*"

"Bang on, old boy. They've got heart. That's why I'm sure you'll get on famously." Munden was puffing, a ridiculous figure in a blue raincoat skipping over muddy puddles to keep up. "You speak the language passing well."

"I don't have the Berliner accent."

"It doesn't matter. The city is stuffed with refugees. You'll pass."

Orris stopped and wheeled on him. "What are you suggesting?"

Munden's chest was heaving. He said: "Best if you settled in here. Went native, so to speak. Find somewhere to live, register for rationing. Help you with papers, of course."

"Did you come alone?" Orris asked.

"Naturally, old boy."

"Didn't bring any muscle?"

"All on my own-io." Munden turned to where Orris was staring. "I can't see anybody."

Somebody, Orris was half-convinced of it. On the Charlottenburger Chaussee, one of the broken lamp-posts had shown a shadow, though there was no sun. Now there was nothing.

Restless, Orris set off again towards the Brandenburg Gate. Ahead was a sign: *Sie verlassen nach 120m das Britische Sektor.* They turned north where crows haunted the gutted ruins of the Reichstag, its fire-streaked walls softened by the drizzle. The building was a grey backcloth to the buzz of the black market. It was as if some giant foot had kicked over their nest: women with prams concealing God knows what under the baby, pale youngsters with dodgy faces and city eyes, men with lumpy coats, handcarts with a dozen beetroot or a treasured piece of Dresden porcelain, veterans on crutches holding out medals. A gaunt figure headed towards them with the limp of an old grey squirrel, thrusting out a hand with two razor blades.

"This is what London wants?" Orris asked. He peered at the faces, edgy. "I'm to burrow into the woodwork?"

"Couldn't have put it neater myself."

"It's a directive? Who from?"

"Eurcon. Who else?"

It was Beamish who'd pointed the way. Berlin, he'd said, run across that field, show yourself to the hounds, I'll watch the leave register, warn the immigration officials. The notion of settling in was a new development.

"Did he spell out the reasons?"

"Hardly necessary, old boy. I mean everyone knows the Russians are coming. With the Red Army poncing all over the Soviet zone, it's as clear as the nose on your face they've got plans for Berlin. Come to think of it, Eurcon did use some such phrase as 'precautionary move in view of anticipated political developments'. You know his half-crown way of putting things. Meant he'd sleep easier knowing we had someone settled in when the time came to haul down the Union Jack and go home."

Orris had turned away from the milling crowd because there were too many unexplained gestures. They were cutting across the Platz der Republik when a car with B.Z. plates passed and drew up by the sentry post. The two soldiers saluted and one of them leaned down to speak through the car window. The car turned round and came slowly back past Orris and Munden.

"You look a bit windy, old boy."

"This directive that I go native and wait for the Russians to march in: it's not your bright idea, it's definitely from the Depot?"

"Extraordinary question. Why do you ask?"

Because I was in Prague when the communists took over, Orris answered to himself, when Dorothy was rolled up. He said nothing, remembering the shadow behind the net curtain and the dark van, like a hearse, that had carried Brouček away.

"Of course, we'd get you out if things became too sticky. Trade you if necessary. The Depot's always got a couple of Russians in the bank, cash them in if it's an emergency."

Stupid tub of lard, it's no bloody good being traded if you're a corpse. . . . The half-thought died. Something made Orris turn his head. Surely there'd been a movement. He sensed that beyond the old woman with the pram and the prodding stick there had been someone else, a man wearing a beret. He couldn't have imagined a detail like a beret.

Orris started walking quickly back through the Tiergarten. He tripped once, his eyes not on the rough ground but watchful for a figure in a beret.

"I say, old boy, hang on a tick. There's a lot we haven't settled. Papers, cover, safety procedures. For God's sake, how do we make contact?"

Munden stumbled a few steps and gave up.

3 April 1948
London

"Spring is a vulgar affair."

There was a row of scowling faces, done in stone, on the façade in Queen Anne's Gate. Scouts from the Treasury, Little Eric had called them. You came in past them, past Tombs or Alderton, up the curved staircase, up the straight stairs, passing through to the adjoining building with its plebs' entrance from Broadway. Still you climbed to one of the attic floors where three rooms had been knocked into one. The Director-General had a view back across Queen Anne's Gate to St James's Park. It was another world. Austerity Britain was a glimpse of paradise when put against the wilds of Berlin.

The Director-General stood at the window, staring out. "Everywhere you look, yellow yellow yellow. There's nothing subtle about daffodils. You were in Paris yesterday." He dropped the remark in the same tone.

"Paris in the spring," Beamish replied. "All tender green and shades of grey and pale blue sky. Nothing gaudy."

"Can't stand the place myself. My father packed me off for leave there before my first posting. Nothing but young girls being dined by fat old men, and songs about dead leaves and dead love. Can't stomach the French at all. If the Resistance had so many heroes, why did the Germans prize a French posting as a rest-cure?"

The Director-General continued to stare out. It was a recent habit, Beamish reflected, talking while he looked at the park, turning his back on the Depot and its problems, counting the months until his retirement, waiting for his 'K'. Sir John and Lady Standing would move to Gloucestershire, the garden would be filled with Roseraie de l'Hay and Rosa Mundi, and they would dispense madeira before lunch on Sundays.

"The Germans have made something of a habit of going to France in recent history," Beamish said. "It explains, if not pardons, the French attitude."

"Whom did you see?" Standing finally left the window for the solidity of his desk.

"One or two people." Beamish was vague. "I had lunch with Jarrière from the Quai d'Orsay. They're full of foreboding about a united Germany."

"And Berlin?"

"Ah Berlin. He was anxious to know our feelings about Berlin."

"Which are?"

"Berlin could not survive a blockade."

"Look here," Standing said, "you are putting forward your personal opinion about Berlin as if it were the agreed policy of H.M.G."

"With respect, Director-General, it is scarcely a personal opinion. I thought it was common ground within the Depot, even if not formalized into policy. Certainly it is my judgement as

Controller, Europe. I have the concurrence of Dayton and Houghton."

The dark gun-barrel eyes bored at Beamish. "You don't speak for the Cabinet."

"If they are vacillating, let us give them our advice. It is what we are paid for."

"I've had Strang on the phone this morning." He took a cigarette from the silver box, the reflex action of a man trying to mask an unhappy memory. "The Foreign Office view is that there is too much defeatist sentiment about Berlin."

"I find it sad," Beamish replied, "that facing facts should be termed 'defeatist'. An emotional word."

"You've read this morning's paper?" There was, for Standing, only one newspaper.

"We don't write *The Times*'s leaders."

"Nevertheless, I smell suspicion of us in Whitehall, ever since Czechoslovakia."

Beamish made no response.

"Talking of which, that's another black area: what progress about the Dorothy Network?"

"I'm following certain leads." Beamish was at his most bland.

"What about Orris? Why have you sent him to Berlin?"

Not for the first time Beamish was surprised at the Director-General's knowledge. Somebody went to the well for him.

"I was not convinced of Orris's complicity," Beamish explained. "I've put him into a situation of maximum opportunity. If he is tempted, we shall know at once."

"If it's not Orris, then who?"

"Orris is not ruled out," Beamish insisted. "He is one of half a dozen possibles. Seven if you include me. Eight if you include yourself."

"Well I'm damned." Standing stubbed out his cigarette with some vigour. The eyes sighted on Beamish. They were fearsome eyes, Beamish decided, because there was so little white to them. They didn't seem part of the face; they were just holes leaking suspicion or anger.

"In logic, you have to be included, D-G." Beamish was earnest about it. "You do see. You have access to files, top-line security clearance, you even made a visit to Prague just before the war."

"If you know that, you'll know I went on government business." Standing sat as straight as the Colonel on his charger reviewing the troops. "Besides, that was nine years ago, long before anyone dreamed Czechoslovakia would go communist."

"A delay-fuse."

"Well I'm damned." The colour darkened in Standing's cheeks like a tropical sunset, pink and mauve with the shadows of his eyes threatening at the edge.

"I'm not being personal. I'm saying that in logic a case could be constructed that you might have betrayed Dorothy. How certain are you of all your contacts?"

"Beamish, I find this grotesque. Are you attempting to interrogate me?"

"Director-General, I'm sure you would not like to be thought of as evading questions." Beamish paused and Standing's colour deepened. "If we were to look in your engagements diary," he suggested, "wouldn't there be a hesitation about one or two names?"

"Well I'm damned. I think you're serious." Beamish made no disclaimer and Standing felt acutely uncomfortable. He was unable to see how the mild rebuke he had intended for Beamish's pessimism over Berlin had been translated into scrutiny of his own behaviour. With Beamish's long face, so critical and compelling, over him, he turned back the page of his diary. "I had lunch on Friday with Grey: he was my successor in the regiment, invalided out in '42, spent the rest of the war in India, where he still has his home; he could scarcely have betrayed our Czech network. Then Murchison, a chance encounter, at school together, turned divorce lawyer, God help him; bedroom keyholes are the limit of his spying. Houghton I took to my club to pick his brains about Iran. Burgess, from the embassy in Washington, about relations with the C.I.A. And finally Monday, Hunt from the Foreign Office." He snapped the diary shut.

"There you are," Beamish said. "Hunt. A conduit to Moscow."

"But damn it, Hunt is known for what he is. We tolerate him because we use him."

"Perfect cover. A minor agent, whom we use for our own ends, secretly somebody very high up. Your control." At length Beamish smiled. "Please, it's not an indictment. Hunt is a pawn and no one is pointing a finger at you. I was just demonstrating that no one is straightforward. Scrutinize any one of us and there'll always be a doubt."

"I think," Standing said, "I need a drink before I go to lunch." Standing poured madeira for them both. "If it had been any other newspaper, we could shrug it off. *The Times* we must take seriously." He turned the paper round to scan the leader. " 'Talk of an airbridge is picturesque.' De-dah de-dah. 'It would be foolish to suppose that, if the worst came to the worst, the allied community and forces there could be maintained by this means alone.' "

"Have they forgotten the civilians?" Beamish asked. "It's what I told Jarrière yesterday. West Berlin uses seven or eight thousand tons of coal a week. How can you fly coal in? And food? And raw materials for industry, or does Berlin simply stop work? I would say the notion of an airlift was *extremely* picturesque."

It was precisely the word Beamish had chosen to use when he ran into Martin Donaghue, leader writer on *The Times*, at the Wig and Pen Club.

5 April 1948
Berlin

First there was the smell.

Smell is the most subtle of the senses, reaching right into the brain to warn of the danger of fire even during sleep. In this case Orris was awake and there was no fire. Instead he was puzzled why the faint smell had been familiar and why it triggered alarm bells. He didn't turn to look, not yet.

A smell, different from the dirt and decay and sweat of the carriage with its chipped red paint.

The train started with a jerk and Orris reached a hand out to the rail for support. The platform was blurring as he caught sight of the blue and white sign: Rehberge. He couldn't remember the next station nor how many there were before the U-bahn crossed into the Soviet sector. Three or four stops, he thought. He couldn't look round at the U-bahn map by the door because the man was standing there.

He'd got on the stop before Rehberge. Orris had noticed him pick his way between piles of sand and stone on the platform to get in the double doors at the centre of the carriage. He was a little shorter than Orris but thick-set. He wore a long grey coat and a grey felt hat. Not a beret. It wasn't that which tripped the wire in Orris's memory.

"Seestrasse."

The train halted at the next station and the platform guard announced the name in a flat voice. Two women got off. A middle-aged man and woman got on. It was after nine in the evening and some fifteen people were in the carriage. Sixteen if you counted the man in the grey coat and hat.

The train started.

The stations were close together in the centre of Berlin, only five or six hundred metres apart. Orris altered his position so he could ram a foot against a seat if he needed to gain impetus. He could see the man now, reflected in a window. There was nothing in the man's face, half shrouded by his hat, just a prominent cheekbone catching the light, a cigarette in the corner of his mouth. He'd come closer, two quick strides if he wanted to move, or if Orris wanted to. If, if.

"Leopoldplatz."

A woman's voice this time. They needed to announce the stations. Only one light in three on the platforms worked. A young woman got off and the train started for the next station.

Orris's thoughts turned back to the man just past his left shoulder. Something was wrong about him, a detail.

"Wedding."

The guard's voice was dead, the vaulted ceiling swallowing all expression.

The man in the long grey coat and grey hat coughed, a dry smoker's cough, and in that instant Orris got it, made the connection, remembered the smell of Russian tobacco.

As the train moved off Orris caught the man's gaze in the dark of the window. There are times when the eyes say everything in a second: love, hate, pity, death. Orris knew, and knew the other man knew: he was an enemy, here at this time and place for one purpose. The knowledge was a stone in the pit of Orris's stomach.

The train swayed as it moved through the tunnel. The next station was the last before the train crossed the line into the Soviet sector. In common with most of the passengers, it was where Orris wanted to get off. He felt the panic of a trapped animal as the other man turned his body square on. The way to the doors was going to be blocked; that squat powerful body would be immovable in the thirty seconds the doors were open; his chance, such as it was, was now.

A man and a woman pushed past, getting ready to leave.

"Just a minute: what time is it?"

Orris spoke loud enough to stop the two. The man half-turned. Like so many Berliners who'd come through the war he carried a memento. One sleeve of his coat hung empty. He looked at his right wrist.

"Ten past nine."

"Is that correct?" Orris raised his voice above the rumble of the train. "Can anyone confirm: is it ten past nine? It's important."

At the very least, he thought, there'll be witnesses and an exact time established.

Faces turned, wan faces, the dullness that comes from poor diet. The faces in London were tired; in Berlin they were etched with exhaustion.

Two agreed the time was correct. A woman in a faded head-scarf maintained it was five past nine.

"Only five past," Orris picked her out. He turned. "What does

112

your watch say—is it five minutes or ten minutes past nine?" He pointed to the broad man with the smell of Russia on him. "I need to know." A dozen pair of eyes were suddenly on the man.

The noise of the wheels changed, the rumble deepening as the train approached the station. Freedom was slipping away. Smoke the man out.

"What's the matter? Don't you have a watch, comrade? I thought Beria gave you a gold watch after five killings."

The man's face with its high cheekbones and upswept eyebrows tilted from Orris to the other passengers, their interest kindled by the emotion in Orris's voice. The man dropped his cigarette, his lips moving silently with some inward curse.

"Don't you speak German?"

The half-light of the station came through the window, flickering rhythmically into the dark of the Russian's eyes. Five passengers remained seated. The rest stood in a group by the central doors, facing Orris and the strangely silent man, intrigued.

When the man moved he was quick, a hand diving under his coat.

"Watch out, he's got a gun," Orris shouted.

A woman screamed.

"Stand still, all you people." He spoke at last, his German thick and ponderous. "This man I am arresting. A criminal, a cheat on the black market, a profiteer." He had his pistol out, the safety-catch off. "Keep back. No one will be hurt."

The train slowed.

Orris measured the distance, knew the Russian's finger could squeeze quicker than he could jump; knew he couldn't reach his own gun; knew that Siberia lay only a couple of hundred metres away.

The train stopped.

"Reinickendorferstrasse."

There was the noise of the carriage door.

"Stop." The Russian was very urgent. "Nobody gets out."

"So I sell butter on the black market," Orris said. "Is it a crime for us Germans to have food in our bellies? What do you want with me, Russian spy?"

"Not spy," he insisted. "I work for the *Kommandatura*."

"Tell me, Russian spy, do you need more Germans for your slave camps?"

"You are a criminal. You must be punished."

"So why do you kidnap all these people? Why is this woman forced to go to the Soviet sector? That one who lost his arm fighting for his country—what do you want with him?"

How many seconds before the door closed? Orris felt the sweat crawling under his arms because there was no time left to work on the sympathies of the passengers. The Russian had his gun on Orris and his back to the window, so that nobody inside the carriage could take him unaware. In the oppressive silence Orris heard a tuneless whistle disappearing down the platform. It was a tableau of hate and fear; it would only be broken when the train arrived at the next station where God knows what welcome was waiting. People disappeared in the Soviet sector; it happened every day; people were swallowed without trace. In his dying seconds of freedom Orris glanced beyond the Russian, out on the platform, his face suddenly eager and his voice loud.

"Guard! Come quick!"

Nobody could resist it. The woman in the faded headscarf, the war veteran with one arm, a woman with a parcel wrapped in newspaper, a gaunt, white-haired man with upturned moustaches in the old Prussian style, a wraith of a schoolgirl with her young brother, a man with paint spattered on his overalls, the Russian with the pistol—everybody turned to this new point of hope. As the gun hand swung away, Orris took a long stride forward and lunged down with the edge of his hand, chopping the Russian's wrist, sending one bullet into the woodwork before the pistol clattered away under a seat. At the same moment Orris brought up his knee, aiming for the crotch, hitting the thigh instead, swinging the Russian off-balance. Orris made a dive past him, gained the door as it started to slide shut. He made it to the platform, and in a jostling scramble behind him out squeezed the woman in a faded headscarf and the Russian.

The doors shut. Nobody else got down. The train started.

No sign of the platform guard. He'd be snug in the box between the two platforms.

There was no time for subtlety or argument or plans. The Russian was reaching for him with killer's hands as Orris got out his own pistol and shot him twice in the chest, the man roaring in agony and surprise, the woman shrieking.

Orris jumped down on the track and ran headlong into the tunnel, away from the shouts and screams, stumbling in blackness, desperate to get back to Wedding station before he ran into the next train. He had luck. He tripped on a sleeper and scrambling to his feet again he saw stars overhead where bombing had destroyed the roof above. The tunnel wall had cracked from the force of the bomb and he fingered-and-toed his way towards the stars. The bricks had sweated moisture in the dank air, or it might have been his hands. He pulled himself clear into the sweet-smelling night.

A faint whistle sounded, like some children's game, behind him.

In the morning Orris bought the *Telegraf*. The front page was full of the crash of a Soviet fighter and a B.E.A. Viking in the air corridor. The Viking had been on a final approach to Gatow when the Soviet Yak had dived out of the clouds and in buzzing under the British aircraft had touched it with a wing. There were no survivors. The Russians claimed the British were flying illegally low over Soviet military installations. Sir Brian Robertson was going to lodge a formal protest with Marshal Sokolovsky.

At the bottom of the page was a paragraph about a body found at the U-bahn station of Reinickendorferstrasse. The man carried no identity documents and had been shot. Unofficially, the authorities were working on the theory that the man had been drunk and in falling had shot himself by accident with his own gun.

Happened all the time in Berlin.

7/8 April 1948
Berlin

In Little Eric's words: "A traitor grips you warmly by the throat but your hands are free to strike back. A fool grasps you by the hand to say hello, and you're finished." The poet-warrior had been in China after his year in Spain but few ever caught the resonance.

The rdv was arranged along one of the tracks that ran through Grünewald down towards the Havel lake. Orris had stipulated time and place and extreme caution, and Munden had retorted that he knew perfectly well how to make a clandestine rendez-vous, old boy, but he didn't see the need for all this boy-scout fol-de-rol. "Just you smell your own sweat and don't bring the dogs on me," Orris told him. Orris had used a call-box at Zoo station but there was no telling whether Munden's phone was secure.

The instructions to Munden were precise. From the Funkturm drive 4.3 kilometres down the Avus. Leave the car by the fire-fighting hut with the besoms and the buckets. Cross the anti-tank ditch and proceed on foot along the track going north-west. There was a wide expanse that had been devastated in the fighting three years before, with shell holes, vegetable plots and homeless families in makeshift huts. After a kilometre the track started climbing and curved due west through an area that had not been completely denuded of trees: there were gnarled pines, birches and sycamores. At the edge of bomb craters the saplings and brushwood grew strongly. Keep moving. Past a dug-out that once contained an anti-aircraft battery. By now you should be bloody certain you've come alone. Six hundred metres and the track dips again. On the left you'll see a huge old tree. That's it. Rdv at ten-thirty. That's ten-thirty ack emma, old boy? Oh Jesus. Orris hung up.

Orris had selected the tree because it was an old beech. Its spread of branches and thick blanket of leaves had smothered the undergrowth, leaving its surrounds clear of cover. Elsewhere was a sea of soft green in sudden balmy sunshine, quivering with early spring growth and birdsong.

Like a leopard Orris clung to one of the beech's branches, waiting for prey.

He was warned of Munden's approach before he came in sight, the blackbirds calling out in alarm in a moving front as the intruder entered their territory. The hat floated through a stand of silver birch. Munden came forward cautiously, his unease plain from the way he checked first over his right shoulder then over his left. His shoes rustled the leaves underfoot. Once a twig snapped and he froze. He made a complete circuit of the beech trunk, checked back the way he'd come, circled the trunk in the opposite direction, and wheeled in terror as Orris dropped to the ground a pace or two behind him.

"Dear God." Munden put a hand up and dabbed at his forehead. The sweat had sprung up with desperate urgency. "You threw a scare into me. Enough to make a brewer's dray win the Grand National."

"Let's go," Orris said.

"No need for jitters, old boy. Me, myself and I were the only ones who came."

"Like last time we met." Orris was savage.

"I don't follow you."

Only bloody scout in Berlin who doesn't. Orris kept it to himself.

Orris led the way along a track that sloped gently west down to the lake. Tanks and guns rusted at the edge, a watery graveyard. He untied the painter from a small boat and rowed out from the shore. Munden sat very upright, like a maiden aunt, his hat on his knees and a pout on his face. Orris dropped the oars and the boat drifted to a slow halt. On the far side of the lake was Gatow, the control tower and radio mast of its airfield rising above trees.

"Unless you brought a tail with a rifle, we're safe here."

Munden was piqued. "I know when I'm being tailed."

"Then how the hell did they latch on to me last time?"

"Who found you?" The pique increased. "Why didn't you tell me? Some pinko been trampling on my patch?"

"I didn't ask for his visiting-card."

There were no other boats, no swimmers. They shared the lake with a scatter of mallards, busy with their own affairs.

"How have you been filling your days, old boy?"

"Making friends, spending money. Beamish gave me a fistful."

"You mean Eurcon. Better if we stick to the rules. More secure."

"You think they've got a midget submarine?"

Munden puffed out his chest with the bravado of a Mussolini. "I don't want to sound pompous but I find your tone distinctly out of court. I am, after all, Berlin Resident and your superior in this field. I don't expect bowing and scraping, old boy, just a soupçon more respect." But he looked away into the distance.

The drakes were squabbling by the shore. Munden stared at them, not wishing to meet Orris's eyes where he knew with certainty he would see no respect. Orris had respected the Czech partisans, while the war lasted. He had respected Brouček. As a raw recruit he'd respected Beamish. And everyone loved and respected Little Eric. But Munden, never.

"I'm going to disappoint you," Orris told him. "My Control for Berlin is Beamish, direct from London. So far as I am concerned, you are a facilities post. I do not report to you, I do not take orders."

"This is my territory." Munden had a tendency to splutter like the bemedalled bullfrog Musso. Spittle flecked his chin. "It is simply not on having you toddle round on your own. We could cross wires, get in each other's hair, trip over each other's feet. . . ."

"Tell me," Orris didn't give a damn about the outburst, "who knew of our last contact?"

"Coding clerk. My secretary, I suppose. They're totally secure." "Switchboard?"

Munden shook his head. "We don't run to luxuries. We're only three men and a dog. Army Intelligence really runs the show in Berlin."

"Who knew in London?"

"Not an inkling, old boy."

"For God's sake, what classification are the signals?"

"Alpha clearance."

"Right. So Beamish himself. His secretary would have alpha clearance. In Signals there would be coding and transmitting clerks. D/Ops maybe. Duty officer on the East European desk."

"I don't know what you're driving at."

"Did you tell the Depot the time of our last rendezvous before we met?"

"Matter of fact, I did. Eurcon asked me to confirm your safe arrival and I signalled our rdv."

Orris concentrated on the blue sky. Beamish, Johns, Hope-Tarrant, Ulyett, Suzman and Falcon. All his paper-chasing had thrown up six names. Like a young puppy in the field he'd expected one of them to come panting after him with a dagger in one hand and a signed confession in the other. Instead he'd got the Russian in the U-bahn. He'd been dreaming in wonderland. He hardly deserved to be alive, gambolling in the spring sunshine.

You're like a dog with a bone, worry, worry, worry, Valerie had said, finishing with her mouth ugly and her voice rising, *only looking up when a bitch passes.*

Now he was making progress. He'd established that Beamish and Eric Johns were still suspects: either could have tipped off the Russian goon squad. Ulyett and Hope-Tarrant were eliminated. The last two were possibles: if Suzman had been coding clerk, if Falcon had been duty officer on the East European desk, at the time in question when Munden had signalled the rdv. The only course was to test the four, clearing them one by one.

"I want you to transmit to London . . ." Orris paused. Somebody was shouting from the lakeside. Two boys with a football. He turned back to Munden. "Eyes only and decode only for Beamish. You'd better write it."

Munden fiddled with the cap of his fountain pen and a small

pad. "Eyes only, decode only. That's alpha-plus clearance, you know. Declaration of war, that kind of stuff."

"Message." Orris was curt. "Fox gone to earth Vonderlagegasse 63. Query: who was duty officer night of 1/2 April. Signed Sladký."

"How do you spell Sladký? Have I got it right? The whole thing seems dreadfully confused." Munden stared at the pad. He read the signal back. "I don't quite grasp it, old boy."

"Encode it yourself," Orris told him.

At five-twelve the following afternoon, Orris discovered the identity of the double agent in the Depot.

Number 63 Vonderlagegasse blew up.

The place had been carefully selected three days before as a safe house where Orris could hide his face if the climate became unfriendly. It had cost him twenty pounds sterling to shift an old half-mad woman. Now he put it to another use. Vonderlagegasse was an insignificant street in the French sector, a couple of kilometres from Tegel airfield; number 63 was an old railway cottage, standing somewhat apart from other buildings and backing on to a cutting that carried the U-bahn track before its final run-in to the Tegel terminus. He'd chosen the cottage because its slight isolation afforded early warning of anyone approaching, also because a window in the cellar was let into the brick retaining wall of the cutting. Five minutes with screwdriver and stone and Orris had succeeded in opening the window. A minute with a piece of soap and the rusted hinges were almost silent.

In the middle of the afternoon Orris hired a van in Waitzstrasse, where anything could be arranged, from a coffin to the body to go in it. He made a play about not having a licence and a driver was produced. Together they transported a tea-chest out to Vonderlagegasse and staggered through the door of number 63, dumping the chest in the bleak front room.

"Piss and shit, what have you got in there? Rocks?"

"You think I look like a *Trümmerfrau?*" And Orris had bunched his fists under his sweater like a grubby boy's impersonation of a woman. The driver had gone off, tickled at the notion of Orris as one of the gaunt females with pick and shovel who shifted rubble from the heart of the city.

The box had, correctly, contained nothing but broken bricks. Orris had used it as a pretext for having the driver flanking him as he entered the house. "The cheapest life insurance is someone else's life," from the gospel according to Little Eric. If the house were already under observation, if his suspicions had struck gold at the very first name, then there could be someone behind a curtain two hundred metres down the street, eye to a sniperscope. Replay of London.

The cottage was two-down, two-up, and Orris was checking an upstairs bedroom when he heard the knock at the street door. He put his nose to the crack in the curtains. A short thin man with the anonymity of a Post Office clerk stood on the front step, head turned to survey the length of Vonderlagegasse. Nothing else out of place. No parked car, no man reading a newspaper, no street-sweeper, none of the little scents the fox picks up. Maybe it was too quiet. He went down, opened the door a crack, pistol hidden but ready.

"Yes?"

"Herr Sladký?" The short thin man had a face that didn't move as he asked the question.

"Who wants him?"

But the short thin man had his own way, like the clerk who turns to the book of rules when faced with an awkward customer. He lifted a photograph, compared it with Orris's features. He dug a brown envelope out of his pocket and passed it through the crack in the door. "From Berlin Resident." He turned and walked away down the street. His limp was the only thing about him that wasn't anonymous. He moved quickly despite it.

Orris inspected the brown envelope. There was no addressee on the front. He carried it to the kitchen, standing back from the window to tear it open.

121

Message begins
Falcon duty officer night of 1st/2nd April Stop Query why you
need information stop XXX ends XXX.

On that evidence Falcon joined the list of suspects.

Orris looked round the kitchen, troubled by something, taking
in the chipped gas stove, the wooden table with the oilcloth
hanging down in awkward folds, the shelf with crockery of sorts,
the blackened kettle, the single frying-pan. Something he didn't
trust, something tweaking at the fox's nose. An alien smell, a
sound, a detail out of place? His glance was nervous, jerky now.

He went back to the envelope, nothing amiss. The sheet of
paper had no heading, no watermark; but no one expected the
twilight brigade to flaunt a royal warrant. No enclosure from
Munden. The message was typed, with the double-S in -*gasse*
rendered by an *Eszett*, but there was every reason to expect the
Berlin Residency to have a typewriter with a German typeface.
The messenger had used the name Sladký, but he had to be
given the cover name to deliver. He hadn't asked for proof of
identity because . . .

Orris hit the door on the way out of the kitchen, feet tripping
to get down the steps, forgetting the light-switch to the cellar,
stumbling across darkened junk towards the grimy light of the
window. A train was clattering through the cutting, the floor of
the cellar trembling to its approach.

Jesus *Christ*, how many seconds of life had he got left? They
knew he was here, knew he would stay in the house, because they
were cunning bastards, they had given him a message to worry
over. The message hadn't come through Berlin Residency at all.
It had been delivered by the goon squad.

The short thin man had checked Orris's face against a photo,
that was why he hadn't asked for proof of identity. But the Berlin

122

Residency didn't carry any photo, and he was damn sure the Depot wouldn't be so sloppy as to post one off.

He had the window open now and tore the sleeve of his sweater hauling himself up. The rear coach of the U-bahn train was disappearing round a bend in the track as he struggled his shoulders out. He was totally unprofessional in leaving the house, crashing his shoulder on the track. There were times when it didn't matter whether you ignored all finesse; survival was the only trick.

Somebody had paid a visit to 63 Vonderlagegasse while he was out hiring the van. That same somebody had waited to make damn certain it was Sladký *né* Orris who'd returned, because he had escaped in Prague, escaped in London, escaped in the U-bahn, and he mustn't escape again.

When the building blew up he was sixty or seventy metres down the track and sprinting hard. In bewildering succession the air pressure wave stabbed his eardrums, he registered a sharp whipcrack, found himself picked up by the blast and hurled to the far side of the double tracks, felt the sting of brickdust, caught a sharp sulphurous odour, heard a hailstorm of falling bricks, tiles, mortar and God knows what. There was a second explosion and he saw the cellar wall fly out, bursting into the cutting.

So Orris knew.

He had drawn the dogs with a vengeance.

He was bruised, his forehead cut. He checked each limb before he got to his feet and ran again down the track, heedless, just putting distance between him and the cottage before they came to check he was properly dead.

All the time he ran the name hammered his brain.

He was so full of the name he almost ran into the train approaching from Tegel. He stood waving his arms above his head and there was a grinding of metal as the train halted. It was close enough to see the anguish on the driver's face turn to anger.

"What the hell game . . ."

"There's been an explosion. The wall's down across the line."

It happened every week somewhere in Berlin, a wartime bomb

unearthed. Disposal experts attached to the Fire Brigade defused most.

Orris went down the carriages, banging on the windows.

"Get out, get out. There's been a bomb."

Afterwards he wouldn't remember shouting. He only remembered being full of the name and a growing hate. Of all six possibles, only one had the knowledge of the cover name Sladký and had the clout to arrange a photo for the identification and would have the contacts to rig the explosion.

Perhaps he wasn't really surprised. It was as if part of him had always known. But there are some things we know and dare not breathe aloud because they are too frightening.

"Get out, there could be another explosion. The gas mains could go up."

It no longer mattered how many of the goon squad came looking now. Orris was able to merge into the crowd stumbling back along the track to safety.

Now he knew the traitor's identity, Orris's task was clear: he had to lure him to Berlin and put a bullet through his head.

10 April 1948
Berlin/Washington

Telecon reference: TT-9341
Classification: Top Secret—Eyes Only
Present Berlin: Gen Clay
Present Washington: Gen Bradley

BRADLEY: At present with our passenger-trains completely stopped, Russians in effect have won the first round unless we find some way to get this changed. Do you see any likelihood? If not, won't Russian restrictions be added one by one which will eventually make our position untenable unless we ourselves are prepared to threaten or actually start a war to remove these restrictions? Here we doubt whether our people are prepared to start a war in order to maintain our position in Berlin and Vienna.

CLAY: I do not believe anything will come from protest to Moscow except rejection accompanied by legal argumentation. Nevertheless I believe that for the record a protest at Moscow is desirable, particularly if it can be given concurrently with similar protests from the British and French governments. Both of them are weakening and apt to give in to the Soviet position.

Why are we in Europe? We have lost Czechoslovakia. We have lost Finland. Norway is threatened. We retreat from Berlin. We can take it with airlift only by reducing our personnel until we are moved out by force. After Berlin will come western Germany and our strength there is relatively no greater and our position no more tenable than Berlin. . . .

14 April 1948
Berlin

There was hardly anything to the girl: a white face under a shaft of light from the street, a thin hand clutching a threadbare jacket across her breasts. She leaned against a pillar, head to one side. In another it would have looked provocative. She looked sixteen, seventeen, so what age was she really? Her life, her despair, her loneliness would age the girl before her years.

It was instinct that signalled to Orris that she was all alone, a child of the storm.

Other churches had been roofed with corrugated iron where God thundered when it rained. This one was open to heaven, the windows blown out, the pews burned, the altar destroyed. At the head of the church someone had daubed a crude cross on the exposed brickwork. Three walls stood intact, one of them with a fire-blackened mural of a saint.

It was the mural that the girl was looking at. Then she moved slowly through a patch of shadow peering at a brass plaque on the wall describing a painting that had vanished.

She was muttering, it could have been a prayer or the inscription, Orris was too far away to tell. When she turned she saw him standing in the entrance from the street. She stood motionless, a statue.

"I didn't mean to disturb you," Orris said.

It had been the whiteness of her face that had caught his eye as he passed the gaping doorway. He had paused to check. It was automatic. Smelling his own sweat.

She didn't respond.

"I thought you might be someone I knew." Or didn't want to know.

She came forward with sleepwalker's steps and stopped in front of him.

"Do you believe in God?" she asked. "A Christian God?"

"Well . . ." It was not a question Orris had considered seriously since puberty. There had been times, in Czechoslovakia towards the end of the war, when he would have said God no longer believed in him.

"Do you believe there's a heaven, with angels and harps, and good people being rewarded? Say you do."

Mesmerized by the tight little face, it never occurred to Orris this was an outlandish conversation. "Why?"

"Because then there must be hell, where evil people are punished."

She passed him into the night.

At the corner Orris caught her up again and she swung round: "What do you want?" He could see her features more clearly now. She hadn't been crying, the pain was too deep for that.

He'd pursued her without thinking. Puzzled, he asked: "Who do you want to see in hell?"

She crossed the road, half running. There was the wall of a cemetery on their right, with broken headstones and drunken crosses. The graves had given up their dead three years ago under the Russian onslaught and the bones had been replaced without ceremony, sometimes two skulls or a couple of extra hips to a hole with the crumbly brown earth shovelled on top.

The girl stopped abruptly and started to moan, rocking on her heels. The sound rose from deep inside her.

"I'm sorry," Orris said, though he never apologized. "I didn't know it would upset you."

"Some of them are dead and some still live. Can you pray? Pray that they burn. Or perhaps hell isn't hot. Perhaps hell is like Berlin."

She went back to moaning, holding on to the cemetery wall.

"Listen," he said, "do you want to sit down?"

"Have you got any money? I haven't eaten." There'd been a harshness in her voice and it changed, a girl again.

He took her to Piepe's, a café that had a back-door supplier. She ate ham and cheese and cleaned up every crumb with a wet finger like an anteater's tongue chasing errant ants. Her nail was bitten to the quick, like a child's or someone desperate. He was content to be silent, drinking the sort of coffee that mordant Berlin wit described as *Blumen Kaffee*: so weak you could see the flower pattern on the bottom of the cup.

She said: "I expect you want to sleep with me now."

Orris was aware of a number of things: that of the four middle-aged men playing cards at the next table, only one turned his face to the girl; that the clock behind the bar was stopped at 6.27; that only two customers were smoking, and one was a young woman with too much lipstick; that the brownish wall had three oblong lighter patches where a group of photographs had been removed; that one window had cardboard in place of glass; that the girl had dark hair, dark eyes and dark smudges under them; and that he was unpractised in dealing honestly with direct questions. She wasn't watching him but she'd gone still.

He said: "Yes."

She nodded. "We'll go to your place." She was straightforward about it.

"Don't you have a room?"

"But there's the dragon. I can't take you. The dragon likes the money I give her, but it offends her to consider how a girl might get money. Yes, even in this city."

Orris played with his cup. "Does she smoke?"

The girl shook her head.

"Doesn't matter. She can sell the cigarettes."

"American cigarettes?"

"English."

They left the café and turned north, cutting across the river Spree and aiming towards Wedding. The route took them back past the church and by the cemetery she pressed herself against him. It was a completely unsexual gesture.

"Where are you from?" she asked.

"South."

"Not from Bavaria?" It would be his accent that puzzled her.

"From Karlsbad. I shan't see home again."

In the night she said to him: "You don't talk much."

"What do you expect me to say? How beautiful you are? How much I love you?" His voice was taut. *Where have your pretty speeches gone now*, Valerie had cried; *you can't talk of love because you think love is weakness.*

"No," the girl said. "Men like to talk about themselves, what they've done, how clever they've been, how someone cheated them of success."

Dear God, he thought, a woman's body, a woman's knowledge. How could I have believed she was a child?

"How old are you?" he asked.

"I don't know."

He turned to her, though her face on the pillow was invisible.

"But everyone knows how old they are."

"I don't know."

"But you must have papers. Birth certificate, identity card, ration book."

"I don't know."

"You can ask."

She began to cry.

"Isn't there anybody you can ask?"

When she didn't reply he reached out a hand and touched her shoulder. She was as thin as a skinned rabbit.

"What's your name?" he asked.

"Rahel."

Orris was quiet. Rahel, the word as much a sob as a name. No wonder there was a kind of madness in her. And her surname? Goldmeyer? Rothstein? He couldn't bring himself to ask how she'd survived. Her family would have gone up the chimney at Belsen.

Orris met the dragon. She had half a dozen discoloured teeth, a lined sallow forehead, hair that was never washed.

She had been standing at the door to her room on the ground floor, waiting in ambush, and Orris got in first before she could upbraid him. Berlin women of her kind had strident voices when they were outraged. He gave her an entire packet of Capstan.

"Just a small gift."

She was overwhelmed. "The gentleman is so kind." And then such generosity made her suspicious. "She's all right? You must understand I take the place of the girl's *Mutti*."

"She seems weak," Orris said. "I'll find her some food." He was looking past her shoulder into her room.

"You must forgive me. There has been no time to clean the room this morning." Nor any of the mornings before. Dust lay thick on the table, there were dirty cups and glasses, a pile of bric-à-brac in a corner could have been collected from bomb sites. She made an effort at a smile, showing discoloured stumps of teeth. One of the canines had a gold filling. "It is not such a nice day as yesterday, is it?"

"Was yesterday a nice day?"

"Don't you remember?"

There was a veritable flurry of signals between the Depot and the Berlin Residency. In Berlin Munden's feelings evolved from aggravation at the meddling from London to pique at Beamish and finally to worry about Orris.

It started routinely enough.

Query what recent contacts with Orris. Query current address. Awaiting earliest. XXX ends XXX

To which Munden replied, before driving to the Tennis Club at Gatow for lunch:

Your 48/BL/112 refers. Last physical contact with Orris 7 April. Two subsequent telephone calls. Orris silent with regard to current activities, reports engaged on work of higher classification than Alpha-plus. No knowledge of current whereabouts. Regards. XXX ends XXX

Munden was greeted by his Signals clerk on return to the Residency. "Can't let a chap digest in peace," Munden muttered, for Beamish's reply was sealed in a brown envelope marked: *Eyes Only, Decode Only, Berlin Resident.* Extra work.

Reference Orris. Fullest information required. My instructions to you were explicit, viz that Orris should go to ground but address known to us and discreet surveillance mounted. Query did Orris give details of his work. Query is it possible to trace telephone calls. Treat urgentest. XXX ends XXX

It seemed to take Munden for ever to encode the reply, for it was three years since his last refresher course in Surrey. He noted Beamish had withdrawn the Berlin File reference from the transmission data at the head of the signal; it was now routed to his personal file. Highly unorthodox and Munden didn't understand it. "Ours not to reason why," he told his teacup.

Reference Orris. His manner made strict adherence to your instructions difficult. Noncooperative at two meetings, refusal to divulge whereabouts, suspicious of all persons, insubordinate in answers. Unable to trace telephone calls believed made public booth. No further details available concerning Orris's work, believed connected with functioning of Depot. No knowledge of Orris's current identity, cover, address. Query do you wish locate through encoded message per Forces Favourites broadcast BFN. As previously minuted, Berlin Residency has insufficient personnel to mount decent surveillance over sustained period. Query should we enlist seek and shadow facilities of American station or British Army Intelligence. Awaiting. XXX ends XXX

Munden sent his staff home at six, settling down for Beamish's reply. He read *Punch* while he waited.

Reference Orris, no further action your end. Specifically no S and S involving Americans or British Army Intelligence. Acknowledge. XXX ends XXX

Munden acknowledged, wondering what the deuce Orris was up to. If the cheeky beggar's whereabouts were so vital, why not get outside help?

Reference Orris, your instructions understood. Will report any approach made by subject, but make no active effort to contact. XXX ends XXX

And sweet bloody dreams, old boy. Munden locked up. The Residency was only manned at night during an emergency. Compared with Army Intelligence they were only a little out-station in the hills.

Next morning Munden instructed his secretary: "If that chap Orris telephones, say I'm in conference and you'll try and hoick me out. While Orris is hanging on, trace the call."

"Lordy." His secretary, disappointed so often by men, pulled a face. "Now what's up? Isn't he on our side?"

The possibility had never occurred to Munden.

Orris found the dragon less intimidating than her reputation. A bottle of gin opened all doors, in this case to Rahel's bedroom. He moved his suitcase in.

His strategy, though it wasn't graced with such a title, was clear. He knew the identity of the double agent in the Depot, who'd sent the Dorothy Network to their deaths, had three times tried to have Orris killed, and practised God knows what other black arts. But the traitor couldn't be certain his cover was blown and would be in agony about what Orris might be discovering. "Put itching-powder in a man's pants," Little Eric counselled, "until he has to scratch to get relief." In the end the traitor would be compelled to take action to ease the tension: he'd be driven to Berlin to seek Orris out.

Then Orris would kill him.

It would take time and he needed a safe house. "I want you to tell me if you see anybody watching."

"Who would be watching?" Rahel queried.

"Or asking questions. Asking you or the dragon or the neighbours."

"What are you afraid of?"

"This is Berlin, isn't it? They run trains to the salt mines from Ostbahnhof."

23 April 1948
Berlin

She was sobbing.

Orris heard the noise as he was passing and knocked. There was no response and he knocked again. The crying had that theatrical quality, demanding an audience, and he put his head into the room.

"Frau Zyber, what's happened?"

The dragon's body twisted towards him. "They carried off Herr de Kowa this morning." The stuffing spilled out of the arm-chair and she picked at it with a claw.

"They? Who's they?"

Orris had increased his standing with another bottle of gin and some tea. She didn't ask where he, Gustav Bode, a supposed refugee from the Sudetenland, had obtained such luxuries. It was not a time for inquiring into others' secrets, for everyone had a ghost haunting some dark corner.

"Herr Bode, they came in two cars. The British. It was terrible."

"What sort of British? Did they show papers?"

"You know how they are. They treat us like vermin." She used an old piece of patterned material as a handkerchief. "I heard fists on the door and when I opened it they came storming in as if it were the war. Oh yes, they had guns out. Guns, in my house, and it's always been so respectable. There were five or six of them, maybe more. The place was overflowing with them, open-ing doors, boots pounding up the stairs. It was poor Herr de Kowa they took. They brought him down with his hands manacled like a murderer. Didn't even give him time to put on a coat. Oh, it was terrible. I wish you'd been here. Suppose they come back."

That was what worried Orris. When the Occupation authorities made a raid, they questioned everyone in the building, checked papers, probed a little deeper. Because where you found one Nazi, you often found others hidden in the woodwork. Orris wanted no one checking his identity as Gustav Bode. When papers were discovered to be forged, the questions turned nasty: What is your true name, Herr Bode? What did you do during the war? Were you posted to an occupied country? Or—and they were deceptively quiet—perhaps one of the camps? There were a hundred thousand still waiting trial.

"Did they search the building?"

"Everywhere, though I told them I only took in little Rahel and poor Herr de Kowa. Naturally I didn't mention you, Herr Bode; you are always such a gentleman."

She raised a glass to Orris. He'd thought it a tumbler of water, but now he caught the stench in the air and the flush in her cheeks.

"Did they ask questions?"

"I told them I don't understand English. And the one who spoke German, well, I laughed in his face. Such German. '*Frau Zyber, untworten Sie uns nicht so unhöflich.*'" She pulled a long face as she mimicked the accent and collapsed in a paroxysm of coughing and laughter. The light caught two glistening tracks where tears had coursed down her cheeks.

A mortar had struck the building in 1945, gouging a hole in the front room on the first floor. As Orris slipped up the stairs, afternoon light showed through cracks in the brickwork. Rain had streaked the wall with damp decay. On the second floor Rahel's room faced the back, de Kowa's room had been to the front.

Rahel lay in bed, smoking one of Orris's cigarettes, doing nothing. She scarcely went out, certainly never in the evening since Orris had moved in. When she was alone she retreated into the past, where the demons were.

"Did they come into this room?"

"Yes," she answered.

"Were they looking for anyone special?"

"Herr de Kowa."

"But he wasn't in this room. Did they ask about me?"

"You were out as usual." For a moment she was peeved by his tone. "I didn't say about you, Gustav."

She'd washed the dirty clothes he'd bundled in the corner. He'd not asked her to. It was a small act of kindness or possessiveness: no difference. Damp socks, underpants and a shirt were draped from the basin. "Didn't they ask about those?"

"It was funny," she replied, animation in her face at last. She got out of bed and crossed to the basin. She was naked, her ribs stark, her breasts small, her thighs slender. She held up one of

134

Orris's socks between thumb and forefinger. " 'And what is this, Fräulein?' 'It is a sock.' 'It is a *man's* sock, Fräulein. Is a man living here with you?' Such a nose he had too, right up in the air. You'd think the sock wasn't clean."

"What did you tell him?"

"I told him I had to live somehow and I took in washing."

"He believed you?"

She shrugged.

"Did he ask for your papers?" Orris continued.

"Papers," she said. "You couldn't get into hell without papers." She put down the sock and walked back across the floorboards. "I told them I only had the International Red Cross document."

"Did you show it to him?"

"Yes."

Orris caught her wrist as she was about to get under the covers. "You got out of bed to fetch it? Just like that—without clothes?"

She wouldn't cry out, though his fingers bit deep. Her eyes blazed with black fire out of a pinched face. She glared, her breasts rising and falling with her breathing, the child's old game of outstaring. It was Orris who turned aside, dropping her wrist with the white grip-marks on it.

"He's gone, hasn't he? He's not after you, is he? It's de Kowa they took away, isn't it?"

"Don't buy my freedom with your body." Orris was furious, not understanding the violence in himself.

She said: "It's my body. I've bought my life with it. You wouldn't think to stay alive was so expensive. I spent my body years ago. Do you understand what I'm saying?"

She stood in front of him, her arms to her sides. She'd never been able to talk before. Even now she had to close her eyes to speak, digging the words out of the slime of the past.

"There were men with demons inside and they needed to let the demons out at night to run. They were ashamed of their demons and that is why I was spared. Because I was a Jew, I was dirt, and it didn't matter letting the demons loose in the presence of filth. They had finally uncovered our family at Potsdam when the war was nearly lost. They came and took away my parents and Grandma; they even took away Ilse because her body might already have been defiled by a Jew. But I was a child, hardly more. I was innocent. They could let their demons run all over my body. Every night I bought my life again." She opened her eyes. "Sundays were worst. In the afternoon, after church."

The words dried up. She got under the blankets and was still, except for her face. She screwed up her eyes and screamed, silently, as in a dream.

Orris sat on the bed. His hand shook when he gave her a cigarette. She'd been in a church when he first saw her. Exorcizing the demons?

"How did they find out about de Kowa?"

"I don't know." The smoke from her cigarette curled up and she stared into it, seeing a leering face or a humped buttock or a leather whip.

"What had de Kowa done?"

"Done?" She echoed him, seemed to be indifferent. "What did any of them do? They killed people, tortured them, were kind to children, loved Beethoven, hated Mendelssohn, refused to eat meat, obeyed their leaders. That is what such people are made of."

"For God's sake, Rahel, he could have been a monster, one who . . ." He didn't finish.

"No, Gustav," she said. "He was a gentle sort of person. One odd thing. He used to put crumbs on his windowsill for the sparrows."

Orris understood that kind of loneliness, waiting day after day for the worst. He said: "The birds would be company."

"He put bird-lime on the sill. He killed the sparrows and ate them. He said four sparrows gave some flavour to the potatoes."

They sat in silence. Through the window came shouts of children. Playing bloody soldiers, Orris realized. Trams clanged down Müllerstrasse.

"Come to bed," she said. "Stop me thinking."

"Gustl, you're not German, are you?"

"I came from south of the Czech border. I told you. Karlsbad."

"You're not German. You weren't here in the war. I can tell. You wouldn't ask questions."

"No," he said, "I wasn't here during the war."

He felt no need to lie anymore. She didn't ask what he had done during the war nor what his game was now. She accepted him, without explanations, simply asking for no more lies.

"Another thing," Rahel said, "there was a label in your underwear. It was English."

It's always little things, Orris mused, too many details to get right. The English cigarettes and gin were acceptable because they were part of the currency of the city. Something so humdrum as St Michael on underpants was not.

"I noticed the label before I washed the clothes and cut it out. The British officer saw nothing."

Orris leaned over to kiss her briefly. His hand lay on her breast, feeling the flutter of her heart. It occurred to Orris, and he kissed her again at the wonder of it, that he hadn't thought of Valerie for a week.

29 April 1948
London

Beamish had written it out in his neat round hand, like a shopping list:

1. D-G
2. PUS at FO
3. For. Sec.
4. PM
5. Depot: restricted to D/Ops, Pol/E, WEX, Sovcon.

In theory eight people apart from himself would share the knowledge. To them should be added one or two cronies whom the Foreign Secretary would consult (Attlee, by contrast, would grip his pipe and tell no one); a Deputy Under-Secretary and two Assistant Secretaries at the Foreign Office; then their Principals and secretaries; departmental secretaries within the Depot; E.O. clerks in Archives; husbands, wives, lovers; within a week the C.I.A.; another day or two and editors in Fleet Street would be asking for guidance.

"We'd appreciate it if you didn't publish. National interest. Yes, it was quite out of the blue, your guess as good as mine. No, our lords and masters don't want to make a fuss about turning out a sinner because it makes us all look fools for harbouring him all these years. Well, the damage is not extensive. All right, he cost six lives, but only one was British."

"I find it damned hard to swallow."

The Director-General was staring across Birdcage Walk to the park. There was no heating in the office, and none was surely needed in late April. Yet he stood in his topcoat as if its warmth was a comfort against the cold wind of treachery. For the first time Beamish noted a slump in the military uprightness of Standing's back.

"We've known for months he was trading with the Soviets," Beamish said. "We discussed it in this very room, oh, it seemed like once every week: should we turn him in, should we let him run free a little longer, should we blackmail him. We'd always appreciated the Russians would penetrate our Intelligence community because we succeeded in penetrating theirs. But we knew it as a matter of logic. Now we are confronted with the flesh and blood results, we find it emotionally unacceptable."

"But him." Standing stared at the bulk of the Foreign Office building rising above the young greenery of the plane trees. "I have known him since Potsdam. I have lunch with him. Been down to his place in Sussex. Met Mrs Hunt. Played tennis with his daughter. Reporting tittle-tattle about the Foreign Secretary, that's all right. But sending men to the hereafter, no."

"It is possible to break bread with someone and be deceived."

Beamish sat in the chair by the mahogany desk, as calm as a judge.

The Director-General had stood immobile for so long it was a shock to see him move, as if an Easter Island statue had come to life. He sat across the desk from Beamish, his hands on the table.

"Even now, aren't you mistaken in the nature of his relationship?" Standing looked up with an appeal in his face. "To betray the Dorothy Network, send six men to their maker."

He couldn't, Beamish noticed, say simply the men had been killed. He searched for euphemisms, feeling guilt for the deaths settling on his shoulders.

"D-G, we misjudged him."

"And we were wrong. For half a year now we believed that Hunt was in the Russians' pocket. We had him followed to Ladbroke Grove, watched the house, observed the safety procedure with the dustbin, saw the contact from their embassy appear. After all, what harm could Hunt do having Russian tea once a fortnight? What dreadful secrets did he have access to in the Accommodation section of the Office, apart from knowledge of where Cyphers were in our embassies? The most we thought he'd do was pinch the used carbons from the typing pool."

Beamish's voice passed in caressing waves over Standing. It was true what Beamish said; they had acted like schoolboys, enjoying the prank. Beamish's voice was very gentle. "We underestimated his capacity for treachery. He deliberately betrayed the Dorothy Network and six people are dead. It would be seven if Orris hadn't jumped clear. Only one of the six was British but they all worked for us."

"If Hunt knew about Dorothy so long ago, why wait over two years before rolling it up?"

"There were seven in the Dorothy Network. How many contacts will they have made during a couple of years? How many pro-West Czechs disappeared during the coup? How many more deaths was Hunt responsible for?"

The Director-General got up and walked, an old man with pain in his joints, across to the shelf where the madeira decanter was. He opened the cabinet underneath and brought out a whisky bottle. Beamish accepted a cut-glass tumbler. Standing drank his in a gulp and poured another measure.

"Time I got out of this game. I accept the logic of recruiting enemy clerks during wartime to find out where the other side keeps its ammunition. I have no taste for the knife in the back. I'm glad it wasn't one of us, at any rate."

"Only Orris still had a question mark against his name. Then he killed a Soviet agent in Berlin, which seemed to rule him out. So I made myself unpopular with Archives and went back to '45, checked who was around when Dorothy was set up. Then I did some legwork. Yesterday evening Hunt did a curious thing. He left the Office, caught a taxi in Whitehall, got out in the Charing Cross Road. After pottering through Foyles he went into the Astoria cinema, alone, with his black bowler and black umbrella and black briefcase. It was a rubbishy film, nothing a man of his education could have wanted to see. Twenty minutes later he reappeared, but the briefcase had turned brown, distressing colour. Ten minutes and a man came out with a coat over his arm, which he didn't put on though it was a showery evening. Under the coat, all but hidden, was the black briefcase. I followed him to a small car in Soho Square. The car is registered in the name of Maleter, Czech commercial attaché."

Standing wandered round the room as if he wanted to imprint it on his brain: a place he wouldn't be seeing soon. There was a group of four photographs on the wall that were never in alignment and he fiddled with one. They showed his Indian days: a dead tiger, a thin woman on the verandah of a house in some hill station, a polo team, a regimental parade.

"He was being shockingly promiscuous, wasn't he?" Beamish remarked. "Unless Moscow had passed him down to the Czechs."

"You've no idea what was in the briefcase he passed to Maleter?"

"Possibly nothing. It could be the briefcase that passed the other way that was important. You know, a stack of dirty pound notes."

Beamish lit a cigarette, taking his time, letting Standing reach his own conclusion.

"All right, I'll make an appointment with the Prime Minister for the morning. What's to be done with Hunt?"

"Premature retirement?" Beamish suggested. "Nervous breakdown, overwork. After all, the last thing we want is some Parliamentary committee baying about lax security and trampling all over our files."

"He sends half a dozen men to their graves and we let him walk out free? God, what a trade we're in."

The sound of Big Ben came faint on the breeze. The Director-General watched pigeons wheel round the park, startled by a dog, the sudden clapping of wings like a peppering of gunfire.

It was April weather, as folklore has it, to the very end. When Hunt walked down the Clive steps from the Foreign Office, the sun shone from a pale-blue sky with fleecy clouds gambolling in the westerly breeze. There'd been a sharp shower some minutes before, sweeping the pavements clear of typists and clerks. The sun had brought them out again and they hurried homewards.

There was a broad patch of glistening purple in the middle of Whitehall, glossy as an aubergine, where a wedge of sunlight caught the wet tarmac.

Hunt passed the Home Office and when he was on a level with the Cenotaph he stepped off the kerb, making to cut through towards Charing Cross station.

He saw nothing.

Afterwards police questioned eye witnesses and wrote down the customary conflicting accounts. On essentials, however, there was general agreement. The cab had swung round the corner out of King Charles Street, following the route Hunt had taken, and had seemingly made no effort to stop. Perhaps the driver simply hadn't noticed the dark-clothed figure.

At the last moment Hunt had swung round and raised a hand to his face, as though that would be any protection.

A woman who worked at the Post Office in Parliament Street

had to be taken to hospital suffering from shock. Hysterically she kept crying: "His teeth, his teeth." As Hunt took the full impact of the taxi's bonnet, his mouth open to scream, his dentures burst out, flying away into the gutter.

His briefcase split open and an exquisite small nineteenth-century Russian icon of St Gregorovius slithered across the road. Police confirmed later that Mr Hunt had been a noted collector of silver.

Nobody agreed on the taxi's number. It didn't stop.

5 May 1948
Berlin

Signal reference: Personal File
From Berlin Resident to Eurcon
Classification: Alpha-plus
Encoded: DM

Reference Orris. He rang Residency again this morning and requested to speak to me. My secretary said I was in conference but she'd get me provided it was urgent. While a clerical officer was activating the phone-trace, my secretary questioned Orris about the urgency of his business. Orris grew abusive saying he wouldn't discuss matters of national security with every girl he picked up. Then apparently suspicious at the delay he hung up. Our only information on the call is that it was made from the Soviet sector. XXX ends XXX

7 May 1948
Paris

Along the Quai des Grands Augustins the lime trees exploded in the wind, fresh greenery in a frenzy, last autumn's seed-heads bombing passers-by. Beamish cursed the convention that Paris in the spring was warm and romantic. The *bouquinistes* had shut up their wooden cases in disgust. Two *croulants* propped themselves against the Pont St Michel, a bottle shunting between them, all's well with the world.

Beamish crossed to the Île, admiring the great globes of the gas lamps in the Place du Parvis. He sauntered as only an Englishman of a certain age and class can saunter past the Café Notre Dame with its deserted terrace tables. A waiter stood counting the francs in his leather pouch and Beamish glanced behind him at the reflections in the café window. Orris would have recognized the symptoms: smelling his own sweat.

On the footbridge crossing to the Île St Louis he paused, leaning on the iron rail, the wind whipping his hair. There was nobody, he was almost sure. He had been almost sure on the boat, the Dover-Dunkirk night ferry, almost sure on the train. Almost sure. It was the doubt that haunted every citizen of their half world: that one day a shadow would turn out to have substance.

Even his own shadow made him jump. The tensions of the past months were exacting their due. Perhaps he could take Janet to Norway for a holiday. His wife was a solid, uncompromising woman who'd frequented the pubs of Fitzrovia in the thirties. They professed themselves Bohemians, free with their love and other people's money. She was a surprisingly good sculptor, with the sculptor's passion to visit Vigeland Park in Oslo. He'd suggest it, in a little while, once this was finished.

Beamish met Jarrière in the Restaurant des Ducs, full of faded plush, slow waiters who looked to be veterans of the Franco-Prussian war.

"The food improves," Jarrière said. "Even in Paris it is possible to eat passably now. In the country, of course, it was hardly a problem until D-Day."

One did not ask a Frenchman what he had done during the war, Beamish reflected. The fact that Jarrière was now a high functionary in the Foreign Ministry signified nothing. He could have been on *tutoyer* terms with Bidault. In the early days of the liberation, collaborators had had their heads shaved; but

France, a pragmatist had pointed out, was running short of razor blades.

"What sort of person comes to this restaurant?" Beamish inquired. It was the second occasion Jarrière had made the Restaurant des Ducs their contact point.

Above his pouchy cheeks Jarrière had pale eyes that darted up and away; as if he were quick to note things, or afraid his expression would betray him.

"It is not close to any quarter in particular so it is a cocktail," Jarrière answered, using the English word. "One or two policemen, from their talk. One or two professors from the lycée, by the chalk on their sleeves. Local government officers from the Hôtel de Ville, antique dealers. Nobody who knows you or me. It concerns you?"

"A habit, that's all. We all acquire habits. I called on an old friend who worked for me during the war. Now he's an estate agent in Dorset. We went to a pub for a drink and he still sat with the wall on his right side. He's left-handed, you see."

"Yes, yes, I like that." The swift pale glance went up to Beamish's face and down again. "We have our habits too. It amuses you Anglo-Saxons to see public men in France kiss each other on the cheek. The kiss is not the point: each man is checking the other's shoulderblades to select the position for the knife."

Beamish gave his attention to the *andouillette grillée*, which he detested for its taste and colour, apprehension welling that he had been given some oblique warning. He didn't know the Frenchman well; the introduction had been effected for expediency.

"That is why," Jarrière seemed to sense his companion's unease, "we also shake hands every time we meet. Every morning at the Quai, I make the rounds of the Europe desk, *bonjour, bonjour*. I shake hands with the Assistant Secretary for the Balkans, the *rapporteur* for the London Conference, Policy Secretary for occupied territories, *bonjour, bonjour*." Jarrière held out his hand across the table, taking Beamish's briefly in his own, releasing it. "You note it is never a long handshake, the warm grip of friendship. It is a brief contact, enough to show there is no knife in the hand."

Beamish looked up and the pale eyes held his this time. They both smiled. Jarrière dropped his hand palm up on the table, as if saying: Look, no knife.

They ate plain grilled sole with a *petit vin* from the Loire. The French have long practice in using culinary skill as a weapon of diplomacy. Beamish reflected that if Jarrière wanted to impress, the fish would have had a complicated sauce and the wine would have been a Montrachet of a good year. To drink a *petit vin* was to show they had progressed beyond the stage of diplomacy, could take pleasure in sharing a minor discovery. Or was it, Beamish's Cambridge scepticism reinforcing his professional caution, simply a more subtle and flattering form of diplomacy?

When a new customer entered, he came with a reminder of the blustery world outside. The wind was felt briefly across the sombre room, enough for every head to turn to the door. Even Jarrière turned once.

The conversation turned by degrees from small talk, through the continuing disasters in Indo-China, to disasters closer home.

"I have to tell you, in strictest confidence," Beamish chose to speak with his chin teed up on his thin hand, "that we have suffered an appalling security leak."

"In strictest confidence, my dear friend, I have to tell you I have already heard. We too have an ear in Prague."

"More serious than Prague. Our leak was not plugged. It was a senior functionary in the Foreign Office. The late Mr Hunt."

"Deceased?"

"But only a week ago."

Jarrière ordered Calvados.

"There has been, which will certainly now be known in the Kremlin, considerable debate behind closed doors in London concerning our position in Berlin." Beamish's rolling sentences, in French, gave his talk something of the flavour of attending a comedy of manners by Molière. "The view which we hold in my department has gained acceptance in the Foreign Office at the administrative level; and the debate at the political level in Downing Street can only go our way. We cannot hold Berlin."

"When we talked a month ago, you gave it as already your government's view."

"I was anticipating."

"Yet it is still not what your government says in public, in parliament."

"Exactly my point. It is a double disaster the Russians should know that what the politicians put out for public consumption, they do not believe in their heart of hearts. My dear Jarrière, there are contingency plans, drawn up by the Army and merely awaiting Bevin's signature, for the evacuation of Berlin in the event of a blockade: first British dependents, then British troops. If we go, it is certain you will go. Berlin will be left to the Russians and the Americans. Truman will not go to war over Berlin: his Generals won't let him. That is known to the Foreign Office and hence, through the late Mr Hunt, to the Kremlin. Berlin would be Russian in a matter of days, without a shot being fired. The big Russian bear has simply to hug and the Little Bear will be squeezed to death."

"You were sent to warn us?" The pouches in Jarrière's cheeks seemed heavier.

Beamish made an open-handed gesture but replied obliquely. "How can you expect politicians to confess they've been sending copies of Cabinet minutes to Comrade Stalin? At least I have no voters snapping at my heels."

Leaving the restaurant, the two men had shaken hands before parting. Beamish was conscious of how the sweat had come and come again in his palms; he'd wiped his hand on the sleeve of his coat and still the clamminess was there. Stigmata. A confession of guilt he couldn't be free of.

He was growing old, Beamish decided with dispassion. You start as a fresh-faced boy, shaking with stage fright. You end as an old man, jumping at shadows. There is only a given measure of years in between. Time to get out, when this was finished.

He'd woken too often recently, in the dead hours, the sweat soaking through his pyjamas. Once in the grip of some nameless terror, he'd started up from sleep and fought with Janet, shouting out in agony, sudden berserk power in his atrophied muscles as they rolled across the carpet.

Over tea and cigarettes in the kitchen he'd tried to explain.

"There was someone there, in the bedroom."

"Who?"

"I don't know. Somebody. I was sure of it. Standing back in the shadows." A ghost. Palacký, Brouček. His hand had spilled tea in the saucer.

Beamish crossed with care towards the right bank, making for Châtelet metro station. He watched the traffic, watched faces, watched feet. There was nobody, he was sure.

"Tell me first about Jarrière."

"He was receptive. I would say he was convinced of the futility of staying in Berlin."

"It must go further than Jarrière understanding Berlin is vulnerable. Will he persuade his government to abandon their position?"

"I imagine so. Oh, I don't know." Beamish felt sudden irritation: he was expected to divine the intentions of a man he barely knew. "You know him better than I. Is he a Party member?"

"Of course not. He is an unwitting tool."

Beamish accepted the rebuke in the other's voice because he realized he was being simple-minded. Jarrière didn't have to be a Party man to further the cause. In any case, it was never a question of paying monthly dues: it was a matter of paying every day of one's life, with all one's endeavours.

They walked side by side along the gravel path through the Bois de Boulogne like two old friends, or a lawyer with his client. Beamish would be the notary: thin, high-shouldered, with the dust of bound volumes of legal cases ingrained in his skin. Polytov was short, stocky, with cheeks that showed a tracery of red veins:

he would be the Norman farmer come to Paris to plead against a cut in the buttermilk subsidy.

"There is every likelihood it will succeed," Beamish said. "He will return to the Quai d'Orsay and speak to the Minister, reporting that the British are preparing to scuttle. The amusing part is they'll swallow it precisely because they've heard nothing from London. They are hungry to believe in perfidious Albion."

Beamish turned to give the Russian a tired smile and checked behind. The man in the dark suit was a steady hundred metres in tow. He might as well have been on a rope, the distance constant. Moscow's top men were skilful but their dogsbodies lacked any element of slyness. It had been the same with the Czarist Cheka.

They reached the horseshoe-shaped lake where people skated in winter. Toy waves snapped at the edge. An alsatian came out of the water with a stick in its mouth and sprinted to a thin young man dressed all in black. At a word of command the dog dropped the stick and stood waiting. In a Europe where people starved, some could still feed a large dog. Beamish caught himself with the thought and couldn't decide whether he was truly shocked at the waste of food or was simply slipping into the habit of thinking in slogans.

"I said," Polytov was looking at him, "we need to have the name of a senior official in Vienna who is vulnerable to homosexual compromise."

"I was considering," Beamish replied. He hadn't heard, his mind far away. He badly needed a break. When this was finished. "I'll have to report back on that."

"Don't delay, please. When Berlin is won, we shall be much concerned with Vienna."

Beamish turned his face aside, letting the wind slap against his closed eyes and his forehead. After Berlin, Vienna. After Vienna, Oslo. It would never finish.

"I have a particular question from Master," Polytov began. "Master" was the cover name for his Controller in Moscow. Odd how the Soviets persisted in using a cover name when from his Depot work Beamish was fully aware that Master was in reality

Mazurov. "Has it been absolutely accepted by the British authorities that Hunt was the betrayer of the Czech network?"

"Yes," answered Beamish.

"He wants particularly to know whether you are quite above suspicion now?"

"Yes. I had made it clear that logically I should join the list of suspects. I stressed it openly to the Director-General and the Foreign Office. Now Hunt is exposed as the traitor with the houseful of Russian silver, my honesty is above suspicion."

"Accepted by everyone?" Polytov insisted. "Master needs to know."

"Yes, by everyone." But Beamish thought suddenly of Orris, who was in Berlin, out of sight, out of contact with London. Orris wouldn't know the story about Hunt. Orris was a problem that would have to be resolved. It was fair enough to get Orris out of London, where he was poking under the carpet, to Berlin, where people were found face down in the Spree every day. But with Orris killing the Moscow executioner and escaping the bomb blast, he was a continuing problem, urgent. What had he been doing in the Soviet sector when he made the phone-call?

"That is excellent," Polytov said. "Because when your Director-General retires, it is imperative you should be above any suspicion."

Beamish stopped short and the Russian was obliged to turn round.

"Colonel, don't tell me you are surprised at the idea?" Polytov asked.

No, Beamish concluded, he'd considered the possibility of succeeding Standing; but drawn back from the consequences. And wasn't there something else, a relic of his honest days? Now, beside a windswept lake in the Bois de Boulogne, he was for the first time filled with a sense of revulsion at himself. That he had sent men to their deaths in Czechoslovakia he had accepted: it was historically necessary. But Hunt, the luckless minor agent, had been killed solely to shield him.

"No, not surprised." Beamish shook his head. "But it's been the custom to appoint the head prefect from outside."

"Head prefect?"

"The top man." Of course it was unreasonable to expect a Russian to fall in with public school jargon, unreasonable to resent him. "I don't know . . ."

There was a bark, just one, and Beamish turned his head. The bodyguard whom Polytov had brought was talking to the man with the dog. They were all dark in colouring, even the alsatian was black, prepared for night work. It filled Beamish with foreboding: already Moscow felt he was so important they scattered muscle round the highways and byways. He looked down the long avenue leading to the racecourse and the man he saw had too heavy a build for a jockey. His life, he saw, belonged to others. As Hunt's had.

"We have reason to believe that this time there will be promotion from within," Polytov said. "Master has his source within the Cabinet Office."

Beamish nodded. He knew a name but didn't speak it.

"In which case," Polytov continued, "it will no longer be possible for us to meet directly. Certain arrangements have been made. You will be informed when the time comes."

The wind had dropped somewhat and Beamish felt the first drops of rain. They started to walk again, inwards towards the city, past two girls hurrying under umbrellas and a tall woman with a nondescript dog on a lead.

"So you think the French will leave?" Polytov jerked their talk back.

"Nothing is guaranteed. Nothing ever is. But it is my judgement that the French, who distrust the British, disdain the Americans and hate the Germans, will be pleased to escape."

"And the British will follow them?"

"No decision has been made at a political level. But the ground is well prepared."

"That leaves the Americans. Stalin wants to get Berlin without war. He would prefer to frighten them out."

"Well, they are demoralized," Beamish said. "What more can you ask?" Beamish was accustomed to controlling others, and did not take kindly to being the puppet on the end of the string.

"You must have a further meeting with their C.I.A. man. Master stressed . . ."

"Oh damn Master. You expect all the world and their dog to jump at His Master's Voice."

"Yes. Yes, Colonel, we do."

They walked in silence. A few of last year's leaves blustered round their ankles. Beamish felt a trickle of wet inside his collar—he'd come without hat or umbrella.

They parted before reaching Porte Maillot.

"I wish you good luck, comrade Colonel."

"Goodbye, comrade." Beamish felt self-conscious using the term. It smacked of draughty soapboxes and dingy meeting-halls with mugs of cocoa after the bright-eyed speaker had shrilled for the blood of the bourgeoisie.

They shook hands briefly. Look, no knife.

14 May 1948
Berlin

The man was blond, but far from the Aryan hero of Nazi dreams.

His hair was in a long sweep down his back and when he shook his head the tresses flared in the light and there was a glitter from the jewelled earrings. He arced a hand and the nails of his fingers were the red of new-spilled blood. His lips were the same vivid hue. Eyelashes like black spiders, eyebrows always asking, eyes from the morgue.

His dress was tied in a slim bow over one shoulder, the other shoulder bare. The material was black because it showed his blond hair to perfection. Black sequins were sewn to the bodice of the dress. Two small spotlights caught every movement, glinting off sequins and hair and jewellery and white teeth as he sang.

"Ich bin eine Frau die nie Nein sagen kann. . . ."

The voice was husky with late nights and whisky and promise.

He'd been introduced in English as Mr Pussy. His real name was Putziger, Putzi to his intimates.

Orris waited, his eyes away from the singer and the pianist in dark glasses. The tables were close together because in Berlin people needed that kind of reassurance. But the two men who'd come in after Orris stood at the bar at the back. They didn't speak; they stared at the gold hair and flashing rings.

And the other faces in the room: Orris considered them. Some older men, pudgy under their chins, weakness showing in their mouths; mostly they had companions, strange hermaphrodite creatures in cute pink and slinky black. A group of middle-aged men and women together, their faces eager to be shocked, hoping for the shiver they'd first felt in smoky cellars a generation before. Half a dozen women on their own; at least Orris assumed they were women. Three Americans out of uniform with three girls of the town. A man with a crewcut by himself, some secret unhappiness in his eyes.

The two men by the bar had checked their coats with the girl at the door. If they were shadowing Orris that would slow them when he left. But he recalled the Russians he'd seen during the time in Prague. They'd always checked their coats because to wear an outdoor coat in an office or a waiting-room was *ne kulturny*.

The song reached its finale. One of the Americans was raucous in his approval. Putzi turned his face in the spotlights, the smile never reaching his eyes. He disappeared through a gap in the curtains.

The pianist was into *Liebling mit dem blonden Haar* and a *Mädchen* asked Orris to dance.

"Later. Is the toilet at the back?"

He paused in the dark of the corridor but no one followed. There were steps up from the cellar and Orris checked the door to an alley. He came back down the steps and through the door marked *Privat*. The curtains to the stage were on the right with the sound of the piano beyond. There were two doors on the left. At the first he heard a man and a woman laughing. He opened the second door cautiously and caught sight of the black dress and the white shoulder and dark eyes meeting his in the dressing-table mirror.

"Heinzi is absolutely going to crucify you."

"Heinzi?"

"He doesn't allow callers backstage. He is so jealous."

Heinzi and Putzi, very nice. Orris paused, letting his senses register. Nothing looked menacing. Smell of stale smoke and unwashed bodies. Subdued piano: *These Foolish Things*.

Orris said: "It's not that."

"Well then?" Putzi swivelled round on the stool. He slipped the wig off and placed it on his lap. It lay like some contented golden cat. "What do you want?"

"I got my identity papers from von Kleist," Orris said. He held up the card he'd bought that morning from the fixer in Waitzstrasse. The light shone on the gloss of the photo, catching the break where von Kleist had folded and refolded it to remove the newness. "He's got a nice touch."

"So?" Putzi ran a hand through his sweaty hair. Without the mane of the wig his face was gaunt, the jaw and cheekbones standing out like a death's head. "What should I do? Applaud?"

The man was aggressive, jerking out the questions in his quick Berliner accent.

"I got the papers but I didn't get a job," Orris said. "Von Kleist told me you had a contact in the Soviet sector employment office."

Putzi fiddled with a cigarette and lit it. He hummed a few bars with the piano, his eyes lifting from the glowing tip of his cigarette up to Orris's face and back again. Orris waited, letting him think.

"I don't know you from a pig's knuckle," he said at length. "Show me the papers."

Orris shook his head.

"Then why the shit should I help you?"

"I expect von Kleist knows the reason for that."

The man was on edge and the thread of control snapped. He hurled the blond wig at Orris who ducked and was on one knee on the floor with his gun out before the other could make another move.

"Keep dead still." Orris's voice was a whisper. His ears caught it now: the door of the next room opening. A voice, a man's. Orris stood upright, backing to the wall. The pianist played a final chord and riffed into the incessant beat of a torch song. There was a woman's laugh from the corridor, very close.

"Who's that?"

"Karin."

"Who is she?"

"Stripper."

Orris wished to God the door had a key.

"The man?"

"Heinzi."

From the sound of it, Heinzi went both ways. The woman's laugh came again, further away.

"Does Heinzi take part in her act?" Orris asked.

"No, dear, he's not like that." But Orris thought he saw insecurity in the other's eyes. Putzi raised his chin. "Heinzi and I do a double act later. He undresses me. If the mood's right, sometimes we do a bit more."

"So Heinzi will be back shortly?"

Putzi shrugged, sighing at the tedium of it all.

The man you question should have the habits of an adulterer. Little Eric's words echoed inside Orris. When he shows indifference it's because his ears are attuned to catch his lover's return.

Orris moved quickly across the bare floor and laid his gun against the powdered cheek.

"Have you seen someone who's been pistol-whipped? It's not a pretty sight. They won't cheer out front anymore. If the gunsight cuts to the bone, the scars will show through powder and rouge. I doubt if Heinzi would fancy you."

"What do you want?" The dark eyes hated Orris.

"The name of the man who gives jobs in the Soviet sector, where I can meet him out of hours."

"There's a bar on the other side, near Alexanderplatz."

"Name?"

"The Donau."

"And the man from the employment office?"

"Kubler. He's got a thirst to support."

Orris wanted nothing more. He hated this place, the people who paid to watch, the tortured souls who performed. He said: "Don't try any fancy footwork," tapping the pistol barrel against Putzi's cheek.

There was nobody in the corridor, nobody on the steps, nobody in the alley. It turned out into Ku'damm by a patched-up shop with a newly painted fascia: Corsetière Marie Thieme. In a city that starved, the fat cats needed corsets. On the far side of the shop was a ruined wall where some officious fool had stuck up a poster: *V.D. lurks in the street*. And in the clubs? And the bars?

Every second lamp was lit down Ku'damm and in the distance was the stump of the Kaiser-Wilhelm memorial church, a shipwreck of man's hopes.

Orris began to walk.

There was no barbed wire or wall.

Someone had taken a pot of white paint and a brush and slapped a line across the road: the limit of freedom.

There was the sound of a late tram coming down Leipzigstrasse. It stopped at the white line to let off a couple of figures, resting quietly while the driver changed ends. It gave a clang of its bell and disappeared back to the Soviet sector.

Orris wasn't alone. He could feel the square breathing while it watched him.

They weren't police: he was certain of that. Police preferred to wait up one of the forbidding long streets, in a cold side alley, and swoop in a sudden burst of fury. It was afternoon and early evening when risk of a raid was highest. Markgraf's police, from their headquarters in the Soviet sector, had orders to put down the "street businessmen".

Here in Potsdamerplatz, where America and Russia and

Britain met in total devastation, was one of the favoured places for the black market. The men with their fibre suitcases offered bacon and cheese, cigarettes and nylons. A piercing two-finger whistle warned of a police *Razzia* and the businessmen vanished in the brickdust of another sector.

The man who stepped out of the shadows had nothing in his hands. He stood close to Orris.

"A dark night, friend."

"It's never too dark for business."

"You're buying?"

"I want a bottle of whisky," Orris told him.

"Whisky?" The man took an interest in the shadows beyond Orris. "Wait here." He took a couple of steps and turned back. "Don't follow me. I get nervous in the dark."

He returned from the ruins of what had once been a shirt shop, carrying a square bottle.

"Look, friend." He had a pencil flashlight and shone the thin beam on the capsule. "The seal hasn't been broken."

Orris caught the hand and flicked the torch over the man's face. He had a mean moustache and eyes that weaselled away from the light. There was a scar on one cheek, the purple weal of shrapnel, a constant reminder that death had once been a step away.

"I know where to find you," Orris said. "Now I know what you look like."

"Stop messing me about. I got mates."

"How much are you asking?"

"Forty dollars."

"You thieving shit."

"Listen, friend," the businessman said, "you can't even lay hands on the stuff in England, where they make it."

Orris dropped the man's wrist and got out two five-pound notes. The stiff paper crinkled as he unfolded them. The torch played over the notes and the man said: "Let me feel."

"Let me feel the bottle of scotch."

There was the sound of a car's engine in a side street and the

156

businessman thrust the whisky at Orris and grabbed the money.

"You're on your own, friend."

He bolted into the ruins with a spattering of mortar rubble.

The Donau was closed. Through the steamy window Orris saw a man sweeping the floor. He rattled the door handle and was ignored. He started to sing, off-key, and the *Kellner* leaned the broom against the wall and unlocked the door.

"Get away from here. Go home and sober up."

"That's no way to talk to a citizen. I have been celebrating. Don't you know what day it is?"

"Go away. We're closed."

"The King of France is dead."

"There is no King of France."

"Executed. Triumph of the people. It's the anniversary. Why aren't you celebrating?"

The barman was looking down the length of the street, for trouble or help.

"Listen to me, citizen," and Orris leaned a heavy hand on the other's shoulder, "if I'm not good enough for you, then screw you, I'm off." Orris turned away and lurched suddenly back. "Where's my old mate Kubler?"

"Gone home. We're closed."

"Kubler, Kubler, Kubler," Orris sang out, peering into the gloom of the bar. "You know what we call him at the office? Do you know?"

"Go away. I'll fetch the police."

"Got no revolutionary spirit, your trouble. Tell me where Kubler lives. I'll drink with him. Do you know what we call him? *Kuhschluck*. Ha! He knows how to drink. Tell me where *Kuhschluck* Kubler lives and we'll celebrate together."

It was two blocks through deserted streets.

"Who is it?"

"Johnnie Walker."

There was a shuffling of slippers and the door opened the

width of a chain. Watery eyes peered at Orris and tried to penetrate the dark behind him.

"I don't know you."

By way of answer Orris twisted the bottle so it reflected the light through the door. Kubler muttered under his breath as he slid back the chain and Orris was admitted.

The room was the lair of someone who had slipped and was gathering speed on the slope. Every possession of value had gone. Anything could have started the slide to dereliction: a wife who'd deserted, a son killed. There were two chairs and a rough wooden table. The lid of a tin served as an ash-tray. An unmade bed was in one corner and Orris thought Kubler had been lying under the covers in his clothes. *Neues Deutschland* lay on the bed, open at an inside page. Kubler had been reading an article headlined: How the Soviet and German peoples will build the future in peace and freedom from imperialism.

"Who are you?" Kubler had reappeared from a further darkened room holding a glass.

"Stolle," Orris replied, giving the name on his latest identity card. Dear God, how many names had he used this year? He was like one of Hitler's ghost battalions in the last desperate days: names on paper without substance.

"Have I met you before?" Kubler asked. "Didn't you come to . . ." His voice trailed away.

"This is the first time we've met. A friend told me where to find you."

"Oh, a friend. Yes." He drank, carefully, holding the tumbler in both hands. "Life would be poorer without friends. Don't you agree? A friend is someone who . . ." The sentence hung in the air.

"Yes." Orris wasn't a fanciful man but an image slipped into his mind: Beamish. It was an extraordinary parallel to have risen in him. Like any professional, Orris was sensitive to the prickling of his skin. Both men were thin, with necks like turkeys, but wasn't it more than physical? There was a sense of some inner purpose sustaining Beamish which clung to this derelict still.

Surely Beamish couldn't end like this: neat spirits in a toothmug and the beginnings of observations he couldn't complete.

He poured whisky into the old man's glass. "We haven't met but my father knew you before the war."

"Stolle you said?" He lifted the glass half way to his lips. "That was it? Stolle . . ." A fragment of a smile touched his cheeks and died. He shook his head. "So many old friends, you understand." He gestured to the empty room and drank.

"And such a long time." Orris felt his way carefully. "Before the Brownshirts, before the boots, before the smashing of meetings."

Kubler began to tremble.

"There was a student called Stolle, I seem to remember. Was your father at Munich?"

It was always the soft accent they noticed. "He spent some time there," Orris replied. Go gently, he told himself, don't rush the fences. Let the whisky do its work. "He was doing research. Not scientific research, he was a philosopher, you remember. He said to me once: physics can smash an atom, but an idea can smash this whole rotten world." Had he gone too far?

Kubler looked up sharply and nodded. "Oh yes, a philosopher." He drained his glass and refilled it. *Kuhschluck*, in Orris's inelegant phrase: Cow-slurp.

"Philosophy can't mend broken heads," Orris said. "There were practical things to do in Munich."

"I was at Heidelberg first; Munich came later. Not just later, too late. The madmen had taken over. Your father talked to you about those days?" Kubler's voice had sunk so low that Orris had to lean across the table.

"Not much. It hurt him to bring the memories alive: Nazi thugs, the rallies, the roaring . . ." Orris had to break off. The old man's hands shook uncontrollably, spilling the whisky on the table. "Also," Orris paused a fraction, decided to risk it, "you were in different cells. It was safer in those days. When the Nazis caught one comrade, others could carry on the struggle."

"There was Schirach. Do you remember Schirach?" Kubler asked the question as if Orris himself had been there. He launched into a disjointed story about Schirach who had penetrated the Nazi party hierarchy in Bavaria and given warning to several Jews and communists. "It was already terrible for us. 1936. Do you remember?" Schirach was betrayed and later found on a footpath with his neck broken, his kneecaps smashed, both eardrums shattered, several teeth extracted. Kubler forgot his glass in the telling of it. Orris let the sentences flow, offering nothing himself but attention. Kubler suddenly broke off: "But you must have a drink."

"I brought the whisky for you. I've been living in the American zone and I escaped to come here. It was a present because you knew my father. Of course, you'd heard he was dead."

"All the best ones are dead. I wish I'd seen Willi before he'd gone." The creature of Orris's imagination had become real in the confusion of the other's mind. He even had a first name now.

Kubler rambled through his underground days, remembering stratagems and petty triumphs and the frightening closeness of violence, stumbling over a name or a date. The whisky bottle had sunk low when Orris said: "I must be going."

"So early?"

"Tomorrow I must look for a job in Berlin."

"But my boy, you have come to the right place tonight. St Lenin must be guiding you." It was Kubler's first attempt at a joke. His laugh turned to a retching cough, and Orris gazed at the pale furred tongue twitching over stained teeth. It was this point precisely that Orris had been aiming for: not just bonhomie with a sot from the employment office, but the opportunity to let a lonely man be generous.

So it was that Orris got his job. No, not the fire service, his chest was susceptible to smoke. Not the milk-bottling factory. What he wanted, Orris held out his hands, was to help build socialism. Well, there was Staaken, the Soviet airforce authorities being in a hurry to extend the airstrip.

Orris trod softly out into the night. It was perfect. All the world said the Russians were coming. And Orris was going to ease their arrival, working on a runway extension at Flugplatz Staaken. It was ideal for his purpose.

27/28 May 1948
Berlin/London

Near the Anhalter freight terminal they had a bright yellow bulldozer out, clearing the ruins by the side of the marshalling yard. It shoved the rubble into heaps near the road where the trucks hauled it off. Far away to the west, on the edge of Grüne-wald, they were creating a whole damn mountain out of the rubble of Berlin. When the bulldozer paused you could hear the banging of the demolition team as they hacked at an old ware-house. Men stood on its sagging walls, attacking the brickwork with picks, stepping nimbly aside as each section crumbled and slid away.

"You might have telephoned, old boy."

"You know what?" Orris turned to look at Munden, and beyond him where the brickdust billowed. "I get an eerie feeling about telephones just now. It's so quiet at the other end of the line it makes me think there are half a dozen people in the room holding their breath and listening."

"What a dotty notion."

"Is it?" It was one of those slow walks through open areas whose sole aim is to frustrate unwanted attention. Orris had known where to come. "Perhaps the Russians have a tap on your line. Perhaps the Yanks are listening, wanting to know when the Limeys are pulling out. Perhaps it's . . ."

"Yes, perhaps it's . . . ?" Munden had the look of an eager recruit on his face.

Well, that tells me all I need, Orris decided, that Munden has been ordered to sniff round me. A second thought slipped into his mind: that Beamish had originally selected Munden as Berlin Resident precisely because the man was so ineffectual. And that Beamish must be regretting the choice now.

There is a fascination about watching the breakers at work on a building. A dozen people gazed, though it had happened a hundred thousand times already to their city. A shout and a bigger crash than usual brought Orris round, smelling his own sweat. One figure, on the edge of the watching group, had his back to the demolition work.

"How long before the Russians march in?" Orris asked the question abruptly.

"My God, nobody has an inkling. A few weeks, a couple of months at best."

"I could have some inside stuff next time we meet," Orris said. "Hot stuff," he added, realizing he had to lay it on without subtlety. "I've wormed myself an interesting job on the other side. Got it through the Soviet administration, for a laugh, lets me keep an eye on their military preparations."

For some seconds Munden didn't reply. His wonder at Orris's ease of penetrating the Soviet administration was swamped with the suspicion that if Orris were one of their boys anyway it would be easy to fix some job. Then doubt crept in: what was the point of a Soviet agent saying he'd got a job through the Soviet administration?

"What sort of job, old boy?"

Orris shook his head. "I'll let you know when they're getting in the red carpet for Uncle Joe."

Orris left Munden standing there, setting off at a pace that made finesse in following him impossible. He went right, left, right, passed the whole length of Kochstrasse before turning up north-east into the Soviet sector. Or as the red-and-white sign had it: You are entering the Democratic Sector of Berlin. He lost his tail, who was a perspiring little man in a fawn raincoat, outside a building with a window display of tinned Russian fish. Orris melted into the shadow of the doorway and out again as the little man overshot.

Beamish put a match to the flimsy and watched it turn to ashes in the ash-tray. Munden had reported another abortive rdv with Orris, who had slipped his tail with his usual careless ease.

He was brooding, that was Miss Lambert's opinion, confided to her mother. Brooding too much these days.

Beamish saw quite clearly now that it was impossible for him to become Director-General. One grubby field agent prevented it. And ominously Orris seemed even to be penetrating the Soviet military establishment in Berlin, if Munden were to be believed.

Beamish brooded on these two facts. Master would have to be told, an unpalatable prospect. Unless, Beamish broke up the ashes with a matchstick, unless he himself went to Berlin and put a stop to Orris.

2 June 1948
Berlin

"I do not understand it. From Robertson I get total commitment. Even from Ganeval I get support. But from London I get this high-pitched buzz of panic. And from Paris . . ." General Clay paused to knuckle his darkling eyes. It was one of a catalogue of gestures he used when discussing relations with the French government: eyes closed, eyelids massaged, sigh, eyebrows raised, scalp scratched, lips compressed, face tilted to heaven, fingers drumming on the desk, deep breath exhaled slowly. Clay's hand dropped back to fondle the dog beside his chair. "The French have asked, unofficially, if we can lend them aircraft. They confess they could not even supply their own garrison here by air."

Lucas chipped in: "That's a fact, sir. What planes they had they've shipped out to Indo-China."

"Let's hear it in words of one syllable," Clay said. He reached for his cigarettes. "And preferably in one minute."

The C.I.A. station head, Wrea, said: "General, I've received a précis from our guy in London—you remember Kordorf?— which you're welcome to read." He proffered it to Clay who shook his head. "Kordorf has had a meeting with two high-ups in British Intelligence: European Controller and Polly."

"Just hold it there." Clay blinked at Wrea. "Polly?"

"Political Evaluator," Wrea replied, deadpan.

"Jesus *Christ*, sir," Garn muttered.

Wrea's eyes never wavered from the General's face. "These two nice folks put to him the following scenario. One, the French are a weak and divided nation, with the communists threatening to seize power; the French cannot hang on in Berlin against the Russian will for fear it provokes riots at home and possible collapse of the Republic. Two, with the French gone, the legal standing of the remaining Allies is fatally weak. Three, with their own left wing snapping at their heels, Attlee and Bevin and company will not risk a critical vote in the House of Commons. They will be unable to act strongly in the face of Soviet provocation here in Berlin. To save face they will negotiate separately with Stalin, run down their garrison quietly, and sneak away while the rest of the world is saying its prayers. Four, we shall be left alone in Berlin facing the Russians, who can pick their time to cut all communications with the city. The President will not go to war to save Berlin and the Russians know we shall simply be starved. . . ."

"Not so fast." Clay stabbed at Wrea with his cigarette. "Truman won't go to war to keep us here. I don't know that. How come the Russians do?"

"About a month ago there was a quote accident unquote in London. The man who was killed was rumoured to be an agent passing top-secret material to Moscow. He worked in the Foreign Office and had access to reports from Washington."

"Jesus H. Christ." It was Garn again.

"Okay," said Clay. It was late and the big central light in his office threw every line on his face into relief. "So if the Kremlin decide we go from Berlin, we go. If they decide we go from western Germany, we go. From Austria, we go. If the communists decide to have a revolution in France, that goes. So long Europe, it was nice knowing you. Will the last G.I. please switch off the light as he tiptoes out. Is that the pattern everyone sees?"

Clay looked from Wrea to Lucas to Garn to Philippides. No one felt it was the moment to speak.

3 June 1948
Berlin

Sometimes she acted mimes for him.

Lying on the bed with his ankles crossed and one arm cushioning his head, Orris drew on his cigarette and watched the girl through the cloud of smoke. The smoke was important, she insisted, like the haze of a final veil. She did her mimes naked.

There were times when she danced, moving in time to the tune she hummed in a little girl voice. There was little erotic about the dances. She would announce: "This is Autumn," or "I am Virtue," or "The Spirit of Greece." She spoke the titles solemnly and started to hum, making long sweeping movements with her arms or little tippy-toey runs.

It wasn't all dances.

If she thought Orris looked tired at the end of the day, her mimes became sexual. She judged his mood. If he needed to be cheered she made it explicit, seducing herself with Orris's jacket, her expression veering from prim refusal to delight to shock, until he smiled. Sometimes suggestion was paramount and she turned out the light. In the evening glow through the window she made love to an invisible man, kissing him, caressing him, feeling the hardness of his body, tensing as she spread her legs and he entered, arching her back, rolling over and over on the floor locked in his embrace, eyes closed in an unvoiced scream until she achieved release. Orris lay spellbound on the bed. Afterwards they were wild and silent together.

There were mimes she did for herself. "*Der Führer*," muttered under her breath. Shoulders rounded, small buttocks jutting out, strutting and preening. Then the tiny clenched fist like a baton conducting the crowd's emotions, lank hair falling forward to lick her forehead, mouth wide as she jabbered nonsense, dark eyes, soul staining her face.

"The Prisoner." The door of the cell swung shut and Rahel held its imaginary bars, the knuckles of her fists white, her eyes on the retreating jailer. She stood, straining out into the unknown, waiting for something, a visit, a noise. It was a sound that came, her head cocking to it, then dawning horror and a shiver of her whole body as blows seemed to be struck in an adjacent cell. She screamed in sympathy, clenching her fists over her ears, and ran to fall on her bunk, hiding her face. She lay still. When the torture next door finished she got up to explore her cell, feeling the walls, the roughness of stone, the window so high she had to jump, the dripping ceiling, the confines of liberty. The torturers appeared in her cell and she shrank in horror. She wasn't physically beaten. They cut off her hair, her fingers scissoring through the dark locks. She was led away naked, unresisting, to the gas chamber. It hissed and was done.

Rahel was unconsolable after this mime. She wouldn't come to bed until the pillow was thrown away.

"You wouldn't understand, Gustl. They used to stuff pillows with hair from the camps."

Her crying had no tears in it. She moaned, rocking her body, face to the blankness of the wall.

Orris never thought Rahel was mad. Just that the demons, long ago in some dark midnight, had run all over her body until they'd found a way in.

"Rahel, Rahel." Orris had hardly ever used her name.

He didn't know whether to touch her body and scarcely knew how to touch her mind. He covered her wracked shoulders with the sheet and perched on the edge of the bed as one would with a sick child.

"I found out a strange thing today," Orris said. She replied nothing, her moaning soft and low. "Shall I tell you about my work?" Her body moved to a secret ache. "I leave here every morning as Herr Bode and take the Stadtbahn as far as Staaken. There I wait for the last of the crowd to leave because I want to be alone at the end of the platform. There is a loose brick and I remove this and change my identity. Herr Bode spends the day behind the loose brick and Herr Stolle strolls out of the station and heads for the control point. I don't know why they are so suspicious at the city limits post but sometimes they are. If it turns out there are a lot of uniforms by the red-and-white pole Herr Stolle goes for a little walk, a detour a couple of hundred metres south where a tree has a branch over the fence. There's an old concrete pillbox that shields Herr Stolle as he clambers over. You understand now why Herr Bode always leaves so early: to give Herr Stolle time to make his little walk, if it's needed."

Orris unfolded it like a bedtime story, as he'd remembered his mother speaking, her voice soothing fears of the dark. The girl's shoulders no longer shook.

"A footpath runs beside a field where they're growing beetroot, and the path rejoins the road a bit before the entrance to Staaken airfield. There are always uniforms there: a sea of khaki, with some airforce blue ones. Not all the airforce uniforms are on airforce men; some are on the G.R.U., the military secret police. So many uniforms. You'd think they'd recognize Herr Stolle by now, but no! Each morning there is a line of men rather like Herr Stolle queueing at the gate, hoping to get in before the bell rings. When Herr Stolle's turn comes three or four of them in their various uniforms inspect his papers. They scratch his identity card to see if it is forged—no, Herr Stolle's card is genuine; it was very expensive. And his work permit—is that in order? Yes, Herr Stolle has a good friend who is happy to give it in honour of his father. The men in uniform rummage in Herr Stolle's bag: 'Is this Dutch cheese with the red rind? How did Herr Stolle obtain Dutch cheese?' Though they do not call him 'Herr', certainly not 'comrade'. I do not think they really like Herr Stolle."

She turned in bed to watch him with deep still eyes.

"But that is only the uniforms at the gate. Inside they like Herr Stolle very much. At first it was because he brought little extras: peanuts or candy bars. Herr Stolle explained he shared a girl with an American sergeant, a man with distressing habits but welcome gifts. Later they appreciated that Herr Stolle was good at his job, very good indeed. They had never known such an electrician. He understood about serial lighting and cut-outs in case of power surges and devised a simple means of testing the inferior Russian wire for its load potential. Oh yes, Russian wire because Staaken is being urgently upgraded to take the latest Soviet planes. Not just big transport planes that need a longer runway but, the wise ones say, the latest night-fighters. Herr Stolle's work on runway lighting is highly valued. Soon it means the Russian Air Force will be able to control the approaches to the British airfield just inside the city limits at Gatow. Also the Russians will be well placed to patrol the air corridor to the American airport at Tempelhof. They'll be able to do it day and night, very soon now."

"Can I have a cigarette?" she asked.

Orris lit one and they shared it.

"Very soon. They're installing radar in the control tower but they won't let a German comrade near that. Never mind. Today I was testing the approach lighting so it was necessary to go into the administration building. First I pass through the main hangar. It is enormous. And Rahel, they say at one time it was used as a film studio. Imagine: fairytale princesses kissed Prince Charming under five-thousand-watt bulbs. Now there are benches and lathes and power-hammers and lubrication ramps. I go on, down to the basement where the main switches and junction boxes are. And that is where I see this weird and wonderful thing. Not the old firebuckets and the dirty bunk beds and the yellowed newspaper with the headline: Führer orders attack on Zhukov. Far stranger. Next to the electricity meter an old plaque is screwed to the brickwork: *In case of emergency, contact Spandauer Area Control at Kraftwerk West*. Fancy that: the Kraftwerk West power station, inside the city limits. The Russians draw electricity for their spanking airfield from the British sector of Berlin."

It was a little nugget of gold Orris had intended to keep to himself. It meant nothing to Rahel.

"I've never heard you talk so much before." She smiled, though the last echoes of darkness haunted her eyes.

6 June 1948
London

Miss Ingle said the Director-General had been asking for him and would he come up at his convenience. The old stand-bys used formalities: it meant jump to it. When Beamish entered the Director-General's office, he turned his eyes towards the window, an automatic gesture.

"Have a seat, Beamish."

The Director-General was behind his desk. There was peace in his face. The post-coital calm, Little Eric had termed it, when a problem that has been itching is resolved. Standing smiled, something Beamish hadn't seen for weeks. In truth, the Director-General might make the same observation about him.

"Not to beat about the bush," Standing said, "I'm handing in my commission. Thought I'd do you the courtesy of telling you in advance."

Beamish felt a terrible numbness. He supposed he must have made a disclaimer—what a shock, reconsider, good of the service—because Standing's droning voice entered his mind, like snatches of talk on a windy day. It was impossible to concentrate on what he was saying: "... increasing burden ... no eagerness for the chase ... none of us gets any younger ... golf, though my greatest handicap ..."

The signs had been there for months: lack of appetite for the battle, weariness with Civil Service intrigue, boredom with details. It had not gone unnoticed in the back corridors of Whitehall, where politicking held more fascination than politics. Who would be the new head? Another outsider? Another General? To promote from inside had always been suspect because an insider had his own little fiefdom that he favoured. But somehow Beamish's name elbowed its way into consideration, growing more prominent in that refined form of gossip known as policy-making. In the way of all gossip, no one knew precisely *how* his name was first mooted: a hint from somebody in the Cabinet Office, perhaps. Beamish is one of us: his tie says it, his taste in claret says it, the allusiveness of his conversation, the perchance wicked way of his tongue.

So Beamish was not unprepared for Standing's retirement. The actuality was still a shock. The possibility had grown to a probability that he would be promoted. Master would expect him to clasp eagerly the opportunity of becoming Director-General. Indeed, Master, with his source in the Cabinet Office, would work to engineer it. Beamish found the prospect intolerable. There was a fluttering of his eyelid. To be Director-General, to be topmost man on the greasy pole, to have direct charge of the espionage and evaluation and support activities of five hundred and thirty-eight souls and indirect responsibility for how many hundreds of smaller fish, to be under the constant scrutiny of his political masters and their bloodhounds in S.B. and Five, to dissemble constantly to his wife and such friends who imagined his job was something cultural, to devote every minute of his working day in furtherance of the King's Ministers, to strive for the enhanced glory of the British Empire; to be seen to do all this, to be accepted without question as straining his utmost while clandestinely, by God knows what subterfuges and betrayals, he sought to serve his Master in Moscow, all this was more than one human could bear. The burden of the job was enough to weary a man like Standing; to embrace the job and plot ceaselessly for the opposite pointed the way to madness.

"Beamish? Are you feeling all right?" The twin gun-barrels of Standing's eyes were trained on his face and Beamish, with a stab, recognized it had already begun: every action and hesitation and inflection of voice was being scrutinized. Had the Director-General stopped talking long before? What had he been saying? Something about a quiet ten minutes with Attlee and a recommendation, though nothing was fixed.

"Yes, D-G. Perhaps a touch jaded after the past few months."

"You took too much on yourself with the reorganization. You

can't run agents on a day-to-day basis and oversee the whole of the Europe desk."

But Beamish could never have allowed any other Controller to run his agents, to know who had been quietly recruited, what they did. So what would happen when he became Director-General? He was going to have to go back through the files, brush across the traces. He was going to have to consider the minutiae of the one big disaster linked to his name: the Dorothy Network. He was going to have to achieve a final solution to its sole survivor who had now burrowed under the floorboards in Berlin.

"It is your only fault, if I may say so." The Director-General was leaning forward. "You must learn to delegate more responsibility. A General cannot fight the battle, he can only direct its course."

"I doubt I would have been cut out to be a General," Beamish said and remembered to smile. "Deciding who to send out to die in battle." Already there'd been Brouček and Palacký and Woodburne and the others, but they'd died for the cause. Hunt had been sacrificed simply to protect his usefulness. Perhaps that was for the cause too. And himself? The cause would claim him in due course? The revolution is bigger than any individual in it.

Standing said: "That is why some Generals only look at the medals and the chins of the troops they're inspecting. It's hard to look men in the eye before you send them out to be killed."

There was a brief intense silence, neither man knowing how the conversation had arrived at this point. It seemed such a desperately personal confession.

"A bit of leave would buck you up."

"Yes," Beamish agreed. "Yes. Get the dust out of my lungs and the real world back in perspective."

"Take a couple of weeks off. The P.M. will canvass my opinion about a successor but I'll hold my fire until you're back. Make the most of your holiday. Once you've moved into this office you'll find your liberty is rationed, as everything else these days."

It was too early for madeira and Beamish declined tea. He

returned to his office, his mind already allocating priorities among the files he would need to launder. One priority was supreme: his break from office duties was going to have to be spent in Berlin. It was unlikely to be a holiday.

8 June 1948
Berlin

There was talk of it in the S-bahn train coming back from Staaken. That was the day when sky met earth, grey piled above grey, and Berliners said God was coming down hidden in the clouds to get a closer look at what the sinners were up to. Now, in the evening, Orris listened to the two women.

"I heard there were sixty or seventy of them."

"More than a hundred. Mark my words, more than a hundred."

"Armed, every one of them. Machine-guns, grenades, the whole arsenal. Who do they think they are? Is it their city? Answer me that."

"What they say is that Berlin is in their zone and they have the right."

"What is true and what they say are church and brothel. It is not their city. It is not their country. Not in a thousand years. Not till the herrings walk on their tails."

The harsh Berliner tones came from a woman with her face in greyish pouches, like a monstrous potato tuber. Her companion wore a black shawl streaked with wet and carried a small cabbage in a string bag.

"They think they can eat up Berlin block by block."

"Hungry as grey wolves. They make us show papers to come to our own city. Now they take over Anhalter. Where will it end?"

"You know as well as I do. Churchill should have given us back our guns. We have to fight them sooner or later."

"I won't be caught again. I keep a knife by the bed."

The strident Neukölln voices fell silent. The women didn't look at each other nor at the other passengers in the carriage. It touched on something no one wanted to talk about but no one would ever forget: how the Red Army had liberated Berlin, guns to the temples of the women they raped and raped again. The Berliners had a word for it: *Plünderfreiheit.* Forty-eight hours when the conquerors did as they wished and any woman who didn't respond to the "*Frau, komm,*" had her throat slit.

Orris walked down flooded streets to the Anhalter freight terminal where he'd met Munden a fortnight before. Blue-grey uniformed police formed a cordon to stop angry Berliners approaching the railway administration building. He could see two Soviet trucks outside the entrance but the soldiers who surrounded the trucks were American. American troops were everywhere and two machine-guns had been set up behind sandbags. Soviet soldiers stood just inside the entrance doors and there were more khaki figures at the windows. They had replaced their workday *Pilotkas* with combat helmets. Nobody moved. The Russians and Americans confronted each other, waiting for the order to fight.

In the months he'd been in the city, it was the first time Orris saw ordinary Berliners put aside their sullen indifference to all their conquerors. Here, in the anonymity of the crowd and knowing that whoever wanted to control the freight terminal also wanted to control their destiny, they were openly hostile to the Russians. Shouts and abuse were hurled; when it progressed to broken bricks, the police moved in.

Orris walked away. The rain fell steadily and the gutters rushed, the water flooding the road where the sewers were blocked. He sensed it was very close, the final struggle for Berlin. Why hadn't Beamish come, God damn him.

13 June 1948
Berlin

"They backed down," said Clay, "because they don't want to go to war. I'm sure of it. The Russians keep pushing and if we push right back, they retreat. We simply have to keep our nerve."

"They don't have to go to war, sir," Major Garn said. "They just breeze in when the politicians have had a bellyful."

"Hear anything from Paris?"

"They're waving their hands and arguing."

"London?" Clay looked down at Wrea, the C.I.A. man.

"Likewise, General, no decision. But Kordorf reports everyone he talks to says we'll have to go. We're not strong enough to resist if the Russians decide to fight, and we've got no answer if they decide to blockade the city."

"Dear Lord, why don't they understand? The Soviets believe they're going to get Berlin without a fight. Everyone else is persuaded of it too. What's happened to them, in God's name? Do we let the Soviets colonize the whole of Europe? Where's Charley?"

"Late lunch," Garn told him.

"Okay, make it a memo."

The army stenographer came in and waited with her pad in her lap, not looking at any of the men in the room.

"To Chief of Staff Gailey. Charles, I want you to send the following cable to Washington."

Clay had scribbled notes and he concentrated on them as he dictated.

"The release of freight at Anhalter terminal followed our ultimatum that we would take over the railway traffic tower located within our sector so that we would be in a position to move these cars with our own locomotives. Situation both there and at border has cleared up now, at least temporarily.

174

"It is quite possible that tightening of controls nearing the weekend resulted from Soviet apprehension that western zone currency reform might take place over the weekend. I am inclined to believe this more likely than a further tightening at the moment to force us from Berlin. That move will come when we install separate currency if it is to come at all.

"There is no practicability in maintaining our position in Berlin and it must not be evaluated on that basis. We can maintain our people in Berlin indefinitely, but not the German people if rail transport is severed. Nevertheless, we would propose to remain until the German people were threatened with starvation if the Soviets did resort to such extreme tactics. We are convinced that our remaining in Berlin is essential to our prestige in Germany and in Europe. Whether for good or bad it has become a symbol of the American intent."

Clay looked up at the stenographer.

"Okay?"

"Yes sir."

"Classify: top secret—though God knows why. By next month the Russians will be reading all the files."

He frowned a moment and shook his head. Even he had caught the fever.

14/15 June 1948
Paris/Vienna/Berlin

Beamish's route took him first to Paris. There he changed trains and changed identities.

Polytov met him in the first-class waiting-room at the Gare de l'Est, sitting down in an adjacent chair and asking for a light. Beamish noted he smoked Gauloises *bout filtre*. It marked the Russian as someone who'd never himself been a field man in a foreign country, only controlled them. "A field man never smokes filter tips because the manufacturer's name is on the filter end and you leave your calling card in every ash-tray." That had been the poet-warrior instructing at the place in Surrey. "Bloody Little Eric's forty hints on staying alive," Waller had muttered. They'd found Waller bumping against the quayside in Alexandria harbour eighteen months later.

"Thank you. Have you read the newspaper?" Polytov asked, holding out a copy of *Le Monde*.

"Not yet."

"I'll leave it with you."

Beamish held the paper folded in his hand. He could feel the outline of documents in it. There was a sheen of perspiration on his forehead and his shirt felt clammy against his back. Nerves, worse than last time in Paris. He fanned his face with the newspaper.

"Humid, isn't it?" Polytov remarked. Opposite them was a stout man with a briefcase on his knees, and a middle-aged woman with a cat-basket sat against the far wall. The woman stared, possibly because they were the only source of animation. "If you have time before your train, perhaps you'd care for some fresh air."

They picked their way round families with old suitcases and squalling children, porters with trolleys, young men with purposeful faces. The loudspeaker boomed unintelligibly against the hiss of a locomotive reducing pressure.

"Master was concerned about this trip," Polytov said. "Very, very concerned."

"He mustn't worry."

"What arrangements did you make in England?"

Beamish felt intense irritation. He was the first person to rise right through the ranks of the Intelligence Service to the very pinnacle and they thought he was incapable of feinting and weaving. "Just a holiday," he muttered. "The D-G's suggestion."

"You had to leave a contact address?"

"Hotel Beaugence near the Invalides. I'll need you to clear it for messages every morning. The desk clerk is all right."

"I'll see to it." They walked in silence while Polytov marshalled his questions. "First, why is it necessary to act at all? Berlin will be ours anyway very shortly. The Western powers are quarrelling among themselves and the French are on the brink of quitting. Incidentally, Master congratulates you, it has been most subtly achieved. Once we have Berlin, Orris is trapped."

Incidentally, he'd said. It made Beamish inwardly angry that the biggest coup anyone had mounted was thrown away as an incidental. He said: "Orris would get out. Run, tunnel, swim. You underestimate his resourcefulness. He'd hitch a Soviet plane to Moscow and walk into the British embassy there. They'd be riveted with a tale of how the heir-apparent to the throne had betrayed half a dozen agents."

"Good enough. But why do you have to go after this man yourself? Master wants particularly to know."

Beamish's irritation didn't lessen. Oh that *particularly*, as if he were a schoolboy to be threatened for a misdemeanour. It wasn't even as if they were immaculate themselves. In training the men from Moscow were formidable: they could tear down a mountain with their bare hands. Of course, a mountain kept still, a mountain had no brain.

"Because your people have tried twice and he's still there. He's a threat." Beamish turned to Polytov for emphasis. A man stood against one of the pillars reading, his face in *Le Parisien Libéré*. Not reading exactly. The newspaper still trembled.

"That is not accurate. Berlin is a city under military occupation and we handed the problem to the G.R.U. They failed again, and that has been noted." The G.R.U. had been under a cloud for years, since Hitler's Barbarossa campaign caught them un-awares. "What is true is that Orris is a genuine threat to your position and you sought to conceal it from Master. Don't try and deny it. We were told a petty criminal needed to be eliminated, not a serious danger."

Beamish hadn't been going to deny anything. To be ruthless with himself, he conceded it an old man's vanity, the reluctance to admit the younger man constantly getting the better of him.

"If Master is dissatisfied with my services, perhaps he would care to cultivate someone else." Beamish's tone was waspish and petulant.

Polytov considered Beamish, sorting out implications and priorities.

"It is true," Polytov said, "you are in need of a holiday. When your business in Berlin is finished, we can drive you to the Baltic coast for a break. You are not thinking straight at the moment. Master has encouraged your climb to the top and can hardly be expected to drop you now. You understand that. You couldn't have the job and *not* work for Master because you are too knowledgeable about a number of our activities."

They'd reached the end of the platform and turned to stroll back. An engine made a mournful cry that echoed under the high roof.

He'd been threatened, Beamish knew. It was quite explicit: your life is the property of Master.

"In Berlin," Beamish said, "I shall want facilities."

"Make your wishes known."

"Also it must be understood that I act entirely alone. Orris is a cunning one. He's dug himself in, running a new identity. The one thing that will make him show himself is the knowledge I'm there. He'll know I'm there, he'll smell it in the wind. He wants me to come, he expects me to come. He's dropped hints, shown himself and backed away. Like a lover, flirting, drawing back because you know you draw the other with you. It's as if we had a tryst, only there's revenge in his heart."

If Polytov felt Beamish unbalanced in his reaction to Orris, it didn't show in his face.

"You're exposing yourself to great danger. You've stressed that Orris is the best man in the field you've ever met."

"What choice is there? He's hidden. Only a prize big enough will lure him into the open. The risk is calculated."

"Master agrees."

"I must be absolutely alone when I meet him. Orris will sense if there's any cover. No Moscow hoodlums, no thick-ankled women with shopping baskets. Is that understood? No men with their faces buried in newspapers."

But when Beamish looked away to the pillar, there was no one.

"If that is the way you want it."

178

"It's the only way," Beamish insisted. "If I see anyone in a shadow, I want to be certain it's someone unfriendly after me."

"Where is your luggage?"

"In the *consigne*."

"It is time you collected it."

It was an eighteen-hour journey to Vienna Westbahnhof.

Beamish stood by the flower-stall outside the station, adjusting a red carnation in his buttonhole. How Moscow adored these conspirator's games! A taxi pulled up and the driver wound down the window: "Are you going far? I am almost out of benzine." He spoke English with a trace of accent, Hungarian Beamish surmised.

"There's never that problem with horse cabs."

Without another word the driver got out and loaded Beamish's suitcase in the boot. He insisted on Beamish sitting in the front seat with him. They drove through the bullet-scarred half dead city and east into the flat country along a pitted tarmac road. The driver spoke once, cursing a stray dog in a village. A couple of kilometres short of Neusiedl they turned off the main road, past an encampment of tents of the occupying Red Army, and on to a military airstrip. The driver showed some sort of pass that was immediately accepted.

The flight took two and a half hours in a droning Soviet transport plane. There were thirty-two seats in the passenger section but Beamish travelled alone. The hammering of the engines gave him a headache.

There were heavy clouds over Berlin, though the air was hot and humid. The aircraft made a single circuit over the disembowelled city before touching down at Schönefeld.

A black car drove up to the plane and a man who gave his name as Martin said he'd been sent to help Beamish. They drove across the puddled tarmac to a makeshift immigration building and Beamish said he would take a taxi from there. No taxis. Well, he'd take a bus or a works lorry—they were extending the runway at Schönefeld too.

"From now on," Beamish insisted, "I do not want to be seen in anyone's company. If your orders have been to shadow me, guard me, molly-coddle me in any way, then check with Mazurov in Moscow. No cover. I don't want my quarry to see you with me and he could be anywhere—waiting at a bus stop, working that cement-mixer."

17 June 1948
Berlin

Orris did a ten-hour stint at Staaken airfield and then, like all the workforce, volunteered an extra hour without pay to help build socialism.

Then he reversed his crossing procedure. It was more difficult in the evening to get the platform at Staaken deserted for the switch of papers. Sometimes he dawdled for fifteen minutes. On the journey back he smelled his own sweat with all the caution of a Wee Free visiting Rome. He established no pattern, getting down at Pichelsberg or Grossmarkt or, on this warm summer evening, at Pankow. He liked to be in the Soviet sector when he telephoned Munden.

"Where are you calling from, old boy?"

"A phone booth. I've got something for Eurcon. Just a whisper, from the cousin of the wife of one of my workmates, but it sounds genuine. There's a Soviet pontoon bridge train crossed over the border at Frankfurt/Oder. This wife's cousin works in Number Two signalbox at Frankfurt and he says the Soviets cleared the station while the train moved through. Headed west. No destination given. Flash it to Eurcon, let him trace it."

"I'll let London know."

"Alpha classification to Eurcon. We don't want a lot of Depot gossip."

"No go, old boy. Eurcon's taking a spot of leave. Just heard it."

Orris had been eyeing a man exercising his dog. Another train had come in on the S-bahn and he shifted his gaze, watching the tired faces come out of the station entrance.

"Tell Eurcon. What contact address did he leave?"

"I suppose I could find out. Leave me your phone number and I'll . . ."

Orris cut the connection. What did it matter? Whatever address Beamish had given, he was on his way to Berlin. At long last Orris had drawn the hound.

18/20 June 1948
Berlin

Orris was a needle.

The metaphor grew in Beamish's mind over the days. At first it was the size of the haystack where Orris was hidden. Two million lived in west Berlin, a million in the east. By the third day the sense had become more active: Orris needled him. Orris had thwarted every effort to silence him, Orris possessed the knowledge that could destroy him, Orris had refrained from telling anyone in authority because he wanted to make Beamish run after him. Orris wanted personal vengeance.

Before he'd left the Depot Beamish had worked the files to death, not just Orris's life-file but the separate operational files. Then with cross-references he'd gone through the files of every agent Orris had been connected with, looking for hints of the kind of man he was, his weaknesses, skills, quirks, patterns of behaviour, prejudices, repeated tricks of the trade. For an agent, like every man, leaves footprints in the sand.

He discovered details he'd never known about Orris: that he detested the smell of fish, was allergic to sticking-plaster, was double-jointed in one thumb. Other scraps were more nourishing: Orris spoke both Czech and German with a Sudeten accent, had made a disastrous marriage as relief (so the Depot's witch-doctor said) after months of self-disciplined isolation, was a political *naif*, had no historical perspective. He was the Depot's best man in the field: he was proficient with gun, knife and hands; when he stood still he went unnoticed; he moved fast without hurrying; he was infinitely plausible when questioned; knowing when to volunteer a morsel in order to deflect a probe, sensing when to display anger or indignation, understanding whether to mumble dumb nonsense or smile transparent truth; his antennae picked up the slightest discordant vibration; he suffered no fool gladly; he possesed all the manual skills Beamish lacked; he was unconscious of the rarity of his expertise and showed no arrogance.

A room had been made available to Beamish in a building past the cemetery in Prenzlauer. Unusually, for security services have a deep-rooted need to mislead, there was no plaque on the wall naming the place as some obscure annexe. A second curiosity was the absence of uniforms, apart from the gatekeeper. Beamish was viewed woodenly by the men he passed on the stairs. Who were they? Refugees from Gehlen? Many in the Gehlen organization had been rumoured to be agnostic during the Hitler period, waiting for what would follow after the inevitable defeat of the Nazis. Some must have chosen the Soviet side rather than go west with Gehlen.

A Sergeant by name Wehlak was assigned to Beamish. The man seemed desperately painstaking, but was that a fault? He'd survived the war. "Have you visited the Soviet Union?" Beamish asked, trying to establish contact. "Yes," the Sergeant answered, considering whether to say more. And then, as if he'd been on a tourist excursion: "I was in a *Panzer* at Stalingrad. We were cut off." "The Soviet army captured you?" "No." There was a pause for more consideration. "I painted a red star on our tank and drove through the Soviet lines back to our division." "You should have given yourself up, avoided fighting for fascism." "I had sworn obedience to the *Führer*," Wehlak said, which ended that conversation.

Beamish had listed every name Orris was known to have worked under: Horaz, Conmar, Sladký, Kellermann, Brownlow; and the first names Giri, Anton, Petr, Curth and Charles Daniel. There was no pattern to them, no trick with initials or talisman with the number of letters. Nevertheless he instituted a search for reference to any of the names at the Rathaus, the military administration, the various authorities for food-rationing, clothing, housing and employment. The names drew blank.

It is not hopeless.

In the sombre hours at the end of another sixteen-hour shift Beamish felt his morale slipping. Not hopeless, he reassured himself. We know a tremendous amount about him. We have a cut-off date because he arrived on March 29th or 30th. We know his sex. We know the narrow band of age he must use. We have his photograph.

Not hopeless.

Beamish and the Sergeant worked at it day by day. They concentrated first on the Food Supply and Control Administration. Orris had to eat. To buy food legally it was necessary to register. There were some eight thousand new registrations since the beginning of April and after two phone calls Beamish was given the further assistance of a pair of clerks. They were searching, Beamish said, for a ruthless war criminal, a man without family, born early 1920s, registered after 29th March. As Beamish anticipated, there were few who fitted the description because it was a generation that had been decimated by war. Colonel Markgraf, former Wehrmacht officer and now pro-Soviet police chief, released twenty policemen to visit the names. Of fifty-eight possibles, all but three were cleared the first evening and the remainder within twenty-four hours.

"Then," said Beamish to the police Sergeant with slow eyes, "he must have *bought* a ration card."

"Very likely," Wehlak agreed. "You can buy anything in Berlin."

"Question them, these people who can arrange anything."

The Sergeant looked dubious.

"Offer them money," Beamish pressed. "They are greedy, anti-social elements. Buy the information from them. This man has to eat, so he needs a ration card and to register."

"They won't tell us. These people continue to do business because they are recognized as the alternative to the official way. To co-operate with us is to destroy that reputation."

"He'll buy black-market food too. Street dealers. Scum with a suitcase and quick legs."

"We'll try showing a photograph. These people are not easy to question."

"Arrest them."

"Difficult if they're in a different sector."

"Kidnap them."

Beamish sank into his own thoughts. He was concerned with a particular problem. But because he was part of the lumpen intelligentsia—his own offhand expression—his mind speculated on the general question: of how we imagine another human being as an extension of our own personality. Abruptly he veered back to the particular problem. Because he himself hated being touched, he'd transferred the same trait to Orris. Whereas the opposite was the truth. He called Wehlak back.

"This man is highly sexed. He has been known to associate with whores. What areas do prostitutes frequent?"

"Until the liberation of the city by the Soviet army it was possible to tell. But now you could walk the length of Budapester-strasse and Kurfürstendamm and have your choice of thousands who ask no more than a cup of real coffee and a cigarette. There is such a shortage of men that even the occupation forces cannot meet. In the districts of Wilmersdorf, Moabit, Schöneberg, Kreuzberg, Wedding, Pankow. . . ."

"All right." Beamish silenced him with a hand. In any case,

after two and a half months Orris would be living with a woman. Not just for comfort but as cover: a man on his own is always more noticeable.

"Is that all, Herr . . . ?" The Sergeant chose not to use the name of the Englishman.

"One more thing. Visit every gymnasium in the city. The man needs exercise to keep physically fit. Take his photograph with you."

"Yes, certainly."

"Is unemployment a problem?"

"There is work for everyone on reconstruction. You have only to look out of the window."

"Then tomorrow morning we start on employment," Beamish told him. "The man would take some kind of job. The neighbours gossip about a man who hangs about all day. We check every male of the right age who has taken a job."

That night was hot and airless. Beamish, feeling profoundly restless, wandered through the long midsummer dusk; past a moonscape of grey rubble; past a window with a picture of Stalin surrounded by red crêpe and a placard: *We salute the father of the Soviet people and the defeater of fascism*; across the foul little Spree river; through the American sector with M.P.s cruising in jeeps; past the man with the valise full of socks, some without holes; past the stump-legged Afrika Korps veteran with the accordion and the cap spotted with coins; threading between couples round Zoo station; under the railway arches at Savigny-platz where a woman hissed at him to share the gloom.

Angry, not at peace with himself, Beamish analysed his emotions. He had every right to be self-critical. Orris had toyed with him, lured him deliberately. Hinting at a job with military connections was such a blatant ploy. Couldn't be true, surely? Tomorrow would tell. Yet even though he'd known Orris was enticing him, still he'd come. And now couldn't find the wretched man. It made him all the more irritable.

It was almost dark in the streets. Sky deep purple, windows

blind. Electricity was rationed and even in summer people had to be miserly by this time of month. Beamish headed back into the Soviet sector, unease pricking at the back of his neck.

Time was running out. He had to return to London but he had to silence Orris first. Beamish frowned: to silence someone. A terrible euphemism. The Dorothy Network had been silenced, Hunt had been silenced, Orris would be silenced. Sometime in the future he himself would enter into that *stille Nacht*.

Beamish peered at faces and saw only darkness and despair. Once, twice maybe, he fancied something was at his shoulder; but when he turned there was nobody.

22 June 1948,
Berlin/London

Before Frau Zyber got to the door the hammering came again.

The man on the step was alone but a second man sat at the wheel of a small car down by Herr Gründgen's building. The man standing in front of her had his fist raised as if about to knock a third time. It wasn't the raised fist that brought the chill to Frau Zyber's blood, it was his eyes.

"I'd like to speak to Herr Stolle."

From his accent he was a local boy not a Britisher. And his eyes, trained to betray no emotion whatever they witnessed, his eyes showed his job had always been knocking on people's doors. He'd kept his other hand in his coat pocket. A coat, on such an afternoon.

"You have the wrong address," the dragon said. "Nobody here called Stolle."

She was closing the door when he reached out his foot to stop it.

"We are friends from work."

Such eyes never had friends.

"We?" Frau Zyber looked away to the little car again. Sometimes the Gestapo had come like this, one alone at the door not to arouse suspicion, another down the street in a car in case the suspect bolted. Of course she was a good German but she hadn't always told the Gestapo everything. In districts like Wedding and Moabit, you stood solid against the rest of the world.

"He hasn't been to work for a week. We're worried in case he's ill."

"I tell you, nobody called Stolle lives here."

"He had an address on his work permit but they hadn't heard of Herr Stolle there either. Then someone remembered he'd talked of his girl, sharing her with an American, a place in this street."

"I have never heard of Herr Stolle. There is no sick man here. I do not run a brothel for American soldiers." She pushed on the door but it held firm. She blurted out: "You're not his pals from work. Look at your hand—that's never done hard work. You smell different. We don't like your sort asking questions round here. Do you want me to shout for Herr Gründgen? He's not young anymore but he knows how to use a half-brick."

The dragon looked through the gap in the curtains half an hour later and the two men still sat in the car.

Summer was best. In summer much of the bulk of the Foreign Office was decently obscured by the leaves on the plane trees on the east side of the park.

The Director-General turned from the window and picked up the letter again. He displayed that magic faith that on a second reading bad news would have changed to good.

The writing-paper was headed Hotel Beaugence in Paris. An attached flimsy carried the translation done by the Babel Room.

Dear Sir,
Mr Beamish, after passing several days here, announced that he was going to pass a week or so fishing in the Vosges region.

He said he had made no reservation, but after he had obtained a hotel he would communicate the address. At this moment we have received no instructions from him. He said that, in any case, he would return by June 25th.

Would you be so kind as to accept, dear sir, our most distinguished sentiments.

P. L. Maheu
Assistant Manager

Fishing? Beamish? It was the first the Director-General had heard of it.

He sat stone still for some time, only a hand moving up to his mouth with a cigarette. Smoke came out of his mouth and nostrils like fumes leaking from a volcano.

His critics in Whitehall maintained that Standing was incapable of thought; which was untrue. Or perhaps that he had no emotions; equally untrue. Or being a product of Sandhurst, had no imagination; which itself showed a lack of imagination. What his critics meant was that Standing despised them as Paperclip Generals.

He told Miss Ingle to send for the Political Evaluator. A week or two later, when Houghton had surfaced and was in circulation again, Little Eric took him down the road to the Two Chairmen and demanded his account of the day the earth stood still. Houghton, still in shock, recollected his meeting with the Director-General consisted mainly of terrible silences while the implications sank in.

"Polly," Standing began, and even the use of that term was unusual, "I've had a priority call from the Foreign Office twenty minutes ago; we're going ahead with the issue of new currency in Berlin. In spite of Stalin's threats."

"So it's war within the week," Houghton said. There was a black silence, the sound of his voice echoing melodramatically in his ears. He expanded: "War if we resist Stalin's threats. Defeat without honour if we don't."

Dark eyes drilled into Houghton's own.

"Is that what you think?" Standing demanded, his voice rumbling.

"Don't you, D-G?"

"I believe . . ." The Director-General lit another cigarette with meticulous care while Houghton waited. "I believe that is what we were intended to think. Which is a horse of a very different colour."

In the silence they heard the soft sound of typing from next door.

"How many years have you known Beamish?"

Houghton, already dreading the course of his audience with this wrathful god, answered quietly: "Since the beginning of the war."

"Do you consider he would make a good and conscientious Director-General? Could he step into my shoes?"

Standing's face was so thunderous that Houghton didn't answer.

"Beamish has gone A.W.O.L.," the Director-General continued relentlessly. "Paris Residency is still trying to trace. Until Beamish is located, until we have a complete and convincing explanation for his absence, his security clearance is cancelled."

"A.W.O.L.?" Houghton said, still trying to take in the implications. "No worse?"

"There is no worse," Standing brushed aside the hesitation. "He was heir-apparent to my throne. The king has no private life."

"But . . ." Houghton was silenced by those gun-barrel eyes.

"At the moment we issue new currency throughout west Germany, at the moment of crisis in Berlin, our European Controller and East European Executive disappears. We do not know where he is nor what he is doing. We do not know that he's sold his soul to the devil. He might even have been kidnapped. But his position no longer allows him any benefit of the doubt. He is to be considered, until proved innocent, a traitor. You will take charge of the East European Desk. You will have full access to all Beamish's papers. Your special responsibility will be Berlin. You will sleep in the office, insofar as you sleep. You will report only to me. You will have access at any hour of day or night. That is all."

Houghton left in another appalling silence.

23 June 1948
Berlin

Nothing happened.

Orris had cramp in both legs from a night in the confines of the blue van and nothing had happened. The whole bloody night those two men in their VW had waited. Five days Orris had spent haunting the ruins and on the sixth he had observed the conversation with Frau Zyber and then he'd gone to negotiate for the van. He'd returned, angling the van into the alley, and waited.

At about ten o'clock one man had gone off and returned with food wrapped in paper. A sausage, Orris thought, from the way they ate. It was hard to see in the soft light from the gas lamp. During the night both men went to relieve themselves in the ruins, and once or twice they walked round the block to get the circulation going.

They were lucky. Orris was afraid when he came to stand that his cramped legs would buckle.

Once, past midnight, both men had tumbled urgently out of their car and while one stood with his hand in his coat pocket the taller had stalked towards the van. Orris pushed back the corner of paper that covered the rear glass panel and waited. Had he made some movement that rocked the van? He heard muffled steps circling, the door handles being tried, then knuckles knocking a tattoo on the side panel like a signal. God, he'd done that very thing in Prague, half a lifetime ago. It had been twenty minutes before he'd lifted the corner of paper again. He hadn't dared smoke and hardly moved again.

He had a lot of time to think and not enough to think about.

What they needed was some kind of marriage bureau, Beamish

and him, to introduce each other. Bloody funny. He was looking for Beamish, Beamish was looking for him. Because the first to get a clear sight of the other would win.

Orris watched while the moon rose, its old light leaning in among the ruins, turning the blank wall of Frau Zyber's building into a pale sheet hung in the night.

The trick had been not to make it simple, for Beamish was too clever to accept a gift. He'd only believe something he worked for. The plan had come all at once, unfolding in his mind like a fist unclenching; and if it had taken weeks to entice Beamish and days waiting for the final act, it was still running precisely as he foresaw.

He'd gone to earth, made use of Munden, dropped a hint or two, knowing Beamish would be compelled to come. He knew too that Beamish would make use of his political masters to help process the trace. He would work through the bureaucratic machine, sifting its files and cards and forms in triplicate, looking for evidence of a Sladký or a Kellermann, not really expecting to find one. Beamish would expect new cover and false papers. He would delve among the bureaucratic byways, looking for the sudden appearance of a man of the right age, searching among ration-cards and police records and hospital admissions and driving permits and clothing coupons and coal rations and the dozen other snares of red tape. There would be a mass of blind alleys and false scents. That was part of it. Make Beamish work, build the tension, because success would be all the sweeter. At some stage Beamish would turn his attention to employment. Among the scores of identities to be checked there would be Herr Stolle, constructing a bloody Soviet air base. Perfect.

Beamish, the clever old controller, had smelled out the fox's earth. With luck he would come in person.

While the fox, most cunning in the field, watched from the hedgerow.

Beamish didn't come.

At eight in the morning the two men were relieved. It was like a shift change at the factory. A second VW drove up with two men in the front seat, they exchanged perfunctory words, the first car drove away.

Orris followed. He scrambled into the driving seat, his knee-joints in agony as they unglued. He kept a hundred metres behind, conscious of how conspicuous he was. There were Occupation vehicles, horse-drawn wagons, buses, some bicycles, but only a handful of privately registered cars and vans. When they turned south-east into Brunnenstrasse and he was sure they were running clear down to the Soviet sector, Orris risked a kilometre on sidestreets where the cobbles had gaping holes. He caught the VW at right angles just before it crossed the white line. The little car immediately turned east and cut a zigzag swathe past block after block of ruins and half-hearted reconstruction. Where the hell were they going? Reporting directly to the Kremlin?

There were traffic signs in four languages but few street names, no district signboards, no S-bahn or U-bahn stations. Orris was lost.

The VW disappeared into the courtyard of a two-storeyed grey building and solid metal gates swung shut. A wall topped with iron railings ran the whole circumference of the building. It stood isolated from its neighbours, a certain pretence to it like the former town villa of a successful surgeon or barrister. Now it had been swallowed by the grey world of bureaucracy. It carried no name, hoisted no flag, gave no hint of what happened beyond the iron railings. The ground-floor windows were hidden by the wall; the upstairs ones were shuttered.

Orris parked the van round the corner. He walked right round the block to stretch his legs and returned to the back of the van. He was hungry and very tired.

He knew with a certainty that had nothing to do with logic that this was the place Beamish had chosen as his lair. The building had the aura, the same all over the world, of too many secrets hidden in filing cabinets, too many secrets dragged into the open, too much pain and too much indifference.

Orris eased open the rear door of the van to check he had a

clear sight of the gate. He double-checked the magazine of the machine-pistol. He settled to wait.

Once the gate swung back and a car with motorcycle escort sped away. Orris eased the safety-catch back on.

He felt more alone than ever before in his life, with that coldness that settles on a man whose only purpose is to kill someone he knows.

He considered idly the notion of driving with brazen face up to the gate and showing a parcel. Special delivery for Beamish. Whisky for the Englishman.

He turned his wrist to check the time. 10.56.

It could only have been a minute or two later that the Volkswagen came from the west and stopped in the entrance, blaring its horn at the gate. Orris frowned, something about the driver's features striking a chord. The gates swung open and the car accelerated forward with a face briefly appearing at the oval back window, a terrified little face taking with it a final memory of liberty, a white face with dark hair and dark smudges under the eyes, a face drawn into the lines of horror he remembered from the mime of the Prisoner. The car passed into the courtyard and the gates swung shut on Rahel.

"Oh, you bastards," Orris whispered.

They could get nothing out of her.

She stood where they had led her, facing the shuttered window. One of the men had pulled her in by the arm, three or four steps into the room, and when he let go she stopped. Her eyes looked wide and drugged, like a refugee's.

One of the men spoke to her and she didn't hear. He slapped her cheek, jerking her face to the right. She stayed in that position, like a doll with its head swivelled, with no thought of rubbing the hurt.

Beamish hurried into the room, taking in the waif of a girl. "Cradle-snatcher," he muttered, and then in German, "Sit down."

193

There was no reaction and one of the men pulled her by the shoulders and forced her into a straightbacked chair.

"You may leave," Beamish ordered. His German was English-accented but correct, learned during an era when German culture was highly regarded. When the two men had closed the door he got out his cigarette packet. His hand trembled a little, but she seemed blind to his eagerness. "Do you want a cigarette?"

She was perched on the chair, stiff and awkward, nothing showing on her face.

"They're English. You must be used to English cigarettes by now. He brings them to you, doesn't he?"

Her silence affected Beamish, making him feel foolish for talking into a void. He took one of the cigarettes and lit it. "Here." He held it out and when she made no move he put it in the ash-tray in front of her. It smouldered and died unregarded.

"We thought he was Herr Stolle but you know him as something different. Herr Bode. I expect you called him Gustav, didn't you? Neither is his real name. Did he tell you he was British?"

The colour had risen to the cheek that had been slapped. The other kept its pallor.

"They talked to your landlady this morning..." Beamish faltered, not knowing the nature of the "talk". He looked back at the girl. "She said your name is Rahel. Do you love this Englishman, Rahel? Yes, I expect he can be quite charming when he wants. Did he tell you his English name? George, like our king. Oh yes, I'm English too, by the way. I've come to Berlin because I need to find George. He ran away from his friends in London, which is really very silly. Now he seems to have run away from his job in Berlin. They are quite worried about him there. But I'm sure he hasn't run away from you. Do you know where he goes during the day now? Does he come back to you at night?"

Beamish got up and stood in front of her. The room was all wrong, with its thin carpet and metal desk and high bare walls. A little luxury might have relaxed her, something soft, hinting at better times.

"How old are you, child? What are you: eighteen, sixteen,

younger? Perhaps George was a bit naughty making friends with a girl so young, but that just shows how fond of you he is."

His eyelid began flickering. It was extraordinary how she affected him. He couldn't stop talking because she wouldn't start. The certainty struck him: she wasn't going to utter a word. The thugs outside would be able to drag no sound from her. The eagerness he'd felt was hopelessly misplaced.

"Child, child," with a leak of irritation, "did it never occur to you he was engaged in something naughty? You must have guessed he wasn't what he pretended. He had a secret, perhaps something too dark to share with you. A lot of people in this city want to conceal their past but he had to hide what he was doing at this moment." He took a breath. "*Now*, with the city in tumult." His hand reached out but couldn't touch her. "I'm not a stern old Prussian *Papi*, I shan't punish you."

No emotion in her face.

"Did you like looking after him? It's good to have someone to care for and when I find George I'll send him back to you. But, of course, I have to know where he is first. Tell me the sort of places he used to go to. He must have taken you out for a drink. A pretty girl like you must like dancing. Would you like to go dancing again with George?"

Silence.

"Say something, Rahel. A word, one word."

In a simple movement Rahel rose to her feet. She stepped round Beamish and stood in the middle of the room. Beamish turned and was transfixed. Without expression on her face she took her clothes off, dropping them in a heap, until she stood naked.

"The Dancer," she said. She started with slow sweeping movements of her arms, tucking her head to one side. She hummed in her little girl voice, her legs and slight body moving to a slow rhythm, drifting like thistledown until she smacked with a physical shock into the unseen bars of her cell. She gripped the air in front of her, knuckles white, staring through Beamish into the past.

"I'm ready for the demons."

She turned her back and crouched on all fours before him, her pinched white buttocks tense.

The uniform was too big around the waist and too short in the sleeves. That didn't concern Orris. People look in a policeman's face, trying to read the future; if they feel guilty, their eyes slip away and are caught by the stripes and insignia of authority. Orris did up the last of the buttons and adjusted the cap.

The policeman's body, stripped to his underclothes, lay in the back of the van. Orris had struck him as he opened the rear doors to satisfy his curiosity. "Sergeant," Orris had protested, "there's nothing in the back but radishes and onions for the Soviet Officers' Club in Karlshorst. I swear it."

The policeman had puffed out his cheeks in disbelief and started round to the back. Then he'd stopped, realizing he'd lose face if he opened the back and this whining young man was proved correct.

"Go on, look. I've not got a dead whore in the back." Orris coughed, the grating of his accent false in his ears, and recovered his nerve. "Are you scared I'll report you to the Comrade Major and you'll make the big trip east?"

With Prussian dignity the policeman continued to the rear, pulled open the double doors and peered into the empty depths. He was turning back with outrage on his face when the heel of Orris's hand caught him under the square of his jaw by his ear. "Only the devil can break a man's neck," Little Eric, more warrior than poet, warned. "You have to go upwards, twisting, brutal. Even then, you need the devil's luck." The spinal column snapped quite audibly. Orris caught the man by the elbows.

"All right, all right, don't take my word, take a closer look," Orris grumbled, easing him into the interior of the van. Orris scrambled after.

Had anyone noticed? A cart pulled by a tattered nag had been passing. The woman leading the horse looked too exhausted to see more than the road stretching ahead.

Beamish slit open the envelope. The paper had a round purple-inked stamp at the top in Cyrillic characters he couldn't read. Underneath in English:

> A report from Paris says our man at the Beaugence Hotel has been questioned about your whereabouts. Imperative you return to London earliest. Contact me. Master. Message ends. Timed 12.18.

"I have to contact my controller in Moscow," Beamish said. "Is this phone secure?"

Sergeant Wehlak shook his head.

"Well, I must go to the Residency," Beamish said.

"The Resident is not there. He's liaising with the city administration at the Rathaus during the crisis."

Liaising, Beamish thought, a nice phrase. "I'll go there. It's closer." He walked towards the door. "Maintain surveillance on Stolle's place." After all, Orris might return.

"And her?" The Sergeant pointed to Rahel huddled in a chair.

"Find her a blanket."

"Is she sick?"

"Yes," Beamish said. "Yes."

There was no second mirror in the Horch or Beamish might have noticed earlier. As they turned out of Elbingerstrasse he glanced back and saw the van some way behind.

"Is that van following us?"

There was a pause while the driver flicked his eyes to the mirror.

"Could be." The driver was grudging. "A blue van pulled out as we left."

It had been six years since Beamish's final flourish in the field, recruiting peasant women and bakers and village mechanics in a long line from Clermont-Ferrand to that treacherous fisherman at San Sebastian. He no longer lived by his wits, trusting no man's smile, choosing loneliness because you were safe from love's betrayal. He studied the van, over a hundred metres behind. The cap was pulled low on the driver's forehead. He seemed a very short man, too short for Orris. Or was he crouching over the wheel?

"Is that a police uniform?" Beamish asked.

"I can't tell."

"Do they use unmarked vans?"

The driver shrugged. The Englishman asked such puerile questions.

Their car was approaching the devastation of Alexanderplatz.

"Shall I do a circuit round the Alex to see if he follows?"

"Yes," Beamish said, peering back. There were reflections of broken clouds across the van's windscreen that constantly obscured the scrap of face. "No, I'm in a hurry. Drive direct to the Rathaus and if . . ."

Beamish was thrown forward as the car braked violently.

"God in heaven," the driver muttered. Three youths with lank hair ran across the square in front of them, bounding away with startled faces. Alexanderplatz was a millrace of trams and buses and people. Young men tore through the crowds, urging, beckoning them to follow. A loudspeaker van blared some message.

"Ulbricht," the driver said.

"Keep going," Beamish told him. "It's urgent."

They could hear it now above the chesty noise of the Horch's engine, the chanting of a disciplined crowd.

"What's happening?" The tension had aged Beamish's face.

"The revolution," the driver said. "The West is trying to force the new Deutschmark on Berlin and the people are rising in protest. A week and the whole city will be ours. By autumn, the whole of Germany."

So it has come, Beamish thought. For days he'd lived with nothing but the problem of tracking down Orris. His view had narrowed to filing-cabinets and buff forms while the world had turned and the crisis had broken. He felt no particular triumph.

Half a kilometre down Königstrasse, massive above the ruins, was the monstrous red brick of the Rathaus, seemingly immune to the worst destruction of the war. A mob surrounded it, surging to hammer on the roof of a car arriving with some local dignitary, chanting "They shall not pass, they shall not pass," and a new cry starting at the far end of the packed street and sweeping through the mass, "Direct democracy, direct democracy, direct democracy."

"You'll never get inside," the driver announced. "I'm not going closer. If they think you're one of the Magistrat they'll smash the car."

"I have to get in. I have to see Voloshky."

"You're mad. Let me drive you to Karlshorst."

Beamish was out of the car and pushing through the edge of the crowd. The faces were intoxicated with it all, the electric thrill of mob-fever, breathing in the smell of power, eyes bright with excitement. They hadn't tasted ecstasy like this since Hitler had put a bullet through his brain.

"Excuse me, excuse me, Soviet Control Commission." Beamish held his grey-and-red identity card forward, pressing at bodies that pressed back, his voice overwhelmed in the roar as windows in the Rathaus burst open and the banner was flung out: *Death to Clay and the Western Imperialists.*

A loudspeaker van was relaying some urgent message over and over. Grötewohl, Ulbricht, there was no identifying the voice, and the words were submerged in the storm of sound.

A voice, harsh with shouting above the uproar of the crowd, bellowed at his shoulder: "Make way for the comrade, let our Soviet comrade pass."

A path opened and Beamish made to turn to thank the voice of authority. He felt the hard metallic pressure in his back and heard the voice muttering in English: "Just keep going, walk as if nothing was wrong, you've got death on your heels if you take a single false step."

In German again Orris shouted: "Our comrade has urgent business inside."

And in English, for Beamish's ears: "Who are you going to see?"

Beamish shuffled forward with hesitant feet, the steps to the Rathaus entrance looming in front.

"Who are you seeing, you poxy bastard, or I'll shoot you now."

"The Resident."

Orris gripped Beamish's arm and jerked him half round.

"The M.V.D. Resident? He's in this building?"

"Yes."

Beamish could see his face now under the police cap, angry eyes staring while he thought hard.

"What's his name?"

Beamish held back, confused by the uproar and the gun in his spine, uncertain how to recover his authority, even how to save his life.

"His name, blast you."

"Voloshky."

There were four policemen stationed at the entrance, not preventing the rioters going in, simply standing and staring. There was agony on Beamish's face and one of the policemen was eyeing them. Orris prodded the gun hard.

"Don't even think of it," Orris warned. "I'm dressed the same as they are." They took the first step and he said, low and with complete conviction: "Understand this. If there's any trouble, any chance of your escaping or shouting for help, any hint that everything's not right, I'll kill you first and take my chances second, so help me God. Get that crystal clear."

They approached the doors and Orris called out: "Comrade Voloshky has sent for him. It's something vital."

They were nodded through.

Colonel Markgraf's orders to his police force had been explicit: there must be no attempt to maintain security. Inside the City Hall the rioting made it necessary to shout.

"Where's Voloshky?"

"I don't know."

"Don't bloody lie."

"I tell you I don't *know*. I've never been here before. I've only met Voloshky once, at Babelsberg. George, listen to me . . ."

"Shut up."

Every door was open. The banquet hall, three storeys high, was a vast cavern of noise. There were milling chanting surging crowds through the hall, the library, the magistrates' courts.

"Your first revolution, isn't it?" Orris said. "You kept away from Prague. What's the matter—got a delicate stomach when the guns come out? Who's on your list for shooting here? Me? Old boy Munden? A few honest little men and a girl who's frightened of demons?"

Beamish made no reply.

They climbed the stairs, Orris to the side and half a step behind Beamish. Above was the council chamber. Young men wearing armbands of the Free German Youth jammed the entrance, chanting and spitting at delegates. The public galleries were packed with demonstrators screaming abuse, anything to prevent the councillors being heard.

It took fifteen minutes through the chaos—"Urgent message for Comrade Voloshky. Where's the Soviet Liaison Officer?"—to find the M.V.D. Resident.

Too many things happened in the first seconds to be taken in all at once. Orris's senses signalled the stream of information, his brain made deductions, his body carried out the actions. It wasn't training that saved him but the reflexes of a young man.

First, that bloody smell. Russian tobacco. He knew even as the door was pushing open they'd come to the right office. He hated the stink of their cigarettes now.

Second, a kaleidoscope of visual impressions.

Voloshky was seated behind the desk, the cigarette abandoned in an ash-tray. He had a sheet of paper in front of him, typed, a list of names it looked. He was putting an X against one of the names, the kiss of death. Voloshky was short and exceedingly ugly, his left shoulder almost hunched, a cadaver for a face with gooseberry whiskers on his cheeks and winter-grey eyes.

It had to be Voloshky because his subordinate was standing. Orris, with the quickness of the hyper-tense to pick out a detail, noticed the scar shaped like a nailclipping on the second man's cheek. He was heavy-set, a man who let his body ask the questions and extract the answers, one big fist pressed to the desk, the other loose by his side.

Their faces turned in unison towards the door.

There was no preamble.

Orris simply shoved his knee into Beamish's haunches, tumbling him to one side. As the thug dived his hand inside his jacket, Orris raised his gun and shot him, crashing him back against the wall.

Third, there was the noise.

The thug was gagging as he tried to speak, sounding as if he were clearing his throat of something. It was blood. It leaked between his lips and dribbled to the floor. He clutched his chest, slid like spit down the wall and lay still.

"Put your hands flat on the desk."

Orris locked the door, laying his ear against the wood. There were sounds of uproar on all sides but not on his account. What was one bullet during a revolution?

Orris spoke German to Voloshky. "I killed him because I can't watch three men at once. Also, when I say what I want, you'll understand I'm not shadow-boxing. Tell Voloshky who I am."

Beamish's voice had grown old. "He's the Englishman I was looking for, Orris."

"It seems," Voloshky chose to speak English, "that he has found you." His left shoulder seemed to draw higher to his head. "Unless, of course, you have changed allegiance, Comrade Colonel."

"Colonel?" Orris looked at Beamish with distaste. "How long have you held that rank?"

A perverse strand of pride wouldn't let Beamish reply. A whole world was collapsing inside him to lie in ruins like the city outside. A lifetime's commitment—the ideals, the acceptance of personal danger and sacrifice, the struggle for a cleaner and braver world—were reduced to this squalid end: that men were killing themselves, fighting like jackals over his carcass. But he wouldn't say how long he'd been a Colonel in the Soviet M.V.D.

"If you haven't come to shoot me," the Russian said, "what do you want?"

From below in the building came the sound of smashing glass.

"I hope your mob doesn't burn the place."

The Russian heaved his shoulder higher. "We're not replaying the Reichstag fire. There's no need. We're the masters now."

His English accent was like Beamish's, honed among the social engineers of Hampstead. There the similarity stopped. Voloshky was content to perform his social engineering with fist and gun.

"Sit over there." Orris prodded Beamish to a chair against the wall. He kept his head averted from the body on the floor.

Orris went to Voloshky and searched him. He removed a small automatic from his pocket and then, for insurance, a cigarette-lighter and fountain pen.

"The situation," Orris said, "has changed. My original aim was simple: Beamish has caused the death of a lot of people who work for my Department; I intended to draw him to Berlin and shoot him."

"Revolutionary justice," Voloshky murmured and showed his teeth in a smile.

Orris ignored him. "This morning he took a girl hostage and is holding her in some interrogation centre. I want her back. I insist . . ." He broke off. There were things inside him he hadn't stopped to consider, feelings he shouldn't display. "She is young and she suffered too much during the war. Let her go free and you can have Beamish." There would be another day of reckoning for Beamish. But Orris didn't say it.

"A girl?" Voloshky asked. "Another agent?"

"She's no business of yours," Orris barked.

Orris was suddenly conscious of the baying of the crowd in the street and the tumult from the corridors and council chamber, and of the utter stillness in the room. The Russian's gaze rested on his hands and he turned them over as if they might have some evidence on their palms. When he looked up at Orris he gave a smile that died before it reached his hollow cheeks. It was, Orris understood, the grimace of someone who'd survived all Stalin's purges.

"I would say, young man, you have a lot to learn. The situation is the exact opposite of what you believe. We hold your girl as a hostage. You are in a building controlled by revolutionary forces, in a city that from midnight will be cut off from the West. The Comrade Colonel is no bargaining counter. Shoot him if you want. He is no use to us anymore. You know the proverb: when you've enjoyed the fruit, what good is the skin? He is finished in London. Do you imagine we are going to keep him in idle luxury the rest of his days? Gratitude of that kind is a bourgeois sentiment. Dispatch him—save us the cost of a bullet. Then go away. I have a revolution to direct."

There was the sound of Beamish retching against the wall, ignored by the other two.

"Your mistake," Voloshky explained to Orris, "is to be English. You think this is all some sort of game, and games have rules. That is why we shall win."

Orris, who had never felt himself particularly English, said nothing.

The afternoon sun hung in the sky. A ray came through the window and crawled across the carpet, sparking on a ring on the dead Russian's hand.

"I should like to smoke," Voloshky said.

"Your cigarettes stink of death," Orris told him.

"George." For the first time since he'd sat down, Beamish spoke. He waited until Orris turned to face him. "George, for all you think of me, accept I'm speaking the truth. I intended no harm to the girl. Despite what Comrade Voloshky says, I'm still useful to them because there's a lot stored up here." He tapped his forehead. He surveyed the Russian without emotion and appeared to draw himself together like a man gathering up the remnants of his pride. "With respect to Comrade Voloshky it is not his business to dispose of me. He is not my superior. I report directly to Moscow. What influence I have there I shall use on your behalf and the girl's. However, you must concede your position is hopeless. Voloshky called your bluff: you didn't shoot me. Making further threats is useless because if you kill us you don't get the girl back. She seems to be of some importance to you, George."

Orris looked at Beamish a long time. They were locked into a hopeless triangle, where the slightest miscalculation threatened disaster. The shouting outside reached a new crescendo. There was the splintering of wood and screams.

Voloshky stared in Orris's eyes, pondering the best way to handle him. He had dealt with hundreds of men and never found any difficulty. There was always a phrase, a nerve.

Voloshky said: "You could, of course, start on me. Start on my foot, go up to a kneecap, a hip. A bullet in those parts is agonizing. I know. I've watched. When I could no longer endure it I would agree to telephone to get the girl to safety. I would lift the phone—and then scream to the guard to come here quickly. Even if I died, it would be all over for you. You must understand, you have manoeuvred yourself into a dead-end street."

Orris said: "I have decided. I'm going to leave here. But you will do two things."

"You are in no position to bargain."

"Then do you suggest I shoot you now and have done with it?"

They held each other's eyes and Orris waited. There was no flicker in the other's face but neither could he find any answer.

"All right," Orris went on. "Use the phone. Find someone who can call off the riot. Tell them they've made their point, they've stopped the city council from functioning. But I'm not walking out through a mob like that because an accident is too easy for you to arrange. Second, get me a jacket and trousers; I'm not going out dressed as a copper."

"What do you intend to do?"

"That is my business."

Voloshky hesitated. "It is a poor deal. The nature of a bargain is that each side gives something."

"I'll tell you what you're gaining," Orris said. "Your life. You can carry on pulling the strings and making your revolutionary puppets jerk. And before you refuse, consider the alternative: you said I can't get Rahel back through you; by your reasoning I might as well shoot you, as I did your thug. Think about it."

Voloshky turned it over in his mind and then heaved his shoulder in a dismissive shrug. He reached a hand out for the telephone.

"Speak German," Orris warned, "or I'll stop you dead."

Within twenty minutes someone in the council chamber had given a signal and the rabble left, chanting the Internationale. In Voloshky's office they heard the falling away of sound and the clamour outside ebbing.

There was a knock and Orris unlocked the door. He stood in the gap, full square in his policeman's uniform, taking the clothes the startled man held out.

"Thank you, comrade, that is all."

He bundled his policeman's uniform and tossed it in the corner and stood in the shabby jacket and trousers.

"Now I'm leaving and Beamish is coming with me."

"George, you are making . . ."

"Shut up."

"Taking Beamish was not part of the bargain," Voloshky pointed out coldly.

"The trouble with you is that you treat it as a game," Orris told him. "You imagine there are rules."

Voloshky's gaze turned from Orris to Beamish. Like most of his country's service, Voloshky had been disgraced sometime in the past and had survived eighteen months in Siberia. His eyes held the cold stillness of a man whose horizons have been snow and ice.

"I wonder what view they'll take in Moscow." Voloshky

glanced again at Orris. "That you kidnapped the brave Comrade Colonel. Or that the traitor left freely."

"Yes," said Orris, standing by the desk. "What does his face show?"

As Voloshky hunched round to look at Beamish, Orris cracked his gun down on the Russian's skull.

Beamish had vomited again. He lay trussed in the back of the van, his face the same grey colour as the corpse beside him.

They drove south-east, through streets suddenly swelled with crowds and police and Soviet troops. The late afternoon sun caught at bayonets and winked at bright cogs in the tracks of tanks. At the Warschaubrücke they crossed out of the Soviet sector. Russian and American soldiers faced each other across the river Spree. A white line was painted across the bridge and the armies were like two teams waiting for the whistle to begin the game. Nobody stopped the van. Nobody demanded papers or an explanation. It was a dirty little half-border where the troops waited for the decision to be made to fight or get out.

Orris drove to the British sector, past knots of people on street corners. British Redcaps and German police patrolled in strength.

He parked the van in the lee of Zoo station and spoke without turning round. To a passer-by he would have looked another of the war-crazy, muttering to himself.

"While I'm away, don't draw attention to yourself. Don't kick the sides of the van. Don't shout. You'd be in God-awful trouble if someone broke down the door and found you with a dead naked policeman."

"George, listen to reason. You're making a terrible error. Can't you see you're backing the losing side? Tomorrow or next week it'll be all over and the Russians will be the victors. It's inevitable."

"We'll see."

"It's what it said in your file, isn't it? No sense of history. You're plain George Orris, the best man in the field the Depot ever had, and you see the significance of nothing. You've no philosophy, no understanding of politics."

"Stuff it." Orris spoke with savage intensity without turning round. He locked the door and walked away through the dusk.

Munden was frightened. It showed in the high register of his voice and the click of the tongue in his dry mouth.

"Old boy, I'm not sure how much longer I'll be at this post. I may get pulled back to Cologne or London."

"You stay where you are or I'll see you're busted so hard they'll never find all the pieces."

"If the Depot says come home, I'm not staying for the Russkies to roll in."

"Who's instructing you?"

"Polly. Apparently Eurcon has gone missing after his holiday."

"Beamish is with me. Trussed like a chicken in the back of my van."

There was a shocked silence.

"You're skating on thin ice, old boy. Where are you calling from, actually?"

"Listen, Munden, you are to send a priority signal to the Depot, Eyes Only and Decode Yourself to the Director-General. Tell him I have Beamish. Tell him that Beamish is a bloody Russian Colonel. Tell him whatever Beamish has been saying about Berlin is propaganda. Tell him to check every statement Beamish made, every contact he went to. Tell him to reverse every bit of advice Beamish gave to the government. Tell him the Russians think we're just going to walk out of Berlin without a fight."

"Old boy, I'm not . . ."

"If you don't do it at once, I'll come and kill you."

He hung up.

It was over twenty-four hours since Orris had eaten and food was paramount. He could feel his body running down and his brain losing alertness. It was thirty-six hours since he had slept but there was no remedy for that.

It took the best part of an hour to find a street businessman who would so much as listen. It wasn't just the old Reichsmarks that were suddenly valueless. All paper money was. It was barter or nothing.

"I can pay in English money." Orris flashed four or five notes in the air. "Pounds sterling."

"See it this way, pal. If the Russians arrive tomorrow, would I want to be caught with English money?" He wore a blue suit with very wide shoulders which he shrugged.

Orris thrust out a pound note. "Take that money and rub it between your fingers. Feel it."

The man took it and Orris grabbed a fistful of his shirt.

"Now you thieving little pig, I want food or I'll run you in for attempting to deal on the black market with me, a member of the Occupation forces."

Orris ate two frankfurters and a Hershey bar with the total concentration of an alley cat.

Orris moved through a restless crowd at Zoo station, constantly pausing to catch reflections in windows, bending to a shoelace, watching eyes, smelling his own sweat. He wedged himself into the call-box.

"Have you done that?"

"Yes." Munden's voice was colourless. "Coded and transmitted the signal myself. I've had a flash acknowledgement. Urgent you give a contact address. Urgent Beamish be fully interrogated. Urgent we know the maximum about Soviet intentions."

"Good, they can have all that. Here's my condition."

"I'm only the damn Post Office. I can but pass it on."

"I'll give them Beamish. But first I must have a squad of British soldiers to fetch someone out of the Soviet sector."

"I beg yours?" Munden's voice was shocked.

"That's right."

"Old boy, you're off your rocker. Sending troops over the line at this moment would start World War Three."

"It started a long time ago for me. Just tell them. My condition. Bloody tell them."

Shortly before midnight Orris rang again. He stood with his back to the wall of the call-box looking at people coming down the steps from the street to the concourse. Someone dropped a heavy case and a score of bodies twitched, bomb-scary.

Munden told him: "I warned you. D-G refused point blank. No raids into the Red sector."

"God, are we running a bloody whelk-stall or a secret service?"

"It's policy: we don't provoke the Kremlin."

"You think they're playing some sort of game? Okay, no one gets to see Beamish." Orris slammed the receiver down. Let the bastards in London sweat a little.

He started to walk away from the station.

At midnight precisely the lights went out. West Berlin went black.

24 June 1948
London

For a long time the Director-General stood staring out across the park. He could see half a dozen lights on the third floor of the Foreign Office building and then in quick succession another five windows blazed. The Berlin working-party was warming up.

Indeed they would be stoking up the fires and getting the irons red-hot.

Beamish had been revealed as a Soviet agent. What the Paris Residency had stumbled on had been confirmed from Berlin. And the Foreign Office, smarting over the Hunt affair, would extract full revenge. It would be noted that the traitor Beamish was being recommended by Standing as his successor.

Standing knew with certainty he would finish his career in

disgrace. Yet the knife that turned in his heart was not because of that.

To have a minor double-agent on your books was one of the risks of the trade. But to have a long-term defector rise through the service until he was poised to take over at the pinnacle was in a completely different category. He knew the reaction in Washington. The Brits weren't simply careless; the Brits couldn't be trusted at all. They'd say the Depot had a structure riddled with dry rot from basement to attic. The Russians mightn't get Berlin now. But second prize was driving a wedge between America and Britain for years.

There was still warmth in the night air coming in through the window. It felt colder at his desk. He picked up the phone.

"Political Evaluator."

"How much longer?" the Director-General asked.

"Hard to tell," Houghton said. "He's been cunning in brushing over his tracks. That's what you'd expect. Unfortunately his secretary was on prolonged sick leave and the replacement kept no duplicate diary during the critical period. We know the people he was talking to at the F.O. and the Cabinet Office. Can't tell his contacts out of school. And then Alan had . . ." Houghton broke off. "Is it right to call a traitor by his first name?"

"Yes," Standing answered. "It could be important."

"In what way?"

"Kindly finish what you were saying."

"Alan had a string of meetings with Kordorf of the C.I.A. He even took me once or twice."

"That was to be expected. A few poisoned words on British intentions that would reach Clay in Berlin. Did you create a good impression with Kordorf?"

"What do you mean? I didn't propose a toast to George III."

"We must exercise extreme caution in dealing with the Americans. We must try to contain the damage. They must never suspect we had a highly placed traitor in the Depot."

"D-G, we cannot simply pretend Beamish has gone missing."

"That is precisely what we can do. Fishing accident in the

Vosges. Death by drowning. Tragic loss. After all, nobody's seen him."

"Orris in Berlin," Houghton pointed out.

There was a silence that afterwards, in the post mortem in the Two Chairmen, Houghton tried to convey to Little Eric. Unfortunately he lacked the poet-warrior's gift with language. A cold silence, yes. A dark silence. A silence that seemed eternal.

"Nobody has seen him," Standing repeated. "Tell me when you have the list of contacts. Tell me what poison he was feeding the Americans. I need to know the extent of the disaster before I face the firing-squad. Bevin, ten o'clock in the morning."

He cut the connection and jiggled the cradle to wake the night switchboard.

"You'll find D/Ops at home and probably asleep. He's to come at once."

That night there were unaccustomed noises of activity in the Depot. Doors, running footsteps, a shout once. The Director-General waited alone in his office. Dawn found him, unmoving behind his desk, sick at heart.

24 June 1948
Berlin

"The stench in here is awful."

Orris sat with his hands on the steering wheel and replied nothing.

"George, I don't think I can stand it much longer. His body's been leaking and it stinks."

"You're alive," Orris said. "You're lucky."

They waited in silence. It was a clouded night, no moon, and Orris's head was a black silhouette against the blackness outside. He sat very still. Beamish had never thought of him as a patient man and was surprised.

"You presumably have a plan," Beamish said. "If you're waiting here it's because you have some sort of timetable."

Orris lit a cigarette. He didn't offer one to Beamish.

"Why are we waiting, George? I have a right to know."

Orris's cigarette glowed briefly, casting an orange glow across the ragged stubble of his chin.

" You intended to kill me," Beamish persisted. "Now you're keeping me alive. You must tell me why."

Orris drew on the cigarette and said: "I'm waiting till your value to London has gone up. They'll meet my price."

"What is your price?"

"A blackface job. Bring the girl out."

"They'll never do it. Never. Send the army into the Soviet sector and it's just the excuse Stalin is looking for."

"That's my price."

He said it with such stubbornness that Beamish stopped. Stalin had a strategy for Berlin, a design for the whole of Europe. Orris had a girl.

Beamish said: "You must love her."

"Love." There was silence in the van. Outside they could hear a shout and running footsteps. The lights of some official car swung across their roof and were gone. "When she's with me in our room, she makes me feel we are the exact centre of the universe and nothing else is of any account."

Yes, thought Beamish, it could be love. The hyperbole, the self-centredness, the lies. Not lies, self-delusion. Orris had once been driven by something quite different: revenge. Now revenge was superseded by fierce obsession with the girl.

It was a city that never slept, afraid of dreams of the past.

At 2.30 a.m. Orris walked down the steps to the station concourse. There were two candles lit and groups stood talking or huddled against the wall. He dialled by matchlight.

The ringing tone continued for a long time before the voice answered: "British Co-ordinating Mission."

"You took your bloody time."

"It's not easy finding the phone in the dark, old boy."

"What do London say now?"

"I haven't the foggiest," Munden said. "Our radio doesn't function without electricity."

"Christ," said Orris. He broke out in a cold sweat.

"Are you still there, old boy?"

"I'm thinking."

Orris stared out at the concourse. It was like the war all over again, people sheltering in the underground. That is what they're preparing for, the first battle of World War Three. And how was he going to get the girl out now?

"Use the radio facilities at Gatow Base."

"I have tried. They won't accept coded signals. I have really pulled every string, old boy. But the bald truth is they are working in the dark, damn near, with an emergency generator, and it's total confusion."

"You mean the British Base draws its power from the Soviets?"

"That is what I mean."

Orris put the receiver down, laughing loudly without mirth. He stopped abruptly.

That night Berlin was a patchwork of gas lamps and darkness, with the dead areas by far the bigger. The city drew three-quarters of its power from the Soviet side, the imposing Kraftwerk West power station having been stripped and virtually all its generating equipment shipped to the Soviet Union.

The van drove along darkened avenues, through Charlottenburg, up north through Siemensstadt, across the Tegel into Spandau. Orris stopped twice to ask the way and finally there it was: the cooling towers and pylons massive in the night. It was a measure of unpreparedness that Kraftwerk West had no police to guard it, just a watchman who limped to the door of his hut.

"Emergency repairs," Orris yelled out.

The watchman peered at the anonymous van and Orris's face, grey in the night

"Papers," he said, as they always said.

"Of course," Orris replied. "Save your leg, I'll bring them over. Got to hurry. Chaos out there."

Orris got out and skipped across to the door of the hut. He hit the watchman hard on the side of the head above the left ear with his pistol butt, found the keys on a big ring attached to his belt and opened the gate.

The power station was an enormous hulk but Orris wasn't concerned with the echoing generating hall and the auxiliary plants the Russians hadn't bothered with. He drove slowly, following twin railway tracks past heaps of coke. The clouds had broken and he left off his headlamps in the starlight. He turned past the generating block, and a low building to the right had lights boasting through all its windows. He coasted to a halt and got out softly. He turned his head, questing, and there was no guard or hint of uproar.

How many engineers would face him inside? Men grew nasty with mates to back them up.

He opened the door and found the answer: three heads turned, only three. And the control panels and dials and circuit breakers looked right. So he walked in, hands in pockets, squinting at the lights and grinning. "Like Blackpool illuminations in here, isn't it?" He spoke English.

No one replied.

Orris moved forward. You always moved forward, nice and steady, get in close, don't give them time to challenge. He said: "Which one's the boss? Chief sparks? Crikey, doesn't anyone speak English?"

"A little." The man wore pens in the breast-pocket of his overalls like campaign medals. He stood against the wall by a diagram of some circuitry.

"Who's the senior engineer?"

"I."

"Good-o," Orris said. "I'm Bristow, liaison officer, Gatow. Major Bristow, that is. The power situation for the whole city is very dicey."

"Please?"

"Very serious. *Ernst, ja?*"

215

"Yes, yes."

"Very little electricity."

Orris had moved directly in front of the senior engineer. He couldn't tell how the man would respond. If he hated all the occupying powers, there was always the gun. The other two were at the edge of his vision, not understanding.

"It is the Soviets who cut off the electricity. They want to drive the Western allies out and kill Berlin."

"What's he saying?" one of the others asked in German.

"He says the Russians want to take the whole city," the senior engineer told him.

"The English are frightened they'll be whipped out?"

Orris half-smiled with the patience of someone who doesn't understand and changed tack.

"The Russians have surrounded the city with tanks," Orris said. "You know, *Panzer*. And they are flying in Mongolian troops."

The senior engineer frowned, trying to grasp it.

"Are you married?" Orris asked. There was a ring on the man's right hand. "*Frau?*"

"Yes," he replied.

"Very nasty," Orris persisted, playing on memories of defeat and rape. "The Russians are sending planes with *Mongolisch* soldiers."

"What does he say about Mongolians?" one of the others demanded.

"The Mongols are flying to Staaken airfield," Orris said. "The runway lights draw their power from here."

There was more talk but Orris's work was done.

At 3.38 they threw the switches and Staaken airfield was plunged into darkness.

The number on the telephone on his desk in the Rathaus had been 20-02-07. It answered at once.

"Voloshky."

Orris supposed no one slept during a revolution. He said: "This is Orris. Can you hear me clearly?"

"What do you want?"

"I have a proposition to put to you. But first you have to understand this is not a game. I am going to put the phone down now and call you back in ten minutes. During that time you will establish what I'm saying is true: the power supply to your new Fighter Base at Staaken has been cut. You can have it back but there are conditions."

Oris depressed the cradle and cut the connection. He leaned his forehead against the cool glass of the call-box and waited.

Munden had gone home to bed. The telephone at the Residency was answered by a young woman who wouldn't divulge his address or number.

Orris pressed his forehead into his hand. There was a humming in his head. It had started at Kraftwerk West and at the time he'd thought it was the hum of the equipment. It hadn't gone away. It was exhaustion. Dawn was breaking and the horizon in the east showed a grey line that throbbed in time to his pulse.

"Listen carefully to this telephone number." Orris read it off the little white card on the instrument. "Wake Munden up. Tell him I shall wait at this number for ten minutes. If he doesn't ring back, they'll shoot him for being a traitor."

Orris waited. One cigarette equalled ten minutes. From the call-box he could just make out in the early light a desolate area where all the trees had been cut for fuel. What would the Berliners use this year? Without coal and electricity and wood, how would they stay alive in winter?

Light and shade had begun to seep back into the world outside. He could make out in the denuded woodland an area some optimist had replanted with saplings. The lines stretched away into the early morning mist like little crosses in a Flanders graveyard.

Orris finished his cigarette and still he waited. He was too tired to move or think of any other plan. The phone rang.

"Who's speaking?"

"Berlin Resident."

"All right," said Orris. "Now's your chance to be a hero. At nine o'clock this morning the power is going to be restored to the British Base at Gatow. I suggest you get in touch with one of the brass there and tell him the news because we have to do something in return."

"I'm listening, old boy."

"Send a detail, it had better be armed, to the Kraftwerk West power station in Spandau and restore power to Staaken, on the Russian side. It's a straight one-for-one swap, understood? And tell the brass this: Gatow will continue to receive power from the Soviets no matter what, because if anything ever goes wrong they simply pull the plugs on Staaken."

"London are going to be very chuffed."

"I don't give a shit. That's half the bargain. Come and pick me up at nine-thirty. I'm at . . ." He peered to make out the name above the station entrance. "Siemensstadt station. I need money."

"About Bea . . ."

Orris cut him short.

He drove the blue van north to Saatwinkel in the French sector, where the road ran down to the Tegeler See. He set the gear lever in neutral, took the handbrake off, and he and Beamish watched the van dip under the lapping waves. Neither said a prayer over the grave of the naked policeman.

It was a four-kilometre walk back. Orris said: "You're not going to be so stupid as to run."

"Where would I run to?"

In the grey morning light the skin on Beamish's face had taken on the transparent hue of the very old or the very sick, the ones close to death.

The S-bahn, under the control of the Soviet authorities, was silent, the station closed. Orris and Beamish smoked the last of the cigarettes, not speaking. There was nothing to say.

At nine-thirty Munden drove up at the wheel of a Standard Vanguard, coming slowly, checking the faces of the people trudging at the side of the road. He stopped close by, his face haggard, showing sudden shock at recognizing the man with Orris.

"Good morning, sir. I wasn't expecting you too."

Beamish shrugged, as much as to say: what hope was there for capitalist societies which employed such buffoons to protect them.

Orris sat next to Beamish in the back seat.

"Money?"

Munden handed back a buff envelope. "A hundred quid. I'd have to get the King's signature for anything more. Do you need a new identity?"

"Oh, I've got papers," Orris said, like an owner might say his dog has fleas.

"How are you going to get out? They've closed the railway and are turning everything back on the Autobahn. There's a plane at midday, another at teatime. Some talk of an airlift."

"Do you think I'd tell you?"

Munden sat very stiff. "Only trying to help."

"Drive to the Brandenburger Tor."

Munden drove roughly, crashing second gear.

"Did you bring any muscle?" Orris asked.

"No. Why should I?"

Orris leaned out of the window. If there'd been a car behind, and he wasn't certain, there was nothing now.

They completed the drive in silence. It put Orris in mind of a funeral cortège, except the body beside him quivered slightly and a mist of sweat had appeared on his brow.

They passed down Charlottenburger Chaussee, the Tiergarten forlorn and decrepit on either side.

"Go slowly here."

Munden cruised gently past the Soviet war memorial, guarded by Russian troops who in turn were guarded by British troops.

"First Worcesters."

That was Munden, filling the tenseness with useless information.

"Stop."

Munden pulled over and put on the handbrake. "You're not going across?"

"Not me," Orris said. He shook his head but the humming wouldn't go away.

"Have you a cigarette?" Beamish asked.

"Of course, sir."

Orris got out to stand by the car. Light drizzle had begun, turning the desolate warscape into a two-dimensional world of grey. The only splash of colour was the blood-red flag above the Brandenburg Gate. Orris was absorbed by a small group in grey uniforms across the white line, sheltering from the rain under the triumphal arches.

"I can't bloody see because of the shadows."

Ten o'clock by Orris's watch.

"The bastard. Where is he?"

Then the car came, the huge Zis of a high Soviet official, and two people got out in Pariserplatz on the far side of the Gate. Voloshky rested his hand on the girl's arm, though she scarcely needed restraining. Rahel's head turned, bewildered.

"All right," Orris told Beamish, "on your way."

Beamish looked at Orris for long seconds. "You know, you won't be ..." He searched for the word: *happy* was wrong; happiness wasn't natural to the human condition; as for *the pursuit of happiness*, it showed how puerile the Americans were. Beamish shook his head, chasing out such senseless Cambridge speculations. And what did Orris want anyway: a cottage, hollyhocks round the door, smelling of boiling nappies? "George, you won't be *fulfilled* with her. She's just a girl. George?"

Orris turned, furious, but all he saw was a man who looked dead already. He said, quite gently: "Goodbye. I'm sure they've got a comradely reception waiting for you."

Orris walked part of the distance with Beamish and then stopped some way short of the white line, not wishing to be near the group of British soldiers when he met the girl again. Beamish stopped too, as if he no longer knew where home was: with the country he'd betrayed or the faith he feared. His cheeks were wet: it could have been rain.

"Go on. Bloody get over there." Orris's voice was less charitable now. "Voloshky's got the champagne in the ice-bucket."

Again Beamish walked, not looking back, not even glancing at Rahel as they passed each other. Voloshky watched the exchange, hunched his shoulder and got back in the Zis.

Rahel, the child of the storm, altered course as she recognized Orris. She was hardly ten metres away when the shot rang out.

Like ants when their nest is kicked, figures ran in every direction. Voloshky's car disappeared towards Unter den Linden. Orders cracked out. Soldiers flung themselves to the ground with their rifles pointing across the demarcation line.

Beamish had halted again, a step or two over the white line. His neck prodded forward, stiff, waiting for a second shot. But no one wanted him that day, no one wanted the embarrassment of his corpse.

In a terrible hush, Beamish took hesitant steps forward. Nobody ever saw what happened to him.

Rahel hadn't wavered.

She walked the last steps and stood over the body of Orris. He lay face down, shot in the back. While the crows away by the Reichstag still called in alarm, she raised her hands to cover her eyes, a blindfold.

"The Execution."

Her Berliner voice hung sharp in the thin rain.

She faced west towards the Tiergarten, where the gunshot had come from. While figures in uniform ran towards her, she began to take her clothes off, draping his dead body.

27 June 1948
Berlin

Cable reference CC4910
Classification: Top Secret—Personal and Eyes Only
From Gen Clay to Under Secretary of Army Draper

General Sir Brian Robertson's Deputy has just returned from London and General Robertson is with me now advising me of his government's position with respect to Berlin situation. His government is determined to stay in Berlin and to make every effort to prevent suffering among the German people as long as possible while ways and means are being considered by governments to break the present blockade. His government has agreed to furnish all possible additional airlift. It believes further that prior to negotiations at governmental level this increased airlift should be laid on and working effectively. In addition his government strongly urges the dispatch of bombers from the United States to selected airdromes in France and England prior to the start of negotiations at governmental level. I am quite sure that General Robertson's government agrees with the view that our departure from Berlin would make difficult, if not impossible, the accomplishment of our mutual objectives in western Europe. I agree fully with these views. I have already arranged for our maximum airlift to start on Monday.

Postscript

Stalin had no doubts. The bear hug could still squeeze Berlin into submission and force the French, British and Americans out.

The blockade began on 24th June 1948. The airlift which no one believed possible followed. It was hesitant, then desperate, and finally increasingly confident. At the darkest hour even Iron Pants, U.S.A.F. General Curtis LeMay, flew in supplies. Throughout the airlift the Soviet authorities continued to supply electricity to Gatow.

On 4th May 1949 Stalin abandoned a blockade which had contrived to make him appear both foolish and brutally inhuman. The airlift continued a further four months, to prove a point and to stockpile food and raw materials. In all, 2,300,000 tons came in by air.

Outside Tempelhof airport in the renamed Platz der Luft-brücke there is a memorial to the American and British airmen who died during the airlift. George Orris has no memorial, none.